THE
RANKIN STREET
RAIDERS

IN HONOUR OF PAT THRASHER 1955-2001

MARK W. MACMILLAN

Please note that this is a work of historic fiction/adventure.
The times and places are real but the characters in this book are
players on a stage and any resemblance to actual people is coincidental.

www.tellwell.ca

ISBN
978-0-2288-4532-4 (Hardcover)
978-0-2288-4531-7 (Paperback)
978-0-2288-4533-1 (eBook)

Table of Contents

"Great is the human who has not lost his childlike heart."

John Leonard

To Wendy MacMillan the architect and love of my life.

We lived in a time of dreams.

Rankin was a tall-treed, leafy street, laden with flower gardens and shrubbery; full of solid, respectable two-storey homes displaying manicured lawns and backyards furnished with swing-sets, sandboxes and patio sets. It was safe and serene. A dozen or so houses on each side, it ran quickly from the main street down to the river. Officially an avenue, we always called it Rankin Street.

Our mothers had frilly aprons and cat glasses and our fathers wore crew cuts and drove flashy cars. Pets were named Corky, Muffy and Buster. Guys rolled up their sleeves and shined their shoes. Girls spent a lot of time curling their hair and painting their nails. Everything was new and improved. Our town was Amherstburg or A'burg. It seemed like any other small community, but it was in a zone of its own. And we knew it.

It was where we raided because there was so much to plunder. The 'Burg and what surrounded it, supplied the lightning for our thunder.

Aside from the woods and fields where we climbed and ran, the creeks and ponds where we fished and swam, there were places, events and changes happening that did not exist elsewhere, anywhere, nowhere on earth. Somehow, we understood that.

A border town, A'burg had been the largest hub of the Underground Railroad, conducting runaway slaves to freedom. This added to its ethnic diversity and culture. It is home to the Amherstburg Freedom Museum that commemorates emancipation and celebrates Black heritage. A Canadian National Historic Site.

Directly across the Detroit River was Boblo, an amusement park that was not only built on its own island but featured the latest in mostly German-engineered thrill rides. Two towering steam-driven, paddle-wheel pleasure boats delivered thousands of Americans to its dock daily. A much smaller ferry transported Canadians from A'burg.

The strong and dangerous currents of the river also supported the largest freshwater commerce system in the world. Freighters longer than Rankin Street passed surprisingly silently by, loaded with everything from iron ore to grain from one end of the Great Lakes to the other.

Fort Amherstburg, later Fort Malden, played a key role in the War of 1812. It was a British enclave to deter American ships transporting troops and supplies along the river. It was a functional fort until 1858, eventually becoming a National Historic Site and museum; a monument to a courageous chapter in the book of Canada.

Pelee Island, a National Park on the southern-most tip of Canada, was just down the road. It had the most bird and plant species this side of the Garden of Eden.

Eighteen miles away was Windsor, housing CKLW, the radio station with the widest broadcasting radius in the country. Windsor had pizza so good it was named after the city and was connected by not only a bridge but an underwater tunnel to the United States.

In Detroit, the Kronk Gym began producing boxers that punched their way to world recognition. Thomas "the Hitman" Hearns and Michael "Mad Dog" Moorer were just two in their illustrious stable of fast and smart fighters with pop. And yes, Joe Louis grew up in the Motor City.

Motown was making hits of its own. From the Four Tops to the Temptations with Smokey and Stevie in between, the number one records seemed to arrive on the airwaves daily, not weekly or monthly.

Detroit TV stations fuelled our nightmares with horror films and educated us with afternoon movie classics when we were home faking sick on weekdays. Johnny Ginger and Captain Kangaroo taught us how to be kind and still have fun.

We watched the Tigers' Al Kaline blast baseballs outta the park and Mickey Lolich keep them in. No one messed with Gordie Howe or Ted Lindsay when they cruised the Olympia for the Red Wings. The grass was green and the ice was smooth.

Mauve Caddies and candy-apple red T-Birds rolled off assembly lines in the Motor City and Windsor like magic machines, with Camaros, Mustangs and Barracudas revving through dual exhausts behind them.

Oh, and the Essex County corn was so sweet it tasted like it came already buttered. The tomatoes were so good people ate them like apples.

The Rankin Street Raiders soaked it all in like pirate sponges.

We climbed inside those dreams, stretched them out and made them real.

Chapter 1

Sixty Seconds to Two a.m.

A young boy was stretched out on a darkened street well past midnight. Beneath him was a rough, iron manhole cover, above him a cloud-moon sky. He was counting in quivering tones, "Twenty-one, twenty-two, twenty-three." The lunar light briefly revealed his contorted white face, frozen by fright. Sweating as the summer heat rose through the pavement and his paisley pyjamas, he seemed to be barring some demon from escaping through the hole with the heavy sewer cap. His counting was keeping the thing at bay. Struggling, robbed of breath, his arms wide out, legs twitching, he continued to call out the numbers.

There were five more of us lurking in the half-light, just out of sight. We had stationed ourselves at each corner of the intersection. Our fifth held the lookout position further up Richmond Street. We were all in our jammies. "It's almost two, he's just about there," one of us hooted from the shadows.

Suddenly, lights appeared in the distance. Two low beams announced a car, heading straight for the youth spread flat on the asphalt. Rolling slowly, as if slumbering, was a long, shark-finned automobile, weaving slightly. Our advance scout arced his flashlight at us—the high sign to abort the operation. We all stared and stiffened.

Our lookout shouted, "Car!"

The boy counted louder and faster, "Forty-eight, forty-nine, fifty."

Unwilling to leave our posts, one of us screamed at him, "Run! A car's coming, give it up!"

"I'm staying till two, I'm not afraid," he hollered back in a strangled voice.

The car drove steadily toward us. To make himself seen, the counter began—remaining on his back—to instinctively flail about, arms waving frantically in the air, legs kicking at invisible attackers but still he counted, now yelling in anguish, "Fifty-six, fifty-seven!"

It was obvious that he wasn't going to give in until he reached the full minute, so we took divertive action to keep our guy from being run over: splaying our flashlights about, directing our beams on store windows, at the car and on our struggling chum. It worked. The car braked and swerved as the suddenly alert driver peered through the windshield trying to determine what he was looking at. Just as our manhole man hit "sixty!" a cloud passed over the starry night and the big boat of a car came to a stop on the side of the street. That was our moment and we all knew it. Without a sound we fled like young greyhounds after a rabbit.

There were four people in the Cadillac, two startled couples driving home from a night out. They were babbling loudly and frantically.

"Goddamn, what happened over there?"

"What's going on, was it a fight?"

"Was someone run over?"

"Can you see any blood?"

"Should we call the police?"

"Let's take a look."

They tumbled out of the Caddy and milled around in the intersection, finding nothing until another auto drove past, honked them out of the way and rushed on with the driver cursing into the suddenly bright night air.

As the couples drove away, the man in the backseat said somewhat grimly, "I think it might have been a kid in his PJs. Pretty dangerous."

"And stupid," the driver added. They headed home, even slower and suddenly sober.

Meanwhile, the six of us were still running silently, spread out on both sides of the avenue, darting into and behind hedges, trees, gardens, fences and sheds that we knew in the blackest of any night. Only our fleeting shadows were erratically exposed above and behind us by sudden illumination from the moon, house lights, beacons from the river and other cars. But no one could see us. We were shades on the run.

When we made Rankin Street, we took turns to carefully scurry into our tent, our flashlights muffled in our pillows as we threw ourselves down on our own sleeping bags. Exhausted, puffing like penguins, we all lay staring straight up, feet akimbo, waiting to speak when the tent zipper was closed to give us the final signal.

We could all feel the glee. We were nervous, happy, proud and exhausted. Giggles and shoulder punches were shared.

"The Rankin Street Raiders rule!" one of us shouted.

"Ssshhh dummy, you'll wake the whole neighbourhood. The cops might be out looking for us."

"The Rankin Street Raiders strike again," we whispered hoarsely and raised our pop bottles into the illumination of flashlight.

"Don't no one dare try to test the best."

"We be burnin' it up down Raider Street—Jeet!"

We hadn't really plundered anything, not being professional privateers, yet but we had saved some swag for the festive outcome of our covert ops.

Each of us had our own horde of snacks and pop: chips and cheezies, pretzels and popcorn, candy bars and sodas. Just like our favourite baseball and hockey players, we each had our go-to treats: Mounds Bars, Arrow, Three Musketeers, Baby Ruth, Mars Bar, Almond Joy, Milky Way, Snickers, Twix and many more. Our favourite sodas were: Coke, Fanta Orange, Tahiti Treat, Royal Crown Cola, Dr. Pepper, 7-Up, Hires Root Beer, Pepsi, Double Cola, Vernors, Cream Soda and Mountain Dew. We were pretty much authorities on these things.

We fell upon our stash greedily, giddy from our triumph. After much laughing, chomping, guzzling and the subsequent belching, we began to feel sleep wrap itself around our triumphant shoulders.

After the hushed celebration began to die down, our new boy, the greenhorn, Gary Baines—who we called Hairy Barry Gains—hadn't said a word; his first successful caper and not a peep.

"Wussup, Pip?" I asked him, "You're not exactly bragging about joining the two a.m. ranks?"

"Yeah man, are you still scared?"

"Or did you piss yer pyjamas?"

"Guys," he said in a kind of surprising whimper. "We might have a problem."

"What the heck are you talking about?" We were all back on full alert.

He eased himself up on his elbows, blinking into the beams of our inquiring lights. We stared and waited, confused and concerned.

"I think that might have been my parents in the back seat of that car."

That let all the air outta the tent.

Of course, there was hell to pay the next day. I was summoned sternly from our little canvas den by my dad and told to bring the "new boy" with me. Not for the first or last time, I was tired and barely remembered the end of the evening as I faced him.

When my father was mad his voice sounded like sandpaper on stone. This not-so-bright morning it sounded like a rasp file grating on granite. I tried to close my ears without moving.

"You are to take this boy to his own house immediately and then return straight here. I am sending the rest of your friends—he crunched the word friends like he was chewing gravel—home after they have cleaned up the usual mess in the tent. Tell them that they're lucky I don't call every one of their parents about this. You are grounded. We will talk about this later, maybe in a week."

We both looked up at the growling parental figure, staring like goggle-eyed dummies.

"Do you understand me?" he bellowed, rasping more granite into my unprotected ears.

We nodded hard, just short of snapping our necks.

Not all the Rankin Street Raiders' missions were completely successful.

Chapter 2

The Arch of Our Covenant

We were making our way to the Arch, our hideout. It was a secluded, sacred place for us, crowded with old trees wrung with sturdy vines, a creek that spawned dark, heavy ponds, thick with undergrowth that made it inaccessible to most. Always wet and dank, full of snakes and leeches, stinging nettles and sawgrass, muskrats and beavers, spiders and biting ants. The Raiders were for it. It was a test just to go there let alone make it our refuge. On sunny days, light filtered in with long, gnarled fingers reaching for us and on cloudy days it was a cave with no ceiling. We loved it and found a strange kind of worship in its jungle-like embrace.

The Arch was an abandoned railway trestle, a great monolith, splashed with ivy and moss and worn with iron stains in the rain, as solid and silent as a pyramid. It overshadowed everything we thought and did there. It seemed to welcome and protect us. We often scaled its sides to gaze upon the history of the still sturdy but rusting tracks, inhale the vintage aroma of the long-steeped creosote that soaked its ties and view the entire countryside above the treeline like kings after a conquest.

We spent so many glorious days there, absent from adult contact and pestering from the dictation and demands of homework, newspaper delivery, lessons, grass-cutting, math, lima beans, pet-grooming, punishment, church, dog shit, relatives' travel slide shows, correcting our attitude and living up to expectations.

Distanced from all that clawed at us and took us away from ourselves, we cooked up some of our best escapades there, and it was rare that adventure didn't happen upon us there in the bargain.

Three of us were on Rankin St. while I lived one house over from the corner. Our fifth pirate was from the other side of town, but he was given special status.

All five Raiders were there on that expedition. We were called by at least three things: our real names, our first names with a "y" hooked on at the end, and our nicknames.

Nicknames were more than common in A'burg—they were pretty much a requirement. So much so that one guy we knew had about four hundred of them. For some weird reason, they just kept heaping up. He was known, among other monikers, as: Creamy-Neck, Buzzard, Shoe-Head, Ear-Wart, Frazzle, Leaker, Tubs, Road-Meat, Slimy, Rat-Teeth, Crusty, Jelly-Legs, Fart-Breather, Yellow-Back, Bean-Turd, Chicken Balls, Burger Queen, Shaky, Flat-Ass, Warp, Little Drummer Boy, Brick-Mouth, Wedgie, Bomba, Sparky, Guts-Face, Swart, Piss-Eyes, Squib, Burnt-Weenie, Moleskin, Toe-Cheese, Rust-Saliva, Garbage and Radish-hair.

Our crew consisted of Gregory, Greggy, G-Man, Rogue, Rogan who was large and barrel-chested with sandy hair and intelligent blue eyes. He had a big head that encased the brains behind many of our operations. He was also the most logical and practical guy in the group. If he thought things might not work out, he'd let us know. Often, we chose to ignore him, but he was usually right.

Scott, Scotty, Scooter, Beluga, Wiry, Whaley was tall and thinner than his surname might suggest with a curly, messy mop of black hair. He was the quietest in the group but was a good man to have in a spot of trouble. Scooter was the only Raider who didn't live on Rankin or 'round the corner. He was a talented bowler and had a strong inner resolve.

After we droned on about whether a prank or a plan was doable or not, he would often break his silence and say, "Let's just do it, Nancys!" If Wiry was in, we were all in.

The smallest and fastest of the group was me: Matthew, Matty, M&Ms, Mighty Mouse, McKendrick. Short with carefully combed dark hair, I was usually well-dressed, which gave me an air of innocence. But I was far from angelic. I was up for any plan because I had an ability to get out of most jams. I could take the worst-case scenario and work backwards from there. In other words, I was sly and had a knack for survival. I always had a Plan B in my jeans' back pocket.

Terrence, Terry, Jarvis Whimple, Skeeser, Thatcher was the funniest of us all, by a wide-open country mile. He was skinny and freckled with unmanageable auburn hair above his rubbery face, which he could contort into anything from a pretzel to an orangutan. He would accept any dare, the weirder the better, and was the bravest of our crew when there was no chance of failure. If stuff went south, he was the first out the door and then long gone, gone, gone.

Finally, we had Leonard, Lenny, Sticks, Celery-Stick, Stanks, Stickwood, a proud and serious kid with wispy blonde hair trailing over his face. He was a tough hockey goalie who would do anything to protect the net. So, Sticks was a natural nickname even though none of us knew what a double entendre was at the time. Some of us might still not know. He refused to show pain or emotion, and he was always a rock when things didn't turn out as we planned. His parents were proper British, so we had to be extra careful around them.

We were all the eldest kids in our families, which wasn't by happenstance. It meant that the vessels we commanded and commandeered were not only buccaneer frigates but hard-hulled icebreakers and ships set on courses of exploration to new lands and experiences. We were the first, slashing through traditions and establishing new standards of daring. We were the Rankin Street Raiders. We took our oaths, secrecy and commissions as seriously as the grave.

And the Raiders were leaderless. We operated as a tactical Even-Steven squad. Each privateer's words and responsibilities were equal to the next. We marauded as a single unit, no man first or last. On a single pair of collective shoulders, we carried our successes as well as our setbacks. We laughed with a loud, shared voice that echoed in our souls. The Rankin Street Raiders opened and gave our hearts to a friendship forged of adventure and trust.

We had foregone our usual Saturday ritual of watching cartoons from 7 a.m. until noon while shovelling back big bowls of Captain Crunch, Tricks, Cheerios, Cocoa Puffs, Lucky Charms, Frosted Flakes, Count Chocula or any other sugary cereal we would beg our mums into buying for us. We ate from TV tables in our worn housecoats. It was tough to give this up, but we were committed.

That morning we were up early and out the back door to meet at the schoolyard before marching off to the Arch. The schoolyard was where we conducted a lot of our business, when we weren't attending classes, of course. It was private and provided us with a fenced-in haven to plot, talk about girls, trade comics, light matches and play on the empty sporting fields. No adults were ever there unless they had wandered in by mistake. In the off hours, the schoolyard was a no-teachers, no-parents, no-problem zone.

We began marching toward our sanctuary as it was a long hike on short legs. We were also lugging slingshots, jackknives, ropes and had packed our own lunches and pops. We never told our parental units when we were on a trip to the Arch, so it was up to our secretive selves when it came to equipment and foodstuffs.

The G-Man had peanut butter and jelly; Beluga had baloney on a bun while Lenny had his usual: Marmite on pumpernickel. That dark, smelly slime was commonly referred to by the rest of the Raiders as rat-shit on death bread. Skeeser and I had made our specialty sandwich. It was always iceberg lettuce, a cheddar cheese slice and ham on white with French's mustard. We loved those sandwiches, so we learned how to create them. The day was fair but with a moist breeze that should have warned us against foul weather. We weren't much on warnings, usually until it was way too late. We always wore jackets, even in summer, because we had to fight our way through the secret path with all the brambles and spiked weeds. Explaining the scratches on our arms wasn't always easy.

The daylight became splintered as we crept nearer to our haunt. It was springtime and everything was lush with green growth. But the pool beneath the trestle was darker and deeper than usual.

"Geez, we gotta wade through that muck," said Rogue.

"Let's push Skeeser in first to see how deep it is," I suggested.

"No way, girls. I'm going the long way 'round," Skeese replied.

"If you're all so chicken, I'll go," Wiry said, already tromping through the green-black water.

"Watch out for snakes."

"Don't drown, doofus."

"I'll eat your sandwich if you don't make it."

The sludgy liquid was only up to his knees, so we all waded in, laughing off our fear.

It wasn't a great idea, even for us, to parade in barefoot. There was always the threat of snakes and not just small garters but water snakes and milk snakes (big boys with nasty bites) and even water moccasins, which were venomous rattlesnakes. How they came to be named after an Indigenous person's deerskin shoe, we never knew. There we also submerged sticks and rocks and once in a while we would dredge up a bottle or rusted can left by some strangers who had invaded our realm years and years before. So, our first project was to string our socks and shoes on the ropes we brought and hang them in shafts of sunlight to dry. Rope always came in handy. It was a rare mission to the Arch that didn't require some type of twine.

There was no real plan otherwise, so we began by finding and whittling walking sticks for the trip back and for attacking one another. We also used them to machete our way through the undergrowth. Naturally separating, we explored the area to see what had changed since our last visit. We foraged and searched under the oaks and elms that hung low with new leaves, glistening in the half-light. Between the boggy bottom of the Arch pool and the latticework of thick hardwood branches there were weeds everywhere, multiplying like vegetative rabbits. Some we knew but most we didn't. The usual clusters of rag, stink and chick weeds as well as golden-rod, burdocks, thistles and fox-tails appeared all over the floor of the Arch. There were also strange plant patches full of prickly ash, dog mustard and thyme-leaved sandwort. Here grew hairy-stemmed spurge and there was goat's beard and spreading dog-bane.

We did know which weeds we could use. We chewed the young purple vines of wild grapes like sweet and sour gum and then spat them out. Milkweed pods were for shaking in the fall like parachute seeds from high atop the Arch. And catnip was employed for freaking out the neighbours' felines that shat in our mothers' gardens. We never tired of watching them become possessed: writhing on their backs like eels in the grass, mewing, contorting and whining, almost laughing. It was worth that alone, watching a pet cat laugh.

We also understood what to carefully avoid like poison oak, sumac and ivy. Usually, we figured that out the hard way. One season, Skeeser managed to cover most of his body with poison oak blisters by scratching his rash like a monkey. Soon after his face looked like a wart hog with a sunburn. After school I brought a group of his friends over to offer their sympathy. This continued until he began to notice them snickering as they walked away and paying me for getting a look at him. It was twenty-five cents a visit. I made a lot more money than I ever did on my paper route by the end of that day.

"Look at the size of this gooey slug."

"Eeeewww, gross."

"Here's an old Cigarillo pack."

"Who cares man?"

"I found a rusted iron spike."

"Great, let's call the *Amherstburg Echo*, we found a railway spike beside the tracks."

"I found a *Playboy* magazine over here."

We all stopped.

"Where?"

"Just kidding."

"Very funny, Spit-Head."

"Hey guys, check this out," Sticks said in a serious voice.

He was up on the train trestle holding a thick, green, vine that was twisted around a tree branch and then trailed down the stone facing. He bent it smartly to show us how flexible it was.

"It's Tarzan time, boys."

"Yeah, right, you haven't got the guts."

"I'm swinging on this vine. It'll take me clear across the pond, and you can bring me my runners."

"You'll never make it because you're too chicken."

"I'm so doing it and then you'll want a try. Last one up here has to carry all our stuff through the bog."

This got our attention. We paused and thought.

"Naw, you're too chicken, Sticks."

"Chicken Sticks! Chicken Sticks! Chicken Sticks!" we shouted.

That did it. With a look in his eye like the one he got when he had to stop the last shot on net to win the game, he stood tall, arched his back like a diver, gripped the vine and swung.

Sticks almost made it. He was part-way over the pool when the branch broke. He collapsed in fright in the ugly water and came up howling. He was holding his foot and it was gushing blood. He just stood there on one foot, screaming and trying not to fall back into that foul pond. Like all of us, he was probably thinking of the leeches that we knew lived down in there. But that didn't stop us. Those invisible blood-suckers might have even accelerated our actions. We were, after all, the Rankin Street Raiders.

Wiry and Rogue, the biggest, rushed in and carried him out. Skeese and I gathered our stuff including the staffs we had cut. We covered his foot with damp socks and wrestled him on one foot through our hidden bramble path of burrs and nettles. It was teaming rain when we reached the road. Gripping our shoulders in turn and leaning on his staff, Stickwood lurched down the road with a tight grimace clenched on his face. In pain and fear, he never spoke.

We munched our food in soggy silence as we hobbled back like defeated troops on rations.

By the time we reached town, all our socks had been bloodied to help our wounded team mate. We decided to pitch them in a garbage can before we propped him up at the front door of his home. We even rinsed his wound at a drinking fountain when no one was looking. Our story was that Stanks cut himself while we were playing in a flooded ditch. He got five stitches and tetanus shot for his troubles.

Despite our schemes, Senior Blighter, his dad, called all our parents in a complete rage. In turn, we were all yelled at and grounded, probably at similar decibels and durations.

It wasn't our best day out at the Arch. But we did manage to squeeze some fun out of it, well, except for Sticks.

Chapter 3

Cub-Bagging 101

Boy Scouts didn't exactly suit the Rankin Street Raiders and the feeling was mutual. Oh, we loved being Cub Scouts: wearing tie-like scarves with toggles, playing games, singing, selling apples and collecting badges. For some reason we couldn't get enough merit badges. You could be awarded a badge for your uniform for almost anything as long as it had some vague relevance to learning. A fried egg and a toasted Pop Tart resulted in a cooking badge. One badge led to another. Stitching your cooking badge onto your sleeve got you a sewing badge. Building and painting a model Mustang muscle car (from a kit) meant a hobby badge. The sky wasn't even the limit. Being able to identify the Milky Way, the Big Dipper and the North Star put an astronomer badge on your shoulder. We couldn't spell astronomer, but we all had that badge. If you could skate, swim, ride a bike or shoot an arrow: badge, badge, badge and badge. Heck, we could even be funny and get an entertainment badge for it. The Cub Scout salute became increasingly difficult because we could hardly bend our arms, our sleeves were so rigid with badges. There might even have been a badge for the most badges. We had more badges than a Mexican generalissimo. We should have been in the Badge Book of Records.

But the best was camping. For the first time, we slept outside somewhere other than our backyards. We got to chop wood with our own personal hatchets that were slung from a cool leather sheath on our belts. Robin Hood had nothing on us. We also carried knives that were supposed to be for whittling and cutting stuff, but we mostly employed them for throwing into trees and playing Chew the Peg. That was a dangerous little game that involved two players standing across from one another. A turn was taken by throwing the knife into the ground near your opponent. If it didn't stick, it was a loss of turn. If the knife stuck, the other player had to stretch to reach it without moving one foot. If he couldn't, the knife was held by the blade tip to whack a twig into the dirt. Then the loser had to pull it out with his teeth. Smart players had their canteens with them to rinse their mouths after a loss. Even smarter players wore boots.

My dad taught me a lot of outdoor lore, but as Cub Scouts we learned things too, usually by mistake or accident because we were suddenly interested in what surrounded us. We had new-found powers of perception. We could identify trees and birdsong. We could identify animal tracks, spoor and sounds. We watched the sun rise and set and felt it move. For the first time, the moon shone on us like a spirit.

Suddenly, we could make hammocks and lean-tos from rope; split wood with accuracy and power by letting the head of the hatchet do the work; tell time by the sun; predict rain by the wind; dry our clothes by a fire; find the sources of streams; feed wild animals; follow trails; use binoculars and walkie-talkies and raise the flag.

We also got to make fires: big, blazing bonfires! We would eat burnt weenies on our sharpened sticks and half-cooked beans from a can. Then we sang along with our Akela around the fire. I don't know if there was a Cub Scout Leader School, but one of the prerequisites must have been playing the guitar and singing like an undiscovered Gene Autry. I mean, our guy could bring it. We hung off every syllable and note. And when it was our turn for the chorus, we shook the sugar maples, buffeted the birches and gave the tamaracks tremors. Finally, it was time for one or two ghost stories that always made us relieved that we were sharing a barracks with other Cubs. They were invariably told in a hushed, creepy voice with an orchestra of crickets, rustling, creaking, hooting and the odd howl behind us in the deepening dark. Some of our favourites were the Monkey's Paw, the Escaped Convict Axe-Murderer, Lost in the Woods, the Ghost Pirate and the Open Grave.

Yeah, Cub camping had it all. Where else could we be fearless and scared silly, tired and wide awake, alone in our thoughts but together in our activities, hungry but satiated by beans, wieners and charcoal marshmallows and under orders, yet proud of our accomplishments?

We were Cubs to the marrow. Badges, toggles, sitting cross-legged in a circle, the three-finger salute, Lord Baden-Powell, the buddy system, helping folks and the annual father and-son banquet; we were for it all. Just add gravy.

But by the time we hit Scouts though, we had enough routine and regimentation in our lives. From homework, practices and lessons to school, church and chores, another burden wasn't worth bearing. Plus, by then girls were starting to take up a lot of our time. Unless you had a woman Scout leader and that was usually somewhat suspect, there was no room for females in Scouts. We no longer enjoyed tying and untying knots like, well, knot-heads. Parading in robotic precision wasn't lifting our adventurous souls into new realms of accomplishment. Sure, climbing a rope was an athletic pursuit, but it was about fifty fathoms below scoring a goal or hitting a homer. Reporting to someone named Tawny Owl or Wolf-Fur was no longer on our dance cards, nor was cleaning our aluminum mess kits with sand until they sparkled.

In short, the Scouting movement had left us ahead.

So, we did what came naturally to us, we became rebel Scouts: riding just beyond or beside the rest of the herd. We played pranks on our fellow Scouts, arrived late and left early, laughed when it was inappropriate and were silent when an answer was required. We even questioned Scouting practices. The great architect of Boy Sprouts was now Lord Bathing Towel and we were throwing him in. The leaders sensed our resistance and began picking on us. There weren't enough newspapers or bottles collected on our annual drives. Our projects were never as good as the others. Our uniforms had to be adjusted constantly. Our shoes weren't shined, and our broad-rim hats weren't brushed. We were becoming a discredit to our troop and an affront to the organization. The Rankin Raider rebels secretly welcomed these rebukes and reprimands. We wore them like invisible badges.

Semaphore was the limit. It drove us over the Scouting cliff. It waved a red flag at our intelligence, was a slap in the face to our self-respect and a special kind of silly. It was in a stupid semester all on its lonesome. It was grandiosely goofy. Standing on top of a hill trying to spell help with two flags seemed to be the first requirement of acquiring your village idiot licence. Take off your shirt, wave it frantically over your head and call it a day. There were no hills near our Scout hall so the Semaphorist had to stand on top of a picnic table while his viewer or reader had to walk over to the other side of the park. Then the convoluted series of signalling began. It was like watching a crazy person baiting an invisible bull. The Scout who was supposedly being communicated with was to take notes and report back on what was said. When it was two of our Raiders' turn, Wiry was the flag-bearer and Sticks was the interpreter. In front of unimpressed Scout leaders wearing grimaces under their Royal Mounted Police hats, Scotty began whipping the two flags-on-sticks around like he was trying to spell out the words rather than signal then. He was corkscrewing, poking and slashing like a swordsman. Lenny was scribbling as fast as his fingers could fly. We other three Raiders laughed like donkeys. No one else moved or spoke. Sticks returned with his message to a silent troop.

"Well, what do you think he said, Master Stickwood?" the Scoutmaster asked harshly.

Stanks looked at his pad without a flicker of a grin and read steadily and loudly, "Home, home on the range, where the deer and the antelope play."

We fell on the ground twisting in convulsions of snorting giggles.

That incident pretty much signalled the start of our Scouting demise.

Not long after, the Scouts and Raiders reached the fork in the path on one last camp-out. It was our Waterloo, our Alamo and our Custer's Last Stand. We might as well have been unfurling the Jolly Roger when we did our Motown March into the encampment the first day. In short, we were both fired and resigned as Boy Scouts after this escapade.

Instead of billeting us among the other twenty Scouts, the five of us we were put in one tent where the leaders could keep us under surveillance. It was a week-long enterprise and for the first couple of days, we did as we were bid, kept our tent area in order, cleaned our equipment, chopped and carried wood, rinsed our laundry, kept the campfire burning and were surprisingly pleasant to all.

In the middle of the third night, we were awakened by a completely unknown sound, a series of splatters on our canvas ceiling. We heard some commotion from the other campers too. Soon the Scoutmaster's lighthouse beam of a flashlight turned the inside of our tent into daylight.

"What have you five been up to tonight?" he bellowed at us. Without waiting for our response, he added, "I knew it wouldn't take long before you started causing trouble. I should send you packing right now."

He hauled us out into the darkness of the forest, other lights splaying throughout the encampment. Standing around, shivering in our jammies, we began to protest and the other Scouts joined us. As the lights began to play over our tents, we realized that we'd all been egged. All the tents, except for the leaders', had been bombarded with a chicken coop full of eggs. Our canvases were covered in raw egg-wash, dripping and sticky in the dewy night. We pointed and pleaded our innocence.

"Alright, alright, settle down, girls," the Scoutmaster chided. "There's a Cub camp down in that hollow. They're just up to some harmless mischief. I'll have a word with their Akela tomorrow. You little darlings can get back to your beauty sleeps."

Grumbles and mumbles could be heard from all of us, not just the Rankin Street Raiders. We knew we would have to clean up the scrambled egg mess in the morning, but it was our pride that had been egged in the bargain. We were the superior beings. How dare these lesser creatures raid us! While the rest of the troop fell back into slumberland, we began plotting. Although we were reclining in our sleeping bags, we weren't about to take this affront lying down.

"An egg for an egg, I say."

"No, that's too easy and they'll be expecting it. We'll end up taking the blame for something they started."

"Why not just storm them with eggs, water bombs and firecrackers?"

"You've got balloons and firecrackers?"

"Well, no, but we have to get those little twerps back somehow."

"We have to make them pay, set an example, teach them a lesson."

"Yeah, no one raids the Raiders."

"It has to be a surprise. We'll be the ones who are prepared."

"And we have to delay our tactics," Rogue announced. "For one thing, they'll be on guard for an immediate retaliation and if we take our time, they'll get bold, thinking we've been told not to do anything because they're just little cubbies. We must make them play into our hands. I've got an idea, but I'm tired. I'll explain tomorrow when we have some time to ourselves."

After a breakfast of gloppy oatmeal and Tang we had to scrub down our tents, take a long hike, collect kindling and were then finally issued a rest period. When had we enlisted in the underage armed forces? We took the opportunity to slip away from the work farm that masqueraded as a Scout camp. Crouching in a clearing hidden from the troop, we listened as Rogan drew out a game plan with a sharpened stick in the dirt.

"Here's the Cub camp below. They have to climb up the hill to get to us and our tent is the closest to their route. About halfway down but a little to the left of the path is an open area that might work for us. It can't be seen from either camp. I say we secretly and quietly, taking turns so as not to draw any attention, dig a pit there, not too deep but not shallow either. Over the next two days, we can throw our eggshells, grease, burnt beans, dish soap and any other cooking crud into the bottom. Then we cover it with light sticks and top it off with pine branches and leaves. After the little punks get their courage back up, they're bound to strike again, and this is a perfect course for them to take if they want to stay out of sight off the path. They'll never see it coming."

He paused and looked at each of us in anticipation. "Well? Whaddya guys think of the camouflaged cub trap idea?"

Well, what do you think we thought? We loved it. We could see it happening. Hear the boughs break as the Cubs tumbled into our underground stink pot. We could feel the rush of pride and power surging through our Raider veins.

"Aces baby, aces!"

"This is gonna be fantastic."

"They'll be like mice in our rotten cheese trap."

"Those puny Cub sprouts won't know what happened until it's too late."

"And they'll come to us. How can we be to blame when they're doing the raiding?"

"Foolproof; a master plan."

"What a perfect counterattack."

"Ok, we start digging today, in twos, always with one as a lookout. Same goes for dumping the garbage. I think we've got two days max before they make their move again," Rogue warned, and we nodded.

Over the next two days, an unseen watcher gazing down from the tree tops would have witnessed a precise series of cagey and vigilant operations performed in unwavering unison by the Raiders. Lord Bathing Towel would have been proud of our manoeuvres, if not for their somewhat vile purpose: using our Scout shovels and hatchets to remove the earth and hack away at roots and vines, whistling warnings when anyone approached and volunteering for Kitchen Patrol duty to hustle the waste away to our secret pit, then carefully replacing and arranging the twigs and leaves on the surface.

When complete, it was about eight feet across and almost four feet deep. A Cub could climb out, but it would be a dirty, stinking struggle. Hard, private tasks were never so enjoyable. We were sowing the seeds in our garden of entrapment. It was alive, growing within us. Seldom was it out of our mirthful thoughts. Biding our time, we winked knowingly at one another. Only we knew why.

After two days we had difficulty sleeping. Every sound the woods produced held potential for us. The snapping of twigs, rustling of leaves and wind in the trees, kept us on alert. Another day passed and some doubt began to itch at us. We were losing ground; time was becoming a burn in our bellies. Our week was running out. And the stench in the trench was mounting. Despite our careful replacement of the foliage over the top, the reek was rising. It began to smell like a dead, bloated raccoon rotting in the sun with an extra odour of sewer gas. Had we misjudged the location? Did one of the Cubs see us creating the trap? Would there never be a second assault?

On the last night, the Raiders climbed into their sleeping bags one part grumpy, one part depressed and one part still hopeful. We didn't talk but each of us stayed awake as long as we could. At some hour in the black early morning, we heard a muffled shout and then a scream and then a longer more terrified scream. We sat up as one like androids coming to life. It sounded as if someone was stabbing a goat. We could hear the fear. There was no doubt, we had bagged a Cub! The camp was alive with flashlights, whistles, yelling, barked orders, scuffling and everyone wanting to know what was happening. Was there a bear? Had some convict from a ghost story broken into the camp? Was there a fire? Was there an accident? We Raiders were well aware of what was going on so we hung back, hiding our smiles in the shadows and watched as Scout and Cub leaders converged to wrestle the frightened little marauder out of the thatched stink pit. Our Scoutmaster took charge. He blew his whistle like a steamboat and sent everyone back to their tents. He told the Cub leaders to take their kid back to their camp, clean him up and make sure there were no more raids that night. They all slunk back down the hill to their hollow, half-dragging the whimpering and snivelling Cub Scout all the way with a few broken eggs in his jacket pocket.

We had our usual Plan B in case stuff really went south and we could tell that was the way the breeze was blowing.

"Check every tent and find out who did this," the Scoutmaster barked.

It might have been a sense of self-preservation despite the odds or just a way to delay our capture that drove us into our back-up mode. The five of us crawled into another tent occupied by junior Scouts. We told them to shut up and we slid underneath them, so it looked like there were only five boys lying in their sleeping bags. We were muffled underneath. Flashlights shone in, the Scouts were questioned and the leaders marched off. The Raiders waited for the hatchet to fall. They would find our tent empty, search the grounds and then eventually re-investigate each tent. It took about an hour. We even managed a few nervous giggles, despite our inevitably grim future. The Scoutmaster himself returned like a police chief with a warrant for our arrest. He commanded that we all come out. It took a few minutes as ten Scouts struggled out of a five-man tent.

There was always at least one geeky-guy Scout leader. He was the type who couldn't throw a baseball, couldn't get a date in high school and couldn't get a job or a life. These leaders were dangerous because they took any affront personally, resulting in an enjoyment of meting out punishment. Our guy was skinny, warty, pimply and probably had Nerd tattooed on his wrinkly ass. He had goggles for glasses and his hair lumped on one side like a dead squirrel. He spoke in squeaks. Bill Brindle was his name, but we called him Beak-Brain.

It was just our luck that he was placed in charge of our torture in the dark hours of that morning—just us and him, adult vermin versus the Rankin Street Raiders. We always took our shots in silence, refused to flinch, show pain or succumb. But we knew this sneaky bastard probably had some special plans for us, and we were right.

First, we had to fill in the Cub trap and that seemed fair enough to us. "Hurry up, I've got more work for you hot-shots before you get to go back to your warm beddy-byes," he whined, alternately shining his light in our eyes.

Then we were martialed out of camp like members of a chain gang. If Beak-Brain had been issued a gun he would have been pointing it at our backs. We came to an open area where our campfire wood was split and stacked; about three bush-cords' worth, eye-high.

"Now move the whole pile to the other side of the clearing, you disgusting disgraces to the Scout uniforms," Beak-Brain chirped at us.

We refused to give him the satisfaction of responding to anything he said and made as brisk a job as we could of it, but it still took us more than an hour. Our slavedriver drank greedily from his canteen and hummed in his high-pitched, nasal way all the while. When we finished, we turned as a group and stared at him.

"Now move it back," he said cheerfully.

After about three hours we had completed our tasks of digging and hauling wood, without a word. But our weasel leader wasn't finished. He was really enjoying his personal persecution.

"Follow me," he said with a hiss in his voice.

We slumped halfway back to camp to our water supply, an old pump.

"Now strip to your undies," he sniggered.

We looked at him with ferocity in our eyes to ensure he wasn't going to try anything he would regret. It was five against one and that one was a weakling. He motioned us to sit under the tap. Then he pumped icy water on us as we each took turns squatting rigidly under the stinging spigot. Everyone was given ten pumps. They felt like ten lashes. We never flinched or made a noise. No one breaks the Rankin Street Raiders. Besides, we knew that would be our last day as Boy Scouts.

Finally, we were allowed to put our clothes on, tramp back to camp and throw ourselves into our sleeping bags. As Beak-Brain flittered away we all finally broke our devout silence. It started as a snicker, grew to a chuckle, expanded into a guffaw and ended as a howl of laughter.

"We bagged a Cub!" we snorted and hooted. "We bagged a Cub!"

Chapter 4

Pirate Pizza

Arrivederci Roma, goodbye Naples and forget Florence. Ignore New York and wave away the Windy City. We had the best pizza in the world. It's called Windsor-style, and the way it's made and even sliced is different than all the rest, even the best of the rest. Right from the first flip, they have to be big pies. This spreads the flavours around, lets them breathe. The light crust is thin, delicious, baked in a dangerously hot oven until crispy but pliable like a flatbread and always seared on the underside. Toppings are few: usually pepperoni but chopped, mushrooms and olives, or peppers and they too are chopped. A sparse tomato sauce manages to be both basic and extraordinary with secret ingredients. Everything is secondary to the cheese. Pure, from the soil, Italian Buffalo mozzarella is the key: so thick you could walk across it, so gooey you could suffocate in it, so full of flavour you could never want to eat again, unless it was a Fargie "zzzza." The final essential is in the slicing. It seems odd, but it makes a huge difference. The pizza must be cut in long, slender strips. This concentrates the savouriness, makes it easier to eat and with so much cheese, helping to avoid a big blob of a pizza slice that is dripping all over your face, hands, clothes and shoes. And they were served with the respect they are due, in Pizza Parlours, not restaurants.

The best "zzza" joint in the whole area was right across from Rankin Street. The planetary-sized pies were created around the side of a pool hall, in a messy, shabby, doughy shop called Fargie's. The genius, Farragamo, who made these heavenly wheels of taste pleasure, was a squat, chubby guy with unkempt frazzles of steel-wool hair and a stubby beard that never seemed to grow. He had tattooed forearms like ham hocks, wore a dirty apron, smoked, swore and never laughed. No one knew his first name because everyone called him Fargie.

Until I ate my first Fargie pizza, I didn't know what pizza really was or could be. My mother, to keep costs down, would open a pizza-in-a-box, use the minimal ingredients and add hot dog rounds for toppings. It was never bacon or pepperoni; they were too expensive. The pies were cooked in two small baking pans. The result looked like red training wheels with chopped wieners caught in their spokes. I often wondered if the cardboard box would have tasted better. I didn't exactly look forward to pizza night.

I finally had my "zzza" awakening late on a Saturday night at Skeeser's house. I was on a sleepover with him. Terry was the oldest so the two of us got to stay up with his dad, who was known but never spoken to as Senior Bowl Cutter due to his preference for home haircuts administered by himself. His real name was Nes, short for Nestor, but nobody ever called him that either, not even God. A tall, dark-haired guy with carefully prepared hair and a corner smile, he seemed to be about six-foot-nineteen to us. He could be both deadly serious and surprisingly funny but there was just a moment between the two. We learned to keep a careful lookout for that moment.

Senior Bowl Cutter was reclining happily in his sleek Barcalounger chair with all kinds of levers designed not only for comfort but to inspire envy in everyone else in the room. Even the Prime Minister would not have been allowed to park himself on that throne. We were camped out at his feet on our sleeping bags, watching an old gangster film full of smouldering cigarettes, hot lead and even more smoking hot dames. Peering into adulthood in the half-light, we were in every scene, watching from the shadows around the corner. When some maroon got shot, we took the bullets, too. When a wise-mouthed weasel squealed we knew he was not long for this world. When a broad got kissed, we felt that flame.

As for the coppers, we were usually against them during our Raider business, but when evil hoodlums were on the lam, we were rootin' for Johnny Law to catch them and throw them in the slammer. When Senior Bowl Cutter laughed with a slight snarl, we followed his spade suit. We didn't know why we were laughing, but it sounded tough.

Our plan was, part-way through the grainy sandpaper of a film, we would announce that we were going into the kitchen to find some snacks. Skeese and I waited about five minutes, not bothering to look for anything. We returned to announce to his dad that all we could find was Vernors, a kind of grown-up soda pop that tasted like beer.

"I'll have one of those," he said, waving us off.

"Do you want it on the rocks or in the can?" we asked in our politest servant voices.

"Rocks," he said in his deep, that's enough of that stuff, I'm watching this movie, voice.

After a few more chortles at the film and a coupla slugs of his Vernors, Skeeser mustered up enough courage to half-mutter, "So, Dad, can we order a pizza?"

More gunplay, more chicks screaming but not a word from the Bowl Cutter of Rankin Street. We watched the movie and waited. There was absolutely no way we were going to make the request again, no point in antagonizing the guy who would be paying. During a commercial break, his combed head began to turn so slowly it was hard to tell if it was moving, especially in the half-glow of the TV. It was wearing that smug smile when it looked down at us from what seemed to be the ceiling.

"Extra-large pepperoni, mushroom and bacon," it said and sank back into the floating caresses of the easy chair.

We darted to the phone, called Fargie's and were back in an instant, in front of the mugs, molls and murder. The doorbell rang about five hours later it seemed.

"Get me my wallet," Bowl Cutter commanded. "Only a fifty-cent tip, and don't drop the pizza."

"Yessir."

"And be quiet. If you wake the other kids there won't be enough for you," he warned, and we heard him chuckle.

Then the ritual began. The prize pizza was placed lovingly on a short side table within reach of the three of us. It was clear that Mr. Thatcher would have the first ceremonial slice. He moved with care and precision. When he opened that lid, I had never witnessed a feast that smelled or looked better. The rich aroma instantly filled the room. The pie was gooey, glowing and steaming hot. It seemed to be moving, undulating, in that giant, grease-soaked box. It made my head swim, my stomach growl and my fingers itchy, until I was handed my first slice. It was skinny but I still needed two hands to secure it and shove it into my mouth. I took my time tasting, for the first time, all the toppings, sauce, crust and cheese as one barrage of flavour. I was chewing all that was good and possible in food. When I looked up, half the pizza was gone. Skeeser and his dad were chomping like racehorses while rolling the next slice up to knock back in one bite. I couldn't believe what I was seeing but it only took a few seconds before I was rolling up and gulping down as many pieces as I could before the whole magic mozzarella kingdom disappeared.

The pizza parade had passed in a few, too-short moments. We relaxed, slurping Vernors, into our distended and satiated bellies. A few burps were heard among the "Blam, blam, blams," barking from the television. The pizza pleasure experience was warm inside us, while we digested it and the mobster movie.

As I slept comfortably in our little encampment of two on the Thatcher family room floor, I dreamt that I was floating lazily in sparkling surf surrounded by mermaids. They were feeding me Fargie's pizza.

The second time I fed on Fargie's pizza was with the Raiders. It was a summer weekday when we were off school. There were four of us sitting around on Rogan's front porch: Rogan, me, Stanks, and Skeeser. Wiry was setting pins in his dad's bowling alley. Wiry's dad had pitched relief for the Tigers and sometimes took us out to catch curveballs. They broke three feet, hissing and writhing like snakes. We called him Senior Hurler. He was funny and soft-spoken with a mass of sandy, curly hair, a wide brow and a stocky build. He was also tough with a fast temper. But he could spin a baseball.

We all had kid-jobs for our savings and a little extra spending money. I had a weekly newspaper route and cut grass for the church. Rogue did some maintenance at his mum's office, and Skeeser had a daily paper route. Sticks always seemed to be in between, beside and behind jobs. Unless it came to hockey, he was short on ambition and cash.

We were wondering what to do with ourselves when we saw Fargie's brother, Joe climb into his old heap of a station wagon that farted oil and creaked down the street. He was a stubbier, shorter version of Farg but meaner if that was possible. Joe was making a pizza delivery and he was never happy about that. He preferred to play pool until he was summoned to do some work at his brother's shop.

"Hey, anybody got any money? Let's order a pizza!" Rogan said.

We all looked up, eyebrows knit, head's being scratched, a big WHAT? on our faces. This had never been thought of let alone done before. We only ate pizza for dinner or late at night. And it was ordered by and enjoyed by adults. But we could smell Fargie's from where we sat.

"What about our parents?" I asked.

"My mother's not home and no one else will know," Rogue said confidently.

"We always eat it so fast, it should be ok, I guess," Sticks said hesitantly.

"We can stash the box in the garbage bin at the park," I added.

"Ok, so who has any moolah?" Rogan wanted to know.

We pooled all our pennies, nickels, dimes and quarters. No one had any paper money. It added up to the lunch-time special large from noon to 3 p.m. with a thirty-cent tip. Sticks was broke but he vowed to pay us later. If the slices were an uneven number, we all knew he'd be short one.

The G-Man ran in to order and was back with some pops from his fridge. His big chest puffed out in pride, "I ordered the free delivery," he announced and then laughed like a jackal.

"But it's just up the street, right over there," Skeese asked him.

"I know, I know, Joe will be really pissed," Rogan replied with a wink.

We sat on the porch and waited for the last train to Pizza Gulch. This was breaking new ground, taking us into a zone we had yet to experience and the first of many clandestine forages for fast food. The successful plan made it all taste sweeter and richer.

I spent half my boyhood waitin' on a Fargie's pizza. It always seemed to take a year and a day because we knew what a delicious experience was coming our way. Soon, pirate pizza would be delivered right to our door. Raise the Jolly Roger!

When dumpy and disgruntled Joe dragged himself out of Fargie's with our pie, we held our breath. We watched him place it on the passenger seat and then step back to read the address. His beady, rat eyes were squinting in the summer sun. He finally raised his head, scratched his dirty hair and looked at the Rankin Street sign. Joe read the address again. He paused, his dumb gaze falling on top of us. We waved like tourists leaving on a cruise ship! We yelled, jumped up, down and around punching one another in the shoulder. Sticks fell off the porch, and I tackled him before he could get up. We watched in glee as Giuseppe Farragamo squeezed himself into his wreck of an auto, slammed the door and drove in first gear toward us, smoke billowing out of his exhaust pipes and his ears.

We could hear him swearing "*A fanabla*" and "*Pezzo de merda*" before he arrived, but we didn't care. We were too top-of-the-world pleased with ourselves. Plus, we couldn't understand a word he hollered.

Rogan paid him quickly in between Italian curses that may have also been directed at our mothers.

"You little bastards try this again, I'll tell Fargie, and you damn kids and your *familia* will be cut off!" A couple more "*Figlio un-Canes*" and he was headed back to his dingy cave of a pool hall.

We feasted like starved demons on that precious pizza pie, soaking in the moment, the flavours and the victory. Then we took the back route, cut through some yards to the park and threw the evidence in the garbage. Another victory for the Rankin Street Raiders. Turned out that the pilot of this plot, Greg Rogan, had roast beef that night for his troubles. He was stuffed but satiated.

From then on, I waged a one-boy war with my dad, also known to us as Senior Drill (Sergeant) because he had a flattop buzz-cut, no one messed with him, and he could snap out orders that would make your thoughts freeze. I was fighting to get him to buy our family's first Fargie's. Per usual, I worked through my mum but when it came to what was considered spending foolish money, I was getting shot down. I tried different tactics. I talked my sister and brother into joining my campaign. I did chores without being asked. I washed Senior Drill's car.

I even managed to reduce the number of windows I broke at home. I had smashed so many panes of glass, all by accident. Some of the missiles I used were chestnuts on strings, footballs, baseballs, hockey pucks, rocks, basketballs, India Rubber balls, peashooters, a bucket, my brother's puppet, a potato, a slingshot, a Frisbee, a water balloon and a boomerang. No matter how accurate I tried to be, these toys and sporting goods had a mind of their own when it came to the McKendrick residence's panes of glass. No bay or picture window was safe. Basement, second story, front, back, side or garage windows all cracked or broke under pressure. I even took out a few screen doors, but that wasn't my fault either.

My personal best in one year was nine. I came to know the glass guy at the hardware store rather well. After a while he started to ask me what I had used each time I broke one. I'd bring the measurements, a shard of the pane in question and 25 cents. He'd whistle and we'd talk about how it happened, then he'd wrap up the new window in thick paper and give me a fresh pack of putty. Except for the shouting and being banished to my room, I kinda enjoyed the procedure. I could have had a successful career in the window trade.

While I was engaged in the lobbying for Fargie's pie, I even stopped throwing things for a time. I was on a mozzarella mission, making pleas for pizza, bargaining against the pizza-in-a-box. I had tasted the El Supremo; how could I give up and settle for less?

One afternoon my dad couldn't take it anymore. He sent me to Fargie's with some cash, but he wasn't happy about it. It was going against his will, and I knew he didn't think it was going to be worth the price. But I didn't care. Swaggering down Rankin Street, in a Fargie delirium, I stopped to pat neighbours' dogs. I moved a tricycle near the road to safety. I waved mightily to old Mrs. Demchuk, sitting scowling at me from her porch under a thatch of frizzled hair in crusty curlers.

"Have a fine day!" I said and then muttered, "You old hag."

I noticed some beautifully arranged flower gardens, appreciated colourful, crisp laundry waving from a clothesline. The world was smiling at me and I was grinning back. With every delighted step, I drew closer to the Promised Land.

When I pushed open the rickety side door, my carefree thoughts were sucked out of my head. Fargie, the pizza virtuoso, was there at the counter, rolling up his sleeves to reveal the tattoos on his muscles and staring at me like I was about to steal something. It was just the two of us. He looked like an angry, smoking, flour-dusted troll.

I shrunk to about four inches and squeaked, "One large pepperoni, green pepper and mushrooms please."

"You got money, kid?" he rasped at me.

"Yessir," I replied shakily holding up some small bills.

"It'll be about 20 minutes. Don't touch anything."

He didn't have to tell me that. I didn't even want to sit on the once-orange and cracked plastic chair that looked like it had been soaked in grime. But I had to and was given a rare glimpse of the master in action. Sinewy arms kneaded the dough into a feathery white pillow. He even spun it and tossed it in the air, giving me a wink. I just sat there like a statue of a scared boy, eyes and mouth wide open. My ears were probably wide open as well in case he asked me anything. Fargie slathered on the sauce, flicked the toppings on like he was dealing cards and then wrenched open the huge, yawning, spark-belching oven. I felt the blast from across the room and wondered if I still had eyebrows.

"Just a few more minutes, kid," he said less aggressively. Maybe he saw the awe in my eyes?

On the way home, I was on a quick march. I knew I had to get that first Fargie's pie back before it cooled. My arms grew tired from holding it like a waiter serving pheasant under glass. So, I turned the box sideways and carried it under one arm like a stack of schoolbooks. I picked up my pace. From one backyard, I saw two kids stop playing catch to stare at me. "They're jealous," I thought. A canary-yellow, rag-top GTO slowed down as it passed me. The two teenagers with slicked hair in the front seat started laughing and pointing.

"I guess everybody loves Fargie's pizza," I was thinking, smiling to myself. Even creepy Mrs. Demchuk started waving and rocking in her chair as I hurried past. I thought I saw the pooch I had patted on the way to Fargie's halt in his tracks, cock his head sideways and yip at me.

When the entire family gathered 'round the kitchen table for this special treat, so much pleaded for, much talked about and anticipated, I was bursting to open the lid and reveal the treasure I knew simmered beneath. What I saw rivalled any horror movie I had ever witnessed. All the pepperoni, mushrooms, green peppers, cheese and secret sauce had rolled into an ugly glob on one side of the bare pizza shell. My heart sank and my stomach churned. Gasping, I was trying to figure what had happened. "Did you drop this expensive pizza?" my pa demanded loudly. "What happened to it?" my sister piped up. "Are they supposed to be like this?" my brother wanted to know. My mother was mum.

The realization came to my father and me at the same time. I thought it, he said it.

"You dumb nut, you carried it home sideways didn't you?"

Usually, I could find a way out of a corner but there was nowhere to turn, no way out, no help for me. I was just thinking that I was glad Fargie didn't know about this atrocious affront to his ministry of mozzarella. I was also thinking that I couldn't have possibly looked more stupid walking home. No wonder people gawked. I couldn't have looked any dafter if I had been walking on my hands and carrying the pizza on my feet.

No one said anything. We sat stonily, glumly watching my mother spread out the dead waste of a pizza. She looked like she was patching a flat tire that would never hold air. The McKendrick household did not order another pie from Fargie's or anywhere else for years. My mum, however, did show the box version the door and began making her own pizzas from scratch. They were pretty good, but no sirens sang to me.

Chapter 5

Buccaneers of Boblo

We sat hunkered miserably over our desks, legs sweaty and welded to our seats, eyes bleary and salty from the heat, brains listless in the humidity, like galley slaves sweltering below deck and the equator, gasping for breath and dreaming of ice-cold drinks. It was math class in late June with less than two weeks to go and we were stuck in a giant two-storey red brick perspiration box with yawning rectangular windows to allow the furnace blasts full reign into the room while the dull flapping of the cracked wings of the brittle old ceiling fan pushed the torrid air down to scorch us further. Mr. Hodgson, from under his slick and greasy grey hair with a comb-over part and behind his steamed twin walls of eyeglass, was snoring out equations. If only there was one for getting out of that school.

But something interrupted him. At first tiny and distant, it swept closer, gaining volume until a sweet, soul sound wafted into our class:

"I need love, love
To ease my mind
I need to find, find, someone to call mine
But Mama said
You can't hurry love
No, you just have to wait
She said love don't come easy
It's a game of give and take."

It was the ice cream coolness of the Supremes, Motown's finest girl group, and according to Scotty Whaley, the Motor City's music machine's finest, period. That summer they released their greatest hit, "You Can't

Hurry Love." And there was no place on earth where it could be heard more often or louder than Boblo Island, an amusement park nestled between Canada and the United States on the Detroit River, just across the channel from the end of Rankin Street. While the Arch was the Raiders' natural shrine and retreat, Boblo was our man-made refuge, ripe for pillaging every year for too-few months. Its annual opening was the surest sign that the summer tide had washed into town.

Like an apparition on a mission, the song swept in upon us, driven by a dozen loudspeakers the size of phone booths, turning the classroom into a cartoon. The seemingly welded clock began to keep time to the beat, while the ancient, battered fan picked up the rhythm. The suddenly animated numbers in our textbooks leapt up off the pages, paired off, held each other close and danced, swirling on air. A refreshing breeze somehow settled on our shoulders. We all hummed the chorus while the Supreme Goddesses gave us a lesson in love. Finally, the music lifted us from our seats and floated us across the river to our island paradise.

Wham! Hodgson's ruler cracked across his desk, dragging us back from Boblo. "We have work to accomplish, ladies and gents, unless some of you would prefer to stay here after school!" He was greeted with a soundless chorus of negative headshakes.

The Motown magic spell was broken. It was a curse and a deliverance. A momentary reverie, a respite from the drudgery and the ever-tightening circle of slow death by numbers, but it was worth it. Summer was here and soon we'd be in fifth gear.

Boblo had everything we junior privateers could possibly hope to plunder from rollercoasters, cotton candy kiosks, a Midway and rubber, shrunken head souvenirs to a roller rink, bump 'em cars, a creepy Funhouse and a zoo with real Bengal tigers. Not to mention two gargantuan Mississippi-style riverboats, the *Ste. Claire* and the *SS Columbia*, that transported revellers from Detroit to the Boblo docks a few times daily. A much smaller ferry, the *Papoose*, made Canadian runs from the 'Burg.

When we set sail to cross the Detroit River's currents of adventure to our island of dreams, we raised the Skull and Crossbones, fired our cannons of conquest and landed with knives in our teeth. We were in a constant state of excitement and exhaustion whenever we visited. We knew that every second we were on that mystic island was bestowed upon us by the twin Gods of Amusement and Adventure.

Boblo was originally called Bois Blanc (White Woods) by French settlers in the area in the late 1600s due to the large population of birch trees made more visible by exposure from the waterways that flowed around the small island, only three miles long and less than a mile wide. Other than some sporadic farming and a Catholic Mission, Bois Blanc was largely untouched until the War of 1812 when the British used it to stage surprise raids on American troops heading up or down the river, to and from Detroit. Eventually a few block houses: sturdy, square, thick-walled structures with tiny window slits to allow for long rifles were built on the island. One survived as an historical site of interest when the Boblo train ride circled the isle. Pock-marked by musket ball fire and strong as a wooden tank, it never ceased to draw some form of attention.

The block house was also a place for young couples to exchange physical pleasantries on moonlit nights, discovered on occasion by the Rankin Street Raiders making their covert rounds, often as surprised as the startled older teenagers.

The Raiders were pretty much born into a life of Boblo buccaneering as their avenue was named after the Rankin family who owned the island in the latter half of the 1800s; first by Colonel Arthur Rankin, a Member of Parliament for the local Essex riding in 1869 and then by his son Arthur Rankin, a celebrated stage actor in New York. Arthur had a palace of an estate built on Bois Blanc that included manicured grounds, game birds, animals and gardens.

Eventually the island was sold to the Detroit, Belle Isle and Windsor Ferry Company. Under that firm, in 1898, it opened with picnic areas, sporting activities, concession stands and its first amusement ride: a huge carousel. For promotional purposes, it was dubbed Boblo and continued as a temple for fun-seekers for almost a century. By the time the Rankin Street Raiders landed on its seemingly always sunny shores, it was at its zenith, one of the largest, diverse and most unusual amusement parks anywhere.

And its attractions seemed endless. Floating serenely between two countries, it was one-part thrills, dancing, roller-skating and raucous laughter and another part spacious lawns, woods laden with lush vegetation and hidden historical discoveries.

Our favourites were, of course, the rides. Technologically advanced, they were purposely designed to magically transform adults into screaming children as they flew mid-air. The German-engineered Wild Mouse or Wilde Maus was the first such construction causing white knuckling, screeching and pleading to bring the so-called ride to a merciful end. A roller-coaster with speed and turns sharper than a Bowie blade, it also induced vomiting. The Raiders all ralphed more than a few times throughout the park either from over-eating or the gut-wrenching thrill rides or both. It was another kind of badge of honour for us.

Although we did eventually invent an antidote: one can of Vernors and you were good for anything Boblo tried to attack your guts with. And it worked. Probably due to the ginger content, but we kept the secret to ourselves, gleefully witnessing many a hapless child or hopeless adult puking in the shrubbery or even worse, letting fly from his or her buckled-in seat on the ride, spraying half-digested hot dogs, fries and milkshakes over the suddenly horrified merry-makers below.

Vernors, a kind of caramel-coloured soda, a cross between ale and beer, wasn't as sweet as other brands which gave it a depth of flavour. It was tough-guy pop to us, a kind of ginger-beer without the alcohol. Invented in the 1860s by a Detroit pharmacist named James Vernor, it is the oldest soda pop still in production in North America. The main bottling plant was in Detroit until the 1960s.

After downing a bottle of Vernors, we would climb aboard every ride we could afford. You had to graduate to the bigger, more aggressive rides based on your height and age. We conquered them all. The Zugspitze was a heavy, low-to-the-ground roller-coaster that ripped people almost out of their skins and when you thought it was over and you had enough, it would repeat the process only in reverse. The Caterpillar scooted around its track with incredible speed and then a canopy would rise over the ride like the closing of a dome and passengers became trapped in darkness as it picked up even more speed whizzing forward in ever-dizzying circles. The Round-Up had you strapped in standing like a moon mission then it spun you up, around and threatened to shake you into next week. The Scrambler cranked riders toward one another then jolted them sideways at the last second, until they felt like scrambled eggs. The Whip, one of the oldest of the fear-enhancing rides, had its own building where it would speed a group per car to one end of the track and then crank them sideways, cracking their backs and brains. Another old and adored ride was the Bug. It would take four or more passengers on a bounding, hilly chase around a mogul track. Part of the fun was seeing strangers begin to gasp and grip in terror beside you. And the Super-Satellite made you feel like jet pilots, rocketing up and around in circles.

While the twin ferry boats, on a mission of joyous diversion, dropped off and picked up passengers by the thousands at the landing pier on the Canadian side, private pleasure boats swarmed the marina on the island's leafy, lazy stretch of shoreline. Swimmers and sun bathers flocked to the other end where a peninsula of white sand beckoned them and fishermen congregated off the extended tip, angling for sweet-tasting pickerel and perch. All the while, the steady traffic of monolithic freighters designed only for the Great Lakes, could be viewed close-up, easing through the two channels, confidently circumventing Boblo like moving city blocks. Perhaps in honour of their daily passing or for show or convenience, an aged Great Lakes freighter, the *Queenston*, was half-sunk in front of the main gates to act as the central dock for the duration.

Known as the Boblo Boats, the *Ste. Claire* and the *Columbia* were custom-constructed at the turn of the century for the sole purpose of conducting excitement lovers 20 miles up and down the river, to and from the amusement park, a task they dutifully performed for most of the 1900s. Triple-deckers, with a fourth, top deck for crew, they were propeller-driven steamships, designed like Mississippi paddle-wheel boats, about 200 feet long and 50 feet wide, with the amazing capacity for 2,500 passengers. Originally coal-fired, they were eventually converted to oil. Designed and engineered by a quietly reserved genius - Frank E. Kirby of the Detroit Dry Dock Company, they were two of more than a hundred vessels he created largely for use on the Great Lakes. Considered one of the United States' greatest nautical architects, his expertise was relied upon during some U.S. international naval transport planning and battle engagements.

At night, especially on the midnight cruises, the Boblo Boats became island icons onto themselves, pleasure palaces lit up with what seemed to be a thousand Christmas trees twinkling above the water with live bands playing Dixieland, Swing, Jazz, Motown and early rock music that lifted and lilted into the evening while couples kicked it up on the dance floor and party people smoked and drank with gleeful abandon. No one could see and hear those statuesque ships pass without wishing themselves aboard.

It was a singular island of plenty, the stuff myths and memories are made of, where millions of Americans and Canadians through the generations gathered to wave bon voyage to their cares, scare themselves just enough, soak up as much delight as possible, dance, laugh, hug, sing and then sail dreamily home under a canopy of stars, in love with life and one another.

Boblo was also a kind of enchanted training ground for the Raiders. Here was a perfect place that begged to be pillaged, offering us so many opportunities for adventure and furtive scheming that it made us woozy. It tested our skills and our ingenuity. When we were first old enough to be allowed to sail to our fair-game isle of plenty on our own, we started small. We soon learned that rides like the Wild Mouse, Round-Up and Ferris Wheel not only turned visitors inside out, but they also turned them upside down, resulting in a shower of coins. We would dart into the open, scoop up as many nickels, dimes and quarters as fast as we could, spurred on by the passengers above shouting at us to stop stealing their money. After being yelled at by one of the ride operators who was threatening to call security, we decided to approach him and a few others and cut them in on our swag. From then on, when riders hollered at the guys operating the rides, they just shrugged their shoulders. For us It was pennies and more monies from Boblo heaven.

But, climbing unsteadily out of their seats, some pissed-off patrons would have at the worker.

"Hey, buddy, those kids just stole all my change. Whaddya gonna do about it?"

"I am sorry, sir but these things happen. It's just gravity."

"Gravity my ass. Those little weasels are thieves and you're letting them get away with it."

"My first concern is for the safety of the passengers, you included. My attention is focused on the proper running of the ride and that people arrive and depart unharmed."

"Why don't you call security? Never mind all this mumbo-jumbo about safety."

"I cannot leave my post. I have to ensure the smooth conduct of the ride and the protection of my clientele."

"Clientele be damned. I'm calling security."

"Certainly, sir. Their building is over there. Ask for Big Nick."

Big Nick was the head of the private force that policed the island. He was about the size of a grizzly bear but with more attitude and altitude. He had the girth of a rain barrel, a megaphone for a voice and a permanent grimace, probably because he had to squeeze in and out of his uniform every work/watch day. Retired from the Navy, he had forearms like fuzzy, boat buoys with anchor tattoos stretched across them. Nick smoked, cussed and spat, all at the same time.

We knew from our first meeting that we had to stay on this guy's good side, if he had one. Often, we would stop by his compact station with an extra ice-cold Vernors or some beef jerky. He always accepted these offerings with a grunt, like he deserved it or we owed him or both. We began to quietly let him know if we saw any older guys acting up or bothering people. Eventually, he would ask us if we'd seen any potential problems that day. When that happened, we knew we had landed Big Nick. But it had taken all five of us to reel him in

Almost all the Boblo workers, from the people running the arcade to the ride operators, ticket sellers, souvenir sellers and roller-rink attendants to the food-service cooks and waitresses, groundskeepers and maintenance employees were from the 'Burg. It was only a five-minute ride across the channel on the *Papoose*. Among the Raiders and our friends, we knew cousins, brothers, sisters, aunts and uncles who were hired to work in some capacity on Boblo. We became increasingly pleasant to them. Skeeser was able to somehow wrangle free passes from a woman on his *Windsor Star* paper route who was a ticket taker. He would often saunter over to her booth on a hot day, ice cream cone or cold pop in hand for her, while we watched from afar.

"Good afternoon Mrs. Dawson. I hope this will help you to cool off on such a hot day," he would say smiling with extra sugar on top.

"Why Terrence, you shouldn't have and aren't you getting to be a handsome young man?"

"Yes, Ma'am, I am and you're still as pretty as those peonies over there."

"I hope you are enjoying yourself and thank you for the prompt delivery of my paper," she said, blushing.

"Yes, Mrs. Dawson. Can I get two tickets for the Tilt-a-Whirl? I really need five for my buddies but all I can afford is two."

"I'll tell you what, my replacement is late today, and I have to use the rest rooms so if you cover for me for a few minutes, I think I can arrange for a few more tickets."

Next thing we know Skeese was selling tickets like he was born for it.

"Step right up, ladies, gents and kids, the best rides this side of Puce. Don't be shy, ask your parents for change. Three for a buck, that's a steal. Thrills of a lifetime for pocket change. C'mon up."

Mrs. Dawson was good for twenty tickets and we were good for the rest of the day.

Working the cold pop or ice cream routine, we would give them to one of our ride- operator cousins once removed. He or she would pretend to take our ticket and, in some cases, let us stay on the ride for an extra trip or two.

With free passes for pillaging and our pockets lined with filthy lucre, we began to branch out into more serious skulduggery.

A mini-putt golf course had been ill-advisedly erected in the heart of the Midway near the Ferris Wheel and the Wild Mouse, two of the most popular rides. We figured out how to get kicked off the course pretty early on by hitting the balls too hard on the outdoor carpet greens and then outside the fairways into the ankles and calves of passersby. After one of us knocked a milkshake out of somebody's hand thirty feet away, the golfing was called to a loud halt.

"Hey, everyone on the mini-putt stay where you are," ordered the scruffy, unshaven course manager under the soiled Boblo Captain's hat, hand-rolled cigarette dangling from his grimy mouth.

He marched from hole to hole and asked every player to show him the single golf ball they had been issued at the entrance. Of course, we five Raiders had zippo to show.

"Ok, you lot, off the course and you're lucky I don't have security throw you on the next boat home, you little bastards."

We slunk away gritting our teeth but by the time we were chugging our next Vernors and chomping on orange Creamsicles, Wiry had come up with a scheme that couldn't fail. The Black Flag would be raised over the ninth hole once more.

"Hey guys, next time we come over, let's bring our own balls and keep the ones from the course. Then, when we get asked, we will always have our original golf ball," Wiry suggested.

"Yeah, and when we go back, let's wait until there's nothing but kids on the mini-putt, then we don't look so obvious," Rogie added.

By ransacking our dads' golf club bags, we solved our sporting and marauding problem. Biding our time on the sidelines, in the shadows, like robbers waitin' on the stagecoach, we checked through when the coast was clear and fell in behind a group of guys older than us.

Soon we were chipping the extra balls in loops over the low fence that surround the putting area. It seemed to be raining dimpled white orbs. We took turns hitting, crowding around so the shooter couldn't be seen driving the ball like Arnold Palmer. Rogie knocked over a creepy sign directing folks to the Funhouse. Sticks chipped one into a guy's lap while he was whooshing by on the Scrambler. Skeese banked one off the goofy Boblo Bear mascot's knee. Wiry lodged one in the rough, taking out a flowerpot and spraying dirt. And I hit the sight-seeing train with a "thonk" as it rounded a corner up ahead of our mini links. And that was just the beginning.

By the time we ran out of our own ammo, there was a lineup at the mini-putt clubhouse. Former adventure-seekers were screaming and yelling blue, red and orange murder. The Raiders waited confidently at the eighth hole, each of us with our club-issued golf ball in hand.

"You rats again," Captain Grimy shouted at us.

"Lemme see the golf balls, every one of you. Right now!"

We all held our alibi's up to him like we were unveiling the winning project at the science fair.

"I don't know how you did it but you better clear outta here before I call security."

"We don't know what you're mumbling about," Rogan said smiling. "Go ahead, call Big Nick. I'm sure he'll be interested in whatever evidence you have that we've done anything wrong."

"Just trying to improve our golf games," Sticks added.

"I'm five under par and am going to finish my championship round," Whaley chimed in. "Have ya got a leaderboard for low scores?"

Grimy balled his fists and stomped back to his station, leaving a trail of dank smoke and sweat in his wake while we congratulated one another with punches to the shoulder and sniggering.

"Par for the course baby, par for the course," I chanted after him.

Self-satisfaction aside, we knew we had to draw light at the mini-putt, leaving a stretch of time between our escapades that day and our next appearance on the fabric greens. Maybe delay it, at least until Grimy had a day off.

We turned our attention to other possibilities that our small God Sport offered us.

One backyard-bonfire-hot day, to cool off and engage in some high-jinx, we all purchased squirt guns in town before sailing to our island Byzantium. They were ray gun models like they used on *Lost in Space*, *Forbidden Planet* and *My Favourite Martian*. We were packin' liquid, alien firepower. After strolling about and covertly soaking and shooting everything we could think of from pompous peacocks strutting about, thanks to Arthur Rankin, forcing them to scream and fan their feathers at us to frightened Fun-house riders thinking drizzle from above was part of the scary experience, we hit upon an idea. A new lemonade stand had been set up near the front gates and the drinks were free that day as part of the grand opening promotion.

"Hey, why not pour some of this stuff into our squirt guns?" Sticks suggested.

This brought an immediate halt to our greedy slurping.

"Yeah, and the refills don't cost anything so we can re-load whenever we want," Skeese said.

"It can be looked at as free advertising for the lemonade," I added.

"Gimme some skin on that one, Stanks," I said.

Our pirate selves left our bodies, wandered out and floated among the happy Bobloites, seeking ways to employ our suddenly enhanced weaponry. Their brigand visions of lemonade bursts from the skies returned to us. Half the rides in the park were airborne. What could be easier, more leisurely and covert than firing our Bueton Nebulizers from above? Until the sweet and sour stickiness set in, the cheerful, unsuspecting victims would think there was a brief rain shower or a mist wafting down on them.

"We have to be certain that no one sees anything, especially security," Whaley said, waking us from our collective dream.

"Shoot from the hip so our guns aren't exposed and only one shooter per ride," Rogeman cautioned.

We marauders marched in a lively, unison fashion toward the lemonade kiosk. The Raiders would be flying high soon, armed and vaguely dangerous.

It was almost too easy. Boblo's excitement machines spun and spiralled with such furious movement that no one on most of the rides cared what anyone else near them was doing.

Usually, they were trying not to look scared while desperately hanging on to save their lives, even though they were buckled into their seats. And our casualties below responded invariably by wiping something moist from their hair or hats, looking up and then around. Seeing nothing, they shrugged and walked on, probably relieved that some kid hadn't released a Technicolor yawn upon their persons. Later, finding stickiness on their daughters' curls or their sons' ball caps, parents blamed it on cotton candy or pop or candy bars.

Our main targets were groups of greaser teenagers with decks of smokes stuck in their t-shirt sleeves, tight, shiny jeans with their empty wallets chained to their belt loops and ducktail haircuts structured with quarts of Brylcreem fashioned with crud-clotted combs. Wiping the syrupy fruit juice from their pimpled faces, cursing and searching, they never even came close to noticing us. This wasn't our first covert ops rodeo.

It was like we were watching our own movie, in charge of the special effects. And it was a sort of slow-motion mayhem, unobserved by everyone but our Raider selves. We could even laugh out loud at some of the Boblo lovers' reactions because no one could hear us above the clanking and cranking of the rides, Motown-booming loudspeakers, screaming and cheerful shouting. Christmas, Halloween, Victoria Day and birthdays all packaged up for us in a gift from pirates' past.

To avoid drawing attention, we took turns getting lemonade refills and reloading our futuristic guns in the shadows, behind trees and shrubs. After about an hour of showering the sticky liquid upon the festive crowd on the pavement paths below, not wanting to push our plundering luck, we hid our weapons and discreetly disappeared into the crowd like the ghosts of swashbucklers.

Before we left the dock to board the *Papoose* to head home, we treated ourselves to a final complimentary lemonade to enjoy on the short but satisfying cruise.

Chapter 6

The Year of the Tiger

Pucks and hardballs, hockey sticks and baseball bats, rinks and diamonds, umpires and referees, skates and spikes, new-mown grass and freshly flooded ice, catchers and goalies, centre field and centre ice, home plate and the net, scoring hat tricks and hitting for the cycle, helmets and ball caps, the blue lines and sidelines, the batter's box and the crease and winter and summer. Hockey and baseball. Baseball and hockey. We played them, watched them on TV and saw our heroes in action live.

Hockey was the Yin to our baseball Yang. They were Rocky and Bullwinkle, chocolate shakes and burgers, t-shirts and jeans. Completely different but they were the twin pillars necessary to balance our sporting lives. We played every game we knew and invented a whole bunch more, but baseball and hockey were the two brightest stars in our sport-fest sky.

The 'Burg was a hot bed for both. There were leagues for every age, from atom through pee wee, bantam and midget up to junior and senior. And there were tournaments throughout the area all the time. We played hard, especially against rival teams from the Detroit area that could draw from a much bigger pool of players, making us Canadians stronger and better. We didn't think of it that way but from early on in our baseball and hockey careers, we had the luxury of playing regularly in international competition. We played baseball everywhere: in parks and playgrounds, our backyards and on the empty schoolyard diamonds on weekends. We played hockey on outdoor and indoor rinks, frozen creeks and ponds, backyard rinks our dads flooded in the frosty cold and dark. When we couldn't get on the ice, we played street hockey in grocery store parking lots with milk crates for goal-posts.

We were bonkers for baseball and wacky for hockey. We carried stats around in our heads and wore scars proudly on our shins and elbows. On our backs were the numbers of our favourite players. We slid home and stole second. We practised slap shots and skating backwards. Our hockey sticks were taped with delicate care and the pockets of our baseball gloves were meticulously rubbed with linseed oil. From the radio, we learned to see games, following every pitch and every pass. Our dreams were filled with flashy scoring and clutch hits. We imagined that we would skate smoothly into the Stanley Cup finals and play proudly in the World Series.

It was a league game, out on the edge of town. One of the last of the season and neither club was heading for the playoffs. The grass was brown and dry, the infield dusty and hard and the harvested corn had been reduced to stalk-spikes beyond the outfield. For the last breath of Indian summer, the sun tried its best to bring a crisp warmth to the day. Although the game was meaningless, we knew we would have to wait a whole season for another, so we were enjoying the autumn embrace and the entire baseball experience of pitching, hitting, throwing, catching, running, sliding, bunting, stealing, spitting and yelling. There was some excitement behind us as the next game was a junior contest to decide which team advanced to post-season play. So, a small crowd had begun to gather beyond the few friends and family that came to see us boot the ball and drop easy fly-outs.

The beloved baseball hotdog vendor Marvin was already setting up his grill, utensils and food. Marv was a stocky ex-semi-pro player with tattoos, a hairy, ape chest and a coupla teeth missing. His voice sounded like a pick-up truck on fresh and crunchy gravel. He always wore an old Tigers ball cap, a greasy, formerly white apron and a toothpick in the corner of his always moving mouth. He was gruff but loved his work, the game and the kids. Years before our time, he had decided to build a collapsible corral that surrounded him while he cooked and served his ballpark franks and sodas.

It was a versatile construction: easily set up and dismantled with narrow counter tops on all four sides for slathering mustard and relish on the wieners, supporting the ice chest for refreshments and the cash box he always kept within close reach and sight. The hotdog stockade also provided a buffer for Marvin so he could work his one-man baseball band magic: turning the dogs, adding new ones, giving change, grabbing more napkins, forking the franks into fresh buns, topping up the condiments from vats he kept at his feet, reloading pops into the ice and commenting on the game and, of course, the Tigers' season. He didn't have a sign for his stall, he didn't need one. The Raiders and everyone else loved Marv's grilled mahogany tubes of summer joy. We swore you could smell them from two cornfields away, maybe three.

Kids were blowing bubbles of gum in the stands, eating and throwing popcorn, yelling at their friends and chattering non-stop. Mums were clasping their hands together in a baseball prayer that their sons would do well and not be injured while dads provided the missing broadcast commentary.

"Get a hit son!"

"Strike this hot-shot out."

"C'mon ump, I know this is little league but let's try to make some good calls for a change."

"Run, run, run, dadgummit, Jimmy, you gotta make third."

"Easy out, easy out."

"You got this guy son, he's outta gas."

"Infield fly rule, right ump? Right ump?"

"Slide, Timmy, slide!"

"What were you thinking, boy, what were you thinking?"

Most of our game was pretty ordinary, a run or so every few innings, a homer or two, a few strikeouts, a close score. Then, that day, everything changed.

"I'm going to bean you or you or you," Randy Darnell Sampson told us when the coaches weren't looking.

Then he grinned and strode back to the other side of the diamond, rolling his shoulders and loosening his shotgun of an arm. D'nell was a big, Black, cocky pitcher who was out to win every game all by himself. He always ignored any signs from his catcher or the bench, throwing whatever pitch he felt like. When the coach took him off the mound and played him on third base, in protest, he would snatch up any grounders that were hit his way and throw curveballs at the frightened first baseman.

His nickname as a pitcher was Strike-Force Sampson but off the mound, he was mostly known as D'nell.

It was late in the ballgame and he had pointed at me, Sticks and Skeeser. We were shivering like shaved rabbits. No one wanted to get hit by one of his fastballs, especially on purpose. The three of us looked at each other in nervous shock, eyes widened by fear, gulping fishes out of water. No one said a word. Our team mates shifted apart from us lepers, not wanting to be near potentially maimed or dead boys. Until we had to take our at-bats we thought of nothing but self-preservation.

How quickly we could get out of the way? How much it would hurt? How to turn our helmets into the pitch if we couldn't dodge it? How not to cry? Could a kid get killed in the batter's box?

When Darnell marched up to the mound, he looked meaner than ever before as he glowered at each of us in turn. He was the giant gladiator, and we were the cowering Christians.

Stickwood had to face him first. As good with the bat as the goalie stick, he was used to being shot at. I don't know about Skeese but I was kinda hoping Strike-Force would hit him, just a graze that would end our baseball nightmare of Russian roulette. He stepped up to the plate, waving his bat in an unafraid stance. *"Bring it on, I can take it,"* he seemed to be saying. D'nell nodded and smirked as though he understood and fired an inside fastball that our Raider fouled off. "Strike one," the ump shouted. The next pitch was an arcing curveball for a ball. The ump signalled ball and Sampson didn't like that, so he took turns glaring at the umpire and the batter. Not wasting any more time, he rose to new heights on the mound and unleashed a rocket. But Sticks was ready for it, the howitzer heading straight for him: he stepped back quickly and in self-defence managed to tomahawk a single over the third baseman's head. I've never seen a guy so relieved. Standing on first, Sticks took off his ball cap, mopped his forehead with his sleeve, pumped his fist into the morning sun and giggled like a little girl. He might as well have hit a grand slam. Then he waved crazily at me and Skeese, like a man risen from the dead.

I was next. Even though he was one of the toughest guys in school, I knew that Strike-Force wasn't all mean and prickly. A couple of years earlier I saw him getting pushed around in the schoolyard by a bigger and older kid. The bully was a friend of mine's brother, so I knew him. I walked over and started talking to him making sure that he understood I had seen what was happening. I asked him about his model car collection, muscle cars that he constructed from kits and painted tenderly. They were displayed like trophies in his room. I told him how cool they were. I managed to divert his attention long enough for D'nell to take off. Sometime later we were playing soccer and Strike-Force, a talented athlete in any sport, was on the other team. I miss-kicked the ball and hoofed him square on the shin. He yelped in pain and everyone froze. He made a fist and came at me but at the last moment he pushed me roughly to the ground. Mrs. McKendrick hadn't raised a fool, so I just stayed down. D'nell went after the soccer ball and the game continued. After that we hung out, shared some comic books, bought ice cream sandwiches and made sports bets with a free lunch as the prize.

I was praying to the baseball gods that he would remember our friendship and spare my life. When I stood in the batter's box, I could feel my legs going weak on me. I looked up at D'nell and he winked, just slightly so only I could see. I saw what Sticks had done so I tried to use my bat to protect myself. He threw some sort of off-speed pitch that sunk over the plate. I flailed at it like I was chopping wood. "Strike one," the ump shouted behind me. I took a deep breath and D'nell floated another pitch with movement for a ball. No sign of the fastball as I fouled off another one and he threw a couple in the dirt. The count ran full, so I prepared for the worst, leaning back, gripping my bat in front of me like a shield. D'nell wound up with purpose and to everyone's surprise threw a lazy pitch over the plate for strike three. I was still shaking when I fell on to the bench, the fear draining out of me like a dissipating fever. I lifted my head and saw him give me that hint of a wink. In relief, I returned it.

When Skeeser walked to the plate, an inning later, like a man facing the gallows, the game was on the line; bottom of the ninth with a 3-2 lead for the other team. There were two outs, but we had a guy on third. D'nell was a mad bull on the mound, kicking and pawing the dirt.

Skeese's whole body was twitching like he had palsy, the bat slipping in his squirming fingers. Before the first pitch was released Skeeser stepped out of the batter's box and held his bat over the plate from a safe distance like he was handing someone a dead snake on the end of a stick. The ball drifted in for a strike.

"Hey, kid, stand up to the plate! Whaddya think you're doin?" our coach screamed at Skeese.

D'nell smiled wide. Skeeser stepped slowly back into the box and then, just as before, backed out holding his bat near home plate. It wavered there like a fishing pole as another harmless, slow pitch sailed easily in for strike two.

The coach was jumping up and down on top of the bench howling at Skeeser with rage.

"Get in there, Thatcher! What's wrong with you? You can't hit the ball from the sidelines. Can you hear me kid?"

His voice was cracking, but Skeese wouldn't even look at him. He had already decided, it was pain and perhaps death versus upsetting his coach. No contest.

By now, some of the junior teams' fans got in on the action. They began booing our skinny pal at the plate.

"Play ball, kid, you're letting your team down," one guy hollered.

"You're letting the game down too," someone yelled.

"Pull that kid, let someone else hit if he doesn't want to," another member of the crowd shouted.

Some little girls could be heard jeering. Other kids were laughing and pointing.

Even Marvin's grating voice sounded from his wiener stand. "It's an insult to baseball! Stand in there, boy! Face up to that pitcher."

"We got a shot at tying this one up and you're it buddy-boy," the coach barked his last order.

For the final pitch, Skeese had one toe on the outline of the box and his back foot as far away from home-plate as he could stretch, over in another county somewhere. Pointing his trembling bat out, he looked like he was trying to feed a carrot on a stick to a Billy goat through a fence. The coach became a human balloon about to burst. Strike-Force softly tossed the ball like he was pitching to his grandmother, and it landed like a butterfly in the catcher's mitt for the final strike and out. Game over.

After the coach stopped yelling at Skeese we all strolled home, the sidewalk still warm under our running shoes, a balmy breeze at our backs. We were happy to be alive. Heck, it was a meaningless game the way we figured it.

And we had good reason to want to live. It was 1968 and it turned out to be the year of the Tiger in Detroit, the team all the Rankin Street Raiders adored. They had not only made the playoffs but the World Series. More than grilled-cheese sandwiches, our bicycles, our model collections of Frankenstein's Monster, Dracula, the Wolf-Man and the Mummy, we loved our Tigers. We knew every player's name backwards: From La Enilak and Mron Shac to Eilliw Notroh and Ynned NiaLcm. All their stats, their feats of baseball brilliance were common information to us. When they slumped, we suffered with them. When the Tabbies clawed their way to victory, we were winners, too. They played in an old-style stadium with an overhang porch seating. It was like my aunt's front porch but about a billboard or two bigger. To the Raiders it was a shrine, a hallowed house of baseball. It was where the members of our team, small gods to us, performed with pride.

The Tigers won 103 games that year and Denny "Pepsi" McLain was responsible for thirty-one of them by his lonesome, the last ballplayer in major league baseball to accomplish that. He was supposed to have downed a boatload of those colas on game days. Mickey "Big Ears" Lolich was the other Tiger titan on the mound. The gentleman's gentleman Al Kaline, also known as "Mr. Tiger," drilled line shots almost through outfield walls. Willie "The Wonder" Horton, an outfielder, had tons of boom in his bat. We could hear the crack on the radio when he homered, which he did thirty-six times. Dickie "Mad Dog" McAuliffe our second baseman was aggressive in the field and at the plate. Small but tougher than the dirt he played on, he backed down from no one and with the help of his foot-in-the-bucket stance in the batter's box he led the league with ninety-five runs scored that year.

Powerful "Stormin'" Norman Cash had a slugging percentage of .487 when he wasn't patrolling first base. Jim "Grey Fox" Northrup could play any field and hit to each of them. He had four grand slams and finished high in the league's most valuable player voting. My favourite player was Bill "The Foreman" Freehan. Tall and chiselled, he was what all catchers should aspire to be: tough and smart with an accurate arm and a hot bat. He cranked twenty-five dingers that year and threw out 971 baserunners out of 1,050 chances, a record he would own for almost 30 years. Oh, and yeah, from behind the plate he helped guide Lolich and McLain to forty-eight wins. "The Foreman" was the rock that anchored the Tigers, the heart in the breast of the beast.

The grinding and surprising Tigers had fought back from being 3-1 in the hole against a St. Louis Cardinal squad, who according to all the stats and odds in the baseball universe, should have won the series easily. They sported an all-star team of players who were household names and/or future Hall of Famers: Curt Flood, Orlando Cepeda, Steve Carlton, Tim McCarver, Roger Maris and the best hurler in both leagues, Bob Gibson. Our team was good. Their team was great. They had won two recent World Series and looked to cruise smoothly to the trifecta. In two of the first four games, they scored fourteen runs while our suddenly human team managed only one. They were kicking the purr out of the Tigers until some lucky bounces, classy fielding, timely slugging and Micky Lolich's arm propelled us to the final. But it wasn't going to be a walk in the ballpark because it was to be played in St. Louis.

Almost as exciting, we had been awarded a pre-game godsend. That afternoon, after surviving the bean-ball threat, we and the other two Raiders had been invited by a woman my dad worked with to watch the game in her rec room on her big colour TV. Lorraine Curran had long, thick, greying and carefully curled hair and sharp blue eyes above a warm smile. She was cute and kind and had two passions in her life: The Tigers and poker. And she lived on Rankin Street. This was a pretty captivating combination in the Raiders' logbook. Miss Lorrie had a regulation poker table that she played on with her gambling group weekly. Octagonal with an emerald felt surface like a pool table, it was framed with mahogany hardwood and even had six recesses for drinks. We had never seen anything so stunning. It appeared to us as an oasis, like a beaming green fountain for fun. As though summoned to a grander world, a royal chamber in another dimension, we gathered there in a giddy delirium, unable to fully grasp our good fortune. Of course, the Raiders all knew how to play poker. We arrived two hours early to play Follow the Queen, Acey-Deucey, Chicago, Kings and Little Ones and, a necessity on that day, Blind Baseball.

Supplied with all the colas and sodas and chips and dip we could consume; we were careful not to let a morsel or a drop touch the elegant and soft surface on which we played. Miss Lorrie distributed the cards with a silky effortlessness like a Vegas dealer.

We razzed one another, tried to bluff, raised too many times and eventually saw the vast ship of experience, which our hostess steered, sail slowly away with all our poker chips. It didn't matter one nit nor flea. We were so excited and delighted.

Then it was game time, World Series final time, Tiger time. The six of us sat in a circle of hope. It was a séance of sporting faith as we watched and absorbed the most crucial contest of our young years. The single game of all games. Clutching our lucky souvenir bats, stuffed tabbies and rabbit's feet, we wore Tiger tees, ball caps and jerseys. On the walls and shelves were Detroit pennants, team photos and autographed posters and pictures, baseballs and bats. Miss Curran had a collection that rivalled Cooperstown, if the Hall of Fame had been dedicated only to the Detroit Tigers.

"Big Ears better bring it today."

"Mick's throwing on only two days' rest."

"Hope he ate his Wheaties."

"Don't worry, Freehan's the man, the Foreman will pluck those Redbirds."

"No way, Willie the Wonder will crush the Cards."

"Forget it, Mr. Tiger will eat 'em up."

"Why don't we bet on the MVP of the game?"

"Sure, money where yer mouth is."

"Two bucks from each of us goes to the winner."

"It's a bet and no welching."

"I never welch!"

"If that means you never pay up then it's true."

"Welch off."

I took Bill Freehan, Wiry wanted Wille the Wonder, Rogie chose Stormin' Norman Cash, Skeese picked The Grey Fox Northrup, Mad Dog was taken by Sticks and Miss Curran selected Lolich.

We watched the first pitch and every one after that. The TV was mounted high on the rec room wall so everyone had clear views. It was the third outing for the two undefeated pitching sensations: Gibson against the Mick. It was the throw down, the duel of the decade. Part miracle, part coincidence but all talent, they would finish with identical .167 earned run averages for the series.

For six scoreless innings we must have looked like Tasmanian Devils on caffeine: twitching, crossing and uncrossing our fingers and legs, chewing our nails, clapping, sighing, shouting and gasping for runs. It was raining on our playoff parade, but we were still hopeful that a rainbow would appear, overshadowing the St. Louis Gateway Arch. That glimmer of light peeked through the clouds in the top of the seventh when Cash legged out a lazy blooper and made it to first. That was followed by a deep single by Willie the Wonder. Two men on!

We all stood when the Grey Fox tapped the plate, waggled his bat and stared purposefully at Gibby. We couldn't speak or breathe. Every Tiger fan on the planet did the same. Northrup took a strike and a ball and then he leaned into a fastball and drifted it deep to centre. We grabbed each other and held on just as Horton and Cash hugged the bases, waiting and hoping with us. Curt Flood went up for the catch, but it somehow got past him.

When the ball dropped, even above our screaming we could hear car horns blare and people shouting in the brisk October air. Cash scored. Horton chugged home too and Northrup made it all the way to third! Two nothing for the downtrodden Detroiters! We jumped and flailed like human puppets almost bouncing off the ceiling.

"That's my boy," Skeeser yelled. "I told you he'd be the man."

Then there was a hush at the game and in the room. My guy stalked to the batter's box. Freehan looked twice his size, a block of granite with grit. We had Gibson reeling on the ropes. The Foreman took a coupla cuts that could have felled oaks. Then he planted himself at the plate. Gibson missed with a curve but on the next pitch our goliath of a catcher rocked him with a hard shot between centre and left. Northrup scored easily from third and Freehan made it to second. All of Tiger Town roared. The walls shook and we danced and fell about in dizzy glee. It was 3-0 for us in the seventh of the seventh game. Baby, baby, baby. Our rainbow had arrived, a beacon of baseball. And that was it, really. The Tigger's Don Wert singled in the fourth run and the Cards' Mike Shannon hit a solo shot in the ninth. It ended 4-1 for the Motor City Maulers. Four at-bats in a few minutes created a monument for us and our heroes.

Mickey Lefty Lolich was the star of the game and the MVP of the series, no question. He won three games and held the St. Louis superstars to one run in the final. He even hit a homer earlier in the series.

"I'm not going to take your money, boys," Miss Lorrie said sweetly. "How's this though," she added. "If you promise to come back to play poker and wash my car, we can call it square?" Now that's what the Raiders called a real fair deal. We never washed and polished a car more thoroughly or tenderly. It shined like the sparkle in the Tigers' World Series rings.

During their reign, the Rankin Street Raiders made a few mistakes and bad decisions, but we must have done something right to be sitting at a poker table and watching the Tigers win the seventh game of the World Series. No pirates were prouder, no buccaneers boasted as much of their victory and no swashbucklers shouted and cheered with such abandon as we did that day, October 5, 1968.

We had knelt and prayed at the Tiger temple and our wishes were granted.

Chapter 7

Robin Hoods of Halloween

One night every year we became desperadoes of the dark, corsairs and crusaders, members of the Mongolian Horde and hallowed highwaymen all rolled into one. The Raiders sailed into the evening waving flags and banners of the conquistadors and buccaneers. Call it what you will: Hallowmas, Devil's Day, Mischief Night or Witches' New Year's Eve, if the Raiders had one day that was theirs' alone it was October 31. That one night screamed at us all year long, a barbaric banshee singing to our souls, spurring us on to new levels of achievement.

Our little hamlet was always unprepared for our pillaging because weeks before we would concoct ways to give new meaning to trick or treating. Rankin was a two-way street as we not only devised unusual tricks, but we found new ways to treat ourselves in the bargain.

But one glorious night we hit our peak, captured the Halloween Holy Grail, reached up and supped from the cup, satiated by the twin rewards of triumph and plunder. It started where many of our successful missions were hatched, at the Arch.

We loved hiking out there in the fall. Under the eclipsing shadow of the great stone and steel train trestle, we investigated everywhere, stepping lightly among the soggy decay of autumn. For the first time in the year, we could see through the woodlands at the Arch's feet. It was eerie yet comforting in the warm glow of sunlight burnishing the fading foliage. All was brown and withering, a retreating jungle yielding to the cold approach of winter. But it was new to us, the youthful, flourishing growth of spring and summer being replaced by the revealing of aging wood, vine and leaf. The fall change carried within it a wisdom, confident knowing that in its decline was its future. The Arch environs would survive to rise from its slumber in the spring. As if in reward for our late season visit, we found thriving new plants hiding under the withering of formerly abundant vegetation. Our favourites were the colourful, clandestine parade of wild mushrooms, interesting, unusual formations with the lifespan of flies. We knew better than to eat any but there was something wondrous about viewing nature's momentary fungal art. And we looked up their names at the library, studying them like magic incantations. There was the early orange mycenae: tiny, capped clusters of glowing armies. Shaggy manes looked like albino corn dogs sprouting up from the forest floor. Meadow mushrooms, not to be confused with meadow muffins, spread their gills into miniature flying saucer shapes. The white elfin saddle was an impossible combination of ghostly tubular curves defying gravity and our imaginations. Bumpy, bright yellow patches opened, almost before our eyes, like leprechauns' umbrellas. Blewits, purplish rotund mushrooms made us laugh as they masqueraded as bent-over cartoon characters with big bums. We found chicken of the woods to be more above-water coral than hens or roosters. We did pluck puffballs, knowing they were harmless, to throw at each other, exploding like alabaster softballs on our fleeing backs.

"Hey guys, check this out!" Wiry shouted, interrupting our foraging. He was holding up a small snake, its body writhing around his arm like an animated vine.

"Where'd you get that?"

"What kind is it?"

"Do they bite?"

"Are they venomous?"

"I found it right over here, and I saw some more."

We all tromped over, looking much more warily at the underbrush. It was a harmless green garter snake about 15 inches long with a checkered green and black back, with some yellow stripes like ribbons along its marbled, smooth scales. The underbody was a polished, yellowish-milky. Its tiny red tongue never stopped darting and seeking. Wiry held it by the head, which seemed wise, it was after all, a snake. It wriggled like an electric wire. "Look, there's a bunch of them," he said pointing. No one had to tell us to try to find one of our own. It was a strange pursuit, a kind of automatic peripheral vision kicked in, providing for forward eye-sight with additional side-sight. We rummaged among the thickets of sticks, leaves and bramble in all directions. Soon we were standing around in a circle, inspecting our own garters like junior snake-charmers. All we needed were baskets, turbans and some flute lessons. Our Arch God, studying us from above, was probably amused.

Skeeser produced a bag he brought for catnip collection, so we stuffed our snakes in it.

"Let's get more." They were everywhere once we learned how to notice them. We searched carefully and quickly for movement, like madmen grasping at shadows in the half-light; seeking something out of the ordinary, not produced by the breeze or our footsteps. Our identical black rubber boots with orange rim tops and soles covered the dank groundcover. Soon, about two dozen of the lively little creatures were captured.

Exhausted from the intensity of the hunt, not to mention the unspoken fear factor at the back of all our minds produced by the potential of stumbling on to a snake the size of a fence post, we slumped together on drier stumps and fallen trees to eat our rations.

"What are we gonna do with all these snakes?" I wanted to know.

"I'm keeping mine as pets," Sticks announced.

"Yeah, like anyone's mum is gonna go for that."

"That's true, mine would scream and faint, my dad would fling it out the door as far as he could and then I would be grounded," Wiry said sadly.

We all nodded and sank a little deeper into our forest chairs. We munched in silence like a defeated platoon.

"Hey, wait a minute. What day is it?" Wiry wanted to know.

"It's Saturday, Dorkus."

"No, I mean what is today?"

A moment passed and Rogan blurted, "Halloween."

"That's right and what do we have planned for our tricks tonight?"

We considered that. Not much more than the usual arsenals and activities of egg and water balloon tossing, soaping car windows, squirt guns loaded with soda pop and smashing pumpkins. We realized that we hadn't really come up with anything new that year.

"Maybe, oh, just maybe, we might be able to combine our tricks with our treats?" Wiry said mysteriously.

We were all ears for that!

"You know how our parents make us give out candy before we go out ourselves? Well, why not give some of the bad kids a little more than they expect? We fill our hands with goodies and then slip a snake into their pillowcases when they aren't looking. But we make sure they're older kids and rude, the bullies that deserve a good scare on Halloween."

Suddenly our Arch park was enchanted with a freakishly fantastic idea. We breathed in the beauty of it. We saw the evil stinkers leap up and away in snake shock. We heard their heart-warming screams. We smelled their pitiful fear. We could taste the success of the caper. We gazed about, lost in the vision of it all like small men, drunk on the idea. We rose together, high-fiving, low-fiving, punching the air and dancing the dance of advance joy.

Wiry was immediately the super star of the day! This was right up the Rankin Street Raiders' alleyway. We would be teaching the mean rats a lesson. Hey, they asked for it. They were only getting their justified desserts. How cool was that?

"Trick or Treat! Trick or Treat! Trick or Treat," we howled up through the Arch's domain. The words had new meaning. This would be an All Hallow's Eve to cherish.

Happy to expound on what was so instantly a devious and dastardly idea Wiry said, "We have to be sure that no one finds out where the snakes came from. We can't tell anyone, no boasting and bragging. We will have to slide them into the kids' bags when no parent is present. And we will wait for dark, daylight is too risky. If one of us screws up we'll all be in trouble, dark and deep trouble."

In a way, that made it even more glorious. We would have to be as stealthy and sly as possible. In our bold Raider's hearts, we knew we would have to do the plan justice. If we failed, the idea would die, too. It was a one-shot at the Halloween harvest moon.

We almost sprinted back to town, careful not to jostle the sack of snakes too much. We wanted them to still have lots of slither left in them when they were employed for our mission.

Heading for Rankin Street we shouted to the clouds like mental patients out on a day pass.

"Snakes alive!"

"We're rollin' snake eyes tonight."

"We been to Snake Town and shook the snakes down."

"You speak with forked tongue, Kemosabe!"

"Trick or Treat, Rikki Tikki Tavi?"

"Want some serpents with your sweets tonight?"

"How's about some reptiles writhing over your rock candy?"

We divvied up our precious little minions of terror, zipping a few each into our jacket pockets or tying them into extra shirtsleeves and scurried home to prepare for the arrival of nightfall.

The previous Halloween we had devised a way to get our favourite treats over and over again. We came up with costumes that could be altered quickly to look like a different outfit then we could return to the best houses, and even restaurants for superior swag. We would visit each of our faves once, change costumes and then after some time had elapsed, loop back to get more. The top three on our list were: old Mrs. Chapman's candy apples, the diner for French fries and the bakery for anything. It was appetizer, lunch and dessert. We didn't even bother with candy; it was beneath our Raider plunder. As the smallest, I would put on a new mask, climb onto Rogie's cloaked shoulders, his face hidden under his collar and pretend the two of us were one giant. People loved that one. We turned our clothes inside out and backward. We slipped our arms into each other's sleeves to be Siamese twins. We brought make-up with us to transform into ghouls and ghosts. We staggered in like zombies strapping tin cans on our feet to be taller. And we bent low to the ground with pillows stuffed into our shoulders to make us hunchbacks. It was presto-chango deep into the evening until the goods ran out. Then we stashed whatever we could, except for the French fries—we scarfed them back right away, as they were no good cold, and then headed out; we gremlins and marauders intent on mayhem.

But before all this we had to perform the formerly boring task of handing out candy, brownies, and jellybeans to little kids while complimenting them on their cheesy costumes. This time, this drudgery would be changed forever, lifted into the lofty realm of nefarious pleasure.

That night no one could stop us from running like dogs to a meat wagon when we heard the little darlings chirp "Trick or Treat." And sure enough, the bad kids, the ones who swore, spat, yelled or pushed the smaller ones out of their way, revealed themselves unmistakably. They might as well have been wearing signs that said, "Put an ugly, slimy snake in my bag, I earned it." We obliged like Robin Hoods of Halloween.

I soon got the hang of it. Before answering the door, I would hold the garter snake firmly by the head and put a little candy camouflage into it with my other hand. Then I'd grab a whole bunch of treats in my free hand. The Trick or Treaters always stared at the handful of candy and ignored the other, which I slipped in while they gawked at their good fortune. It really was serpentine sleight of hand.

Once our trick or treat duties were completed when the costumed kids slowed to a trickle, we gathered under a Rankin Street light to compare tales. It was a giggling, glorious success. Happy as hobgoblins, we flitted off into the dark to take care of Halloween phases two and three.

My mother got a call from Wiry's mum the next afternoon after church. They were friends and both nurses. Mrs. Whaley had heard from some parents about snakes being slipped into trick or treat bags. Wasn't it awful? In detail, she told of one kid who spilled all his Halloween harvest out onto the living room rug while his family looked on. A snake wriggled out, frightened the family and then disappeared into a heating grate that led to the basement. The boy could hardly bring himself to eat some of his Halloween swag, but he managed while the father nervously spent an hour reptile-hunting in the cellar, with no success.

"Was it venomous?" my mum asked.

"No, they only saw it for a minute, but it looked to be a little green garter snake," Wiry's mum replied.

"Did they have any idea which house it came from?" Mum wondered.

"No, but that creepy old Mrs. Armand over on Alma Street has always been the main suspect when something like this shows up," Wiry's mum suggested.

"I heard she hates kids. I tell mine to stay away from there, especially on Halloween," my mother added.

"Who knows, it could be some crazy old man who doesn't mind handling snakes," Wiry's mother replied.

"I guess it's better than razor blades in apples?"

"Or horse manure in brownies."

"What will they think of next?"

They nodded over the phones.

A few days later, my mother heard from another friend over coffee that there had been several Halloween snake sightings, almost an epidemic.

"There was a bunch of them," I heard her telling my disinterested dad. A few garter snakes were hardly a big deal to a guy who did prospecting in the wilds of Northern Ontario in his youth. He pretended to listen anyway. In the next room, I was much keener to hear what she had to say.

"It turns out at a house over on Laird Avenue when a snake squirmed out of a boy's bag, the dog snatched it up in his jaws by the tail and shook it until it's neck snapped," Mum told Dad in a whisper so we kids couldn't hear.

"Isn't a snake's whole body the neck? Or isn't it just a head and a body and there is no neck?" my father laughed.

"Be serious. I hope this won't happen every year," Mum said with worry.

In a loud voice, my father stated, "Oh, I doubt that it will happen again."

My mother learned later that the snake that slithered down the grate enjoyed a long life in the basement, eating spiders and ants and surprising family members on occasion. Eventually he was killed by their cat. Other serpent stories continued to circulate around the community but eventually the tales shed their skins, slinked off and were never heard from again.

None of our parents or anyone else ever found out who was behind the All Hallow's Eve reptilian rampage. Only the proud Rankin Street Raiders knew the truth and, well, maybe my dad.

Chapter 8

Demolition Derby Part One - the Brightside

Our class was crouched in the stairwell that led to the school basement, peering around and above the brick topped-with-concrete enclosure that surrounded the entrance were thirty-six eyes, including those of Mr. Burnham, our teacher. They were watching us preparing to light a sixty-foot fuse that led to a small powder keg lashed to an old stump at the edge of the playground. Gunpowder isn't hard to make if you have the right ingredients, in the exact measure, with the proper packing. An actual school project, we were in the process of demonstrating the operation and use of an essential part of Canada's history. Bringing our past to life by blowing stuff up.

The Canadian Pacific Railway (CPR), completed the last spike on November 7, 1885, connecting the country for the first time for travel and shipping. It boasted some 10,000 miles of track and the use of more than 25,000 workers. Sir William Cornelius Van Horne was the human engine that drove the CPR, Canada's cross-country railroad, to completion. And it needed a lot of blasting to be built. That's where we came in.

Mr. Burnham, a shorter guy with spectacles and a squint, looked a little soft but he had a megaphone voice and the hairiest chest this side of King Kong. He was tough, yet fair, like an umpire who you could trust to make the right call. As a result, he was fine by us. The class project called for four students to work together. We got to choose sides, so it was me, Lennie, Whaley and D'nell—three-quarters Raiders and one-quarter Strike-Force. How could we lose? It had to be something based on the completion of the CPR. Some classmates were working on the hardships of thousands of Chinese "Coolies" on whose backs the tracks were laid while being over-worked, ill-housed and paid pittances. Others were researching the difficulties of carving rail lines through the Rockies, the mountains of money it took to accomplish this seemingly impossible task, the politics of geography involved with the provinces and the United States and even the structure of the trains, tunnels and tracks.

I came up with the idea of the gunpowder because my dad was a miner. The four of us practised our pitch to Hairy Burnham. We were desperate to get the green light, so we came up with a quadruple approach to show solidarity, different viewpoints and a strong argument. Finally, after some assurances from my dad that he would help and some studying up on black powder, we were called in to make our presentation. We took turns. Two shots each.

"There was a lot more blasting than probably anything else to get the CPR made so we want to demonstrate how it worked."

"We'd be using hands-on preparation for this project."

"It'll be an actual re-creation of what the CPR used to help build the railroad."

"Kids would be able to see and hear first-hand the effects of a powder charge going off."

"With a note from the school, we can get the proper amount of ingredients from the drug store."

"This is part of what our country was built on."

"Too many projects are just written from research. This would be real, with an essay to back it up, of course."

"My dad said we could do a practice run out at the Brunner Mond quarry."

"You're always telling us to come up with our own ideas."

There was a long silence. Then Mr. Burnham exhaled with a weird whistle in his breath.

"Let me get this straight. You're suggesting that I let you blow something up in the schoolyard?" he said, like we were asking him to jump off a cliff, accompanied by his teaching career.

"It'll be completely safe. My father knows the right distance and he can supply the proper fuse."

"We can use a small amount, a low explosive; just enough to give the class an idea of what it was like."

"I don't know about this," he said peering carefully at us. "I'm going to have to check with the Principal. In the meantime, I want a written outline of exactly what you gentlemen are proposing," he told us.

That was a yellow light. We were half-way home to kablooey.

Sticks looked up the raw materials: sulphur and charcoal for the fuel and potassium nitrate or saltpetre as the oxidizer to allow the mixture to blow. He figured the right amounts for each ingredient for a small blast.

D'nell planned the best location in the schoolyard, deciding on a tree stump, which allowed some protection if we tied the charge to the opposite side while still providing a clear view for students from the stairwell. He did the measurements for the wick, too.

I worked with my dad to get an idea of what type of container would be best to use and how to make it bomb-worthy. He suggested the smallest-sized, six-ounce frozen orange juice can. One hole could be drilled to serve a few purposes: draining the thawed juice, stuffing the can with the powder mixture and inserting the fuse for blast-off.

Wiry wrote the explanation for Mr. Burnham, emphasizing the CPR connection, Canadian heritage, the safety of the experiment based on my dad's and the druggist's involvement and the importance of the demonstration as a first-hand learning experience for us and our fellow students. He also included all our suggestions for the assignment. It was a good report and thorough. We submitted it and waited.

A few days had passed when we were finally called in to see Mr. Hairy Chest after school.

"I'm not going to lie to you boys, I've got some real problems with this project," he started in. "And so does the Principal."

We fidgeted and slumped and slumped and fidgeted.

"I'm not sure that all the students' parents will be as certain about the safety as you gentlemen are."

We looked down at the floor and exhaled. Exhaled and looked down at the floor.

"But, as you know, I am all for my students showing initiative, coming up with new ideas."

We sat up straight and swallowed. Swallowed and sat up straight.

"And your submission was excellent, the best one I received from the entire class. Well done."

We held our breath and held our breath.

So, here's what I counter-propose to you," he said with a gleam behind his glasses. "I will send a note home to parents to get them to sign off on their children attending your exhibition and those who don't have permission can stay inside. Here's the prescription for the drug store. But you have to test your gunpowder project and report back to me with the results before it can happen here. Am I clear?"

We stood up, said a quick, "Yessir!", grabbed the note and made for the door.

"And I want the druggist's signature on the chemicals," he called after us.

Our first order of business—alright, our second order of business, after jumping on each other's shoulders, crashing around and yelling, "Yippee" and "Hot dang" —was to get the gunpowder ingredients. We had already done the math, and I ran it past my pa, so we were ready to burn. We needed two batches, one for the trial run and another for the real thing. We drew lots for who would deal with the druggist because we didn't like that guy. Mr. Parthon always looked down his ski-slope nose at us like we were termites in his personal house of cures. He all but accused us of stealing every time we went into his stinky shop and followed us like a house detective. The only time he was happy was when we showed up for a prescription that he knew would taste bad or hurt us in some way. He wore his lab coat like a Brigadier's dress uniform, pompous and proud. He had a greasy mouth, drooped on one side in a grimace. He was also bald and belligerent. We called him Wide-Part Parthon or Prune-Face Parthon. Knowing he would give us a hard time with this unusual and potentially dangerous request, we decided to play him out a little, like a pharmacist fish. We would hang back and let him get all worked up.

D'nell drew the short popsicle stick. Better and better, Black kids were even worse than us heathens in Parthon's rotten mind. They were thieves, first, second and always, in his biased book.

Strike-Force strutted in like he had just bought the place, letting the door slam behind him. We viewed from the window. Wide-Part's head snapped up like he'd been slapped. As he watched our operative striding toward the proprietor, his eyes narrowed, his teeth clenched, and his hands tightened into fists on the counter.

Before Prune-Face could say anything, D'nell smacked a list down and said, "I need salt peter, charcoal and sulphur and in these amounts." Then he stood back, crossed his arms, daring the druggist.

We thought Parthon's shiny head was going to explode before we got a chance to detonate anything ourselves.

"You, you, you've got to be crazy coming in here for these chemicals. You think I'm going to let you blow up my drug store?"

D'nell just smiled and continued to glare up at him.

"Is this some kind of holdup? I'll call the police you hoodlum. You'll go to jail for this you bastard." White, foamy, spittle was forming at the corner of his lopsided mouth.

The pharmacist continued crabbing, pounding his fists until D'nell slowly reached into his pocket, unfolded Mr. Burnham's note and lazily dropped it on the counter.

Wide-Part Parthon glowered at the slip of paper like he was reading hieroglyphics, then stepped away, arched his back, shook his head side-stop, side-stop, in rage and then stalked over to his jars of potions.

When they were ready, D'nell told him he had to sign the teacher's note, or he wouldn't pay up. Prune-Face growled and scratched his signature like the pen was a dagger. Strike-Force paid, turned on his heel as though were on parade and quick-stepped it out the door. Before it slammed, we all made sure Wide-Part could hear us cracking up at him: "*AAh, ah, ah, ha, ha, ha, ha!*"

I was in the passenger seat, the rest of the crew of Project Powder Keg were sitting in the back and my father was at the wheel when we pulled up to the barbed wire-lined gates of the outer reaches of the Brunner Mond quarry. It was open pit, and everything looked like craters on the moon. My dad jumped out and using a giant's key opened the pie plate-sized padlock, drove in and carefully closed the gates and re-locked them. Everything was quiet except for the gravel under his feet. We felt like we were on military missions before, but this was high up there where our Jolly Roger fluttered. We might as well have been there to blow up the Hoover Dam.

He took us up to a scrubby ridge that overlooked some empty rocky flats. He had given us instructions on the way. The idea was that we would do the work, but he would guide us through the steps required in order to set up the explosives so we could follow them precisely when it came time for the boom show and tell at school.

First, we marched off the distance to the ridge to be sixty feet. This was easily done by having Wiry, the tallest, take twenty long strides, counting for a yard each. Then we pushed a couple of medium-sized stones together and taped the powder-packed-tight canister to one of them. Looking down at that juice can we silently hoped that it could level an entire orange grove. Then came the third-best part, my dad let D'nell and Sticks reel out the thick, white fuse. Hunched over and careful as surgeons they rolled the extended wick out, steady, smooth and straight to where we waited by the mini boulders. There was no wasted movement, like they were preparing to collapse the canyon entrance before the bandits caught up with us. My father showed us how to insert the fuse and then tape it securely in place.

Our jitters increased as we came a few steps closer to blast-off. We all hunkered down on the other side of the short bluff. We did rock, scissors, paper for who would strike the match. Stickwood won the lottery. Then came the second-best part, we all counted down from ten, rocket-ship style (except for my dad) and with a shaky wrist, Sticks lit the fuse. Eyes an inch above the ridge, we watched as the spark side-winded and hissed toward the rocks. We lay sprawled, like robbers waiting for the train's safe to blow. We counted out the timing. It took about eight elongated seconds. Then we saw a black cloud appear above the bomb for half a second, the thunder before the lightning and then everything, including our guts shook with a cracking *"Pow!"* It was an air-ripping sound we had never heard or felt before. Gravel, dust and dirt fell from above and around the detonation site. One of the stones had been blown sideways. We stood to investigate but my father motioned us to stay where we were.

"You've got to wait a few minutes in case there's any powder left to burn," he said. "Plus, it'll be hot over there so just be patient, boys."

Eventually, he waved us on, and we scrambled over the hill like prospectors striking it rich. The ground and the two rocks were scorched, and the orange juice can was blown clean at the top and bottom with burst out gashes in the sides. It was hard to believe that power and sound could have happened in much less than an instant. And it got the attention of all five of our senses.

"Whoa, now that's what I call a blast."

"That was wild, off the charts."

"Project Powder Keg has lift-off."

"Here's to the big blow show at school."

"Slam dunk people, slam dunk."

"I think we're lookin' straight at an A-Plus for this assignment, right guys?"

"Damn right, we are."

"Hey, watch your language and make sure you follow the exact same procedure when you're at school, otherwise it might not work or even worse, it might work too well."

"You bet. Thanks, Mr. McKendrick."

"Yeah, thanks, Dad."

"You're welcome. Now, let's clean everything up. I brought a metal pail for it all in case anything is still smouldering."

Our exhibition was scheduled for the following Monday. This gave us the chance to meet at my house, prepare everything including packing our mini keg and collecting all the things we would need. We ran this all by my dad and we were ready for the big blasterino the next morning at 11 a.m.

"Don't be cocky, and check every safety measure you can think of, twice," my father added with an oddly warm look in his eye.

We decided to wear slightly similar blue shirts, so we looked like a uniform bomb squad. We were even allowed ball caps (the Tigers) because the presentation was outside the school. At least we looked like we had some idea of what we were doing, handling explosives and all.

While our classmates watched from their stairwell bunker and half the student population craned their necks through the windows on the north side of the school, we taped the black-powder-stuffed juice can to the stump, rolled the fuse reel out like we had done that one hundred and ten times before, inserted it into and taped it to the can, and then turned as one to wave at all the kids and teachers. I think I even caught sight of our Principal, peeking out from behind his office curtains. The whole thing was an exciting mixture of fear, anticipation and not a little doubt.

We four Project Powder Keggers stationed ourselves behind the far corner of the school, about a dozen yards from Mr. Burnham and our class. We awaited his signal like racehorses at the gates.

"Light the charge and everyone keep your heads down," he shouted.

Sticks scraped the wooden match on the pavement and lit the wick. As before, it crackled and snaked toward the target. We heard some kids say, "Whoa!" Then it slithered up over the stump and disappeared over the far side.

Out of sight and silent, nothing happened. We clutched each other's arms and took a deep breath, prepared to hold the air in until something blew the heck up. Very still and nothing. Time was standing around and waiting, clipping its nails. Then a single spark appeared followed by a fizzle. Black smoke rose like a puffball and then the crack burst out wracking the air like a sledgehammer on an anvil, shaking the windows, the ground, our ears and chests. Birds exploded out of the trees beyond the fence, flying blind in all directions. Dogs yelped and whined all over the neighbourhood. A cat sprinted out from under a bush like it had been scalded with boiling water. Stump splinters fell among the smoke and soot.

When the echo of the sound and sight of the blast subsided, we stepped out from the side of the building to be greeted by another, more unexpected roar. It was the clapping, shouting, windows banging and feet stamping of the students and most of the teachers. As the consummate demolition experts that we suddenly were, we removed our ball caps and took a bow. That was met with cheers and yelling. Mr. Burnham looked more relieved than proud, but the hint of his satisfaction was there.

We jumped up and down, waved like we were being issued Oscars for our performance and then ran over to inspect the explosion. There was hardly anything left of the OJ can and the stump was shredded and charred, the asphalt scorched blue-black. The area looked like an ogre's campfire minus the burnt bones. We looked up to see the teachers herding their charges back to their desks. Our moment in the sun and smoke had ended, or so we thought.

"Clean it up and then report back to class," Hairy Burnham shouted sternly at us. "And guys," he added with a smile, "Nice work. You did a good job."

That meant an A with a plus like a cherry on top.

It was our first and last school spike. Even Sir William Cornelius Van Horne would have been proud.

Chapter 9

Sapphire Starlight Night

The Raiders were too young and busy to have much time for girls. Oh, we all had mums, sisters, cousins, aunts and grandmothers for female influence. And we had the odd hot teacher, a few pristine check-out chicks and some drive-in dolls that we had on our radar because they issued us little choice. That left girls at school and there were plenty that we were kinda keen on, but we had little money and a lot of our efforts and energy were channelled into plot planning and mission manning. In other words, we were ramping up to dating. It was on our to-do list but not at the top yet.

When we weren't watching Saturday morning cartoons in wintertime, we could usually be found helping Pucky prepare the local outdoor rinks. The only ice surfaces in town, they consisted of a series of five-foot, somewhat water-tight boards erected and dismantled annually, a smaller side rink with short planks to keep the ice in and a bunkhouse, reserved only for winter use. In it, skaters could change into or out of their boots, warm up to the stove in the corner, drink hot chocolate and use the washrooms 'round back. It was dingy, the floor was sliced into wood-shavings from our skates, the benches were hard, and the lights were dim, but we loved it. It was our own ski-chalet and the Puckster's pride. In fact, the whole operation was solely Pucky's domain. No other authority figure ever showed up unless it was parental units dropping off or picking up their kids. He was the rink master, custodian, human Zamboni, maintenance man, lighting and heating controller, groundskeeper, guardian and he had the final say on when the rink opened and closed, depending on the weather or the condition of the ice and probably himself on some days.

He didn't look much like the emperor of the ice park. Medium height but stocky, his face, neck and head all seemed to be one murky mass of gnarled hair and grit. If a bull had hands, they would have looked like Pucky's. He walked hunched over as though he were shouldering all the skating pleasure in A'burg. And he was. His eyes were dark and penetrating, revealing that a life-form did indeed exist behind the tousled hair and dingy cap with ear-flaps. Pucky had two voices, one muted murmur when he spoke to womenfolk and a coach's bark when he snapped at anyone else. He wore one uniform, a set of originally blue overalls, worn to a greasy grey on the outside and plaid flannel on the inside, exposed at the sleeves and collar. He moved so slowly and assuredly that those coveralls seemed frozen in motion like the ice they tendered: arms akimbo, legs in step. They could probably have carried on his duties without Pucky inside.

But you never even dared to spend an inkling thinking about thwarting Pucky. That would be like crossing the street against the lights in downtown Detroit. His few words were law. He never tacked up a list of rules in the bunkhouse, as everyone was expected to know them, passed down by siblings and friends from year to year. There weren't that many, but they were ice-clad: no smoking, no swearing, the side rink was for little kids and there were times for shinny games when hockey sticks were allowed on the main rink; otherwise, it was public skating only. Disregard for these edicts or bad behaviour was met with one punishment—banishment for the season. Any exiles who attempted to sneak in were caught long before the toe of their skate touched the rink. Plucky Pucky presided, and nothing got past him.

No one ever saw him during the other three seasons. Maybe he went south for the summer or hid out somewhere in the wilds of Comber? People had theories, but there was never an authenticated sighting during the off-skating season.

He usually performed his private ceremony of mending the boards, shoring up leaks at the edges, cleaning the ice and then flooding it with a firehose that he was granted use of from the nearest hydrant in the mornings in case it snowed overnight. Knowing that he was a worthy ally, the Raiders showed up to assist the skating Czar. Besides, it meant that we might be the first to hit the newly minted ice. He had two large shovels that he welded together to form a makeshift plow, so we volunteered to use those to scrape the previous-night's skate-shavings off as well as any snow. Some of us helped him clear the corners and the gates and throw the frozen crud over the boards. We also mounded and packed the low areas with snow to keep the surface even. Then it was time to hose it all down. Only Pucky sprayed the rinks. We never tired of stepping up on the wooden struts that supported the boards to watch him, a professional frost-polisher, at work. It was like watching a wizard waving a giant wand, transmuting mere water into a crystal sheen.

He directed the flow methodically with the same pattern: drenching the far end first, soaking the edges and keeping the main areas level with side-to-side sprinkling. Then it was time to wait. No one stepped a skate on ice until Pucky pronounced it ready. Puddles had to freeze. Cracks had to fill in. The bottom of the boards had to be solid. Sometimes crystals would form above low-lying areas while the water below stayed liquid. Those sections, if they were large enough, had to be re-sprayed. Skating too early could ruin his efforts for the entire surface to harden as a single shell with no weak points, divots or bumps. Once complete it was as smooth as any indoor arena, maybe even in the National Hockey League.

We played hockey, tag with no touchbacks, crack the whip, chase the hat, free the bunch and raced in circles. We were speed merchants weaving in and out of traffic without brushing anyone. We skimmed the ice up and down, sideways and backwards, on one blade then the other. The Raiders skated dizzily around, on and above the rink, twisting, leaping and coming to long stops to shave the surface into long sheets of freeze-spray that snow-coated others.

Often our games involved girls and guys with some jostling that would take place between the two, sometimes inadvertently, sometimes advertently. This interaction provided both sides with informal contact minus the worry or embarrassment of having to ask one another to have a skate together. On Friday and Saturday nights that's what happened. Under a series of lights, strung expertly over the rink like a twinkling trellis, men and women, teenagers and boys and girls would glide glove-in-glove or mitt-in-mitt about the glacial oval to the sounds of rock 'n roll, Motown and crooning favourites of yesteryear. Only replacing the radio and music with gramophones and waltzes would have changed anything from generations earlier, couples slicing along the crystal surface, side-by-side in the Alps beneath the mountain-framed heavens.

It was an odd Thursday, so much so that it was really a Friday. School was off the next day for one of the periodic teachers' conventions. Our instructors would have to sit around all day at meetings listening to, and expected to absorb and put into practice, new teaching techniques dreamt up by non-educators to make a living. Often these tactics never survived past infancy as they attempted to apply invented and untested theories directly to students' brains. The results were usually haphazard at best, more hazard than hap. We, on the other hand, were free as sparrows to flit and fly where we willed. During the afternoon, Skeeser and I had been bumping into, purposely or not, two girls we thought were pretty neat. He had his eye, shoulder and elbows on Jeanette "Jean" Smullens and I was leaning into Beverly "Bev" Denton.

They were both from out of our surrounding neighbourhoods. Jean was cute, petite and all big blue eyes with an alluring, mischievous grin. Bev had a cascade of long, dark hair down her back, eyes that sparkled in the day and night, and a certain fetching, female grace.

After we played skating games, knowing that Pucky knew when to keep the park ice open for music free-skates in the evening based on these school-free Fridays, Skeester and I had decided to reach down deep into our guts to wrench up enough courage to ask the girls back for the night skate. To our astonishment, they both said yes. As we watched the skaters leave for the day to allow Pucky time to clear the ice, Thatcher and I nervously congratulated each other on the success of Phase 1.

"Wow, I never thought she'd say yes!"

"Me too, this is major man."

"Primo."

"Outta sight."

"Righteous."

"Slip me five without the jive."

Being Raiders to the bone, of course, we would then implement Phase 2. Our idea was to have our mums make up extra-large thermoses of hot chocolate without letting them know that we would be sharing them with girls. Oh, and there was a Phase 3 too! That's why we were hanging around like rink-rats after everyone was gone. We skidded over to Pucky to ask him if he needed help preparing the surface for the second shift, knowing full well that he did.

"Sure," he said, obviously puzzled by our sudden kindness. "I don't have a lot of time to clean and flood."

We nodded, got behind the big snow plow and pushed it like mules. The two of us, exhausted and getting chilly, cleared the ice in half the time. We knew we had to get home, get cleaned up, have supper and get back ahead of the girls. We hadn't done a lot of this dating stuff, but we at least knew better than to keep a woman waiting.

When we finished, as he was sloshing about in his big, buckled, black rubber boots spraying the surface, he thanked us, unusual for the rink master. Time for the third phase. Walking unsteadily on our skate-guards, we wobbled over to him.

"Pucky, we got a favour to ask."

"Yeah, it's not a big one."

"What?" he wanted to know, peering at us sideways with one eye.

"Well, we know the lights are on a timer and we thought that…"

"We were hoping you could leave them on a few minutes after closing."

"You know, after everyone is gone."

"But us, that is."

"Now why would I want to do that?" he demanded, rubbing a frozen glove against his stubble.

"Ah, well, 'cuz we're skating with some girls tonight."

"And we thought it would be cool if we had the rink to ourselves for a bit."

We stood a little wilted, looking up at him like twin puppy dogs waiting for a treat.

Then Pucky did something strange. He grinned. Out from under all that grizzle, blinked, ever so briefly, the whites of his teeth. The moon might as well have been shining right at us, it was that rare a sight.

We part ran, part stumbled and part skied home.

Smelling slightly of our fathers' aftershave, axe-cut parts in place, hot chocolate in tow, we returned to our ice palace. Our knees were shaky, but our hopes were up there somewhere among the frosty branches.

Bev and Jean arrived about the same time at opposite ends of the ice. We each cruised over to meet them like we invented skating. We might as well have been wearing tuxedos and top hats. The gals looked like radiant ice princesses. We collected them, helped lace their skates, stashed our thermoses and eased out into the frozen dance hall we had helped stage. It was tough going at first. They had figure skates with toe-picks and precision-solid blades while we wore banged up tubular hockey skates with dents from slapshots and more scuffs than soccer balls. They seemed to float while we struggled to surface without our hockey sticks to prop us up. Eventually, we reached some form of unison. We began to drift together now cross-armed, then hands on winter coat hips and shoulders and finally as a foursome like some wintry movie musical. We warmed ourselves with the hot chocolate, laughed, pitched the odd snowball and fell a few times, usually into each other.

After about what seemed like three days, Pucky began ushering everybody out. We plopped down on the steps and swigged the last drops from our canteens. Bev and Jean began to loosen their laces, but we asked them to wait.

Sure enough, after the last person left, I caught Pucky heading out, too. He didn't look back but waved at us over his shoulder.

"What's going on?" Bev asked.

"Looks like we got the joint to ourselves," I said.

"But everyone else had to leave?" Jean wondered.

"Yeah, we got an in with the man in charge. Everything's cool," Skeese said with a laugh.

"Shall we, ladies?" I asked.

We slipped out onto the ice and realized that the music was still playing. The lights seemed to be flickering in tune. Pucky must have had the radio on the timer, too, that old rascal. The speakers were pounding out "Do You Believe in Magic?" by the Lovin' Spoonful. Oh, we believed alright. We grabbed one another's hands and danced on the frozen surface like Bobby and his full four were playing just for us. And they were. That was followed by the Temptations' "My Girl." Then came Martha Reeves and the Vandellas' "Heat Wave".

We lost track after that. The four of us swooped about, releasing and catching one another at the next bend. We bumped each other backwards.

Splayed our arms forward like speed-skaters. We shimmy-shook and camel two-stepped. We hully-gullied and bony-maronied. We swayed and twisted, churning out new moves thanks to the slick, illuminated dance floor.

Somehow, we knew that our time was almost up when the Beatles started into "Yesterday". It felt like yesterday and tomorrow at once, all wrapped up in the power of song and skate and life and energy and boy meets girl. We slow-dance-skated till Paul McCartney hummed the last few bars. Then everything switched off except our hearts.

"Oh no, the lights are out. We'll have to leave," Jean said, hugging Skeese.

"I'm afraid we might fall getting off the rink," Bev said, squeezing me.

"Don't worry, we'll be fine," Skeester said quietly and firmly.

"We got you covered girls," I added confidently.

Time for Phase 4. Did I mention Phase 4?

Skeese and I leaned into the girls' warmth and flicked on our flashlights. We suddenly were in twin spotlights, centre ice. The barons and baronesses of the ball. We took their hands, cut our beams and swirled them into the sapphire starlight. The only sounds were our skates and our breathing. We glided on the glimmer beneath our blades. Sky and ice reflected. We were skating on mirrors. No one spoke. The wind whistled a tune just for us. We were alone under the bowing, spiralling galaxy. Following the shadow-patterns in the ice we slid in and out of shimmering moments of wonder.

But Time rang its relentless clock chimes, and we had to leave. We escorted the girls to their doorsteps and, as we compared cheat sheets when wandering back to Rankin, we found that we each had received a moist peck on our flushed cheeks for our efforts.

I crawled hazily under the covers, switched off my night-light, turned and looked out my bedroom window just in time to see the crescent moon beam me a crooked smile.

Chapter 10

Bobby the Dog

A boy was prone, his cheek crushed against the sidewalk. His body contorted as though he had been dropped from high above. His reddish hair was matted over a ghostly, freckled face. An elderly lady approached, steadying herself on her cane. She stepped uneasily in her sturdy oxford shoes, a light veil covering her eyes. Birds sang and flitted in the Waterworks Park behind them at the base of Rankin Street. It used to function as a water filtration plant but had long-since been taken over by more modern machinery and moved. Under the walnut trees that adorned the park the grass and leaves lilted in a soothing breeze. As the lady neared the lad, she could see that his torso was over the walkway, but his legs were strapped to a fire hydrant, his knees at the ground, feet squirming at the top. She lifted the lace from her face and gasped, unable to perceive what was happening. The kid tried to roll up on his side, but his bonds held him in place. His moist eyes pleaded silently up to her for help. A gleaming, aquamarine Ford T-Bird cruised by, sleek and smooth. As she bent closer to look, whitish foam began to dribble from the corner of the kid's mouth. Then it started to pour out, bubbling in the summer sun. A sudsy lava streamed onto the sidewalk and into the gutter, a torrent of milky lather. She shrieked and almost fell on top of him.

When the flow finally ceased, blinking into the sunlight like a mole, he managed to whine, "Help me. Please untie me."

"What is wrong with you?" the wrinkled senior wanted to know. "What have they done to you?" she asked soothingly.

"Bad boys put me here, I didn't do anything. I'm sick."

"Alright, let me see what I can do, young man. These boys must be cruel."

The venerable matron stooped to release his ties when in an instant the boy wriggled loose, was up on his feet, clapping his hands, whistling and laughing like a circus clown.

As a man released from prison, Skeeser ran briskly down the street waving and hooting, cackling at the heavens.

Raising her walking stick like sword she shouted, "Come back here you scoundrel! I'll give you a caning on your backside for scaring me. You'll regret this disgusting prank of yours!"

"*Eeee-heee-Orreeette!*" he screeched to the skies. His own singular scream of victory. "*Eeee-heee-Orreeette,*" echoed through the park and down the street.

She chased him but it was in slow motion compared to our Raider hero of the day. Our boy Thatcher was already out of earshot, celebrating one of the greatest performances of his life. We other four Raiders clutched our sides in convulsive giggles behind bushes not far away. He had discharged new life into the Waterworks Park that bright day.

Skeese had invented his classic "foam-gobber" a few weeks earlier but he had to work on getting it up to maximum effect, which took some practice and a lot of saliva. This was its very promising public unveiling.

Spitting was part of our daily activities. It wasn't to be crude or even cool, we just found it relaxing and natural. And there always seemed to be some sort of competition that grew out of it.

We would spit on the ball diamond, the soccer pitch, the football field, the schoolyard when teachers weren't looking, the street and the sidewalk. We spat from our bicycles, into cricks and ditches, into ponds and cisterns, into the sky and into next week. It wasn't as if we were spraying spittle everywhere we went. We certainly didn't spit in church, the classroom, at home, at the movies or in a restaurant or grocery store. We never spit at people, pets, storefronts, muscle cars or into the wind. We knew when to hold our phlegm and when to release it. The RSRs had some pride and dignity.

There were four basic types. It started with the slobber gobber, the lowest form with the most dribble and least distance, like when you are brushing your teeth. You just kind of let go of what is in your mouth by pushing it to the front with your tongue and huffing outwards. This is how we all start, but sadly many do not advance beyond this messy stage. The second least impressive on the spitting scale is the blow-fish technique, the act of gathering saliva on your tongue and then blowing it out your mouth, away from your body at some distance. Unfortunately, the mucous tends to spray like a shot gun spread rather than stay concentrated like a bullet from a rifle. This, too, is inaccurate and sloppy and looks pretty cheesy, like you think you know what you are doing but you don't, and you probably have body odour and stink-breath. The third most difficult and widely used loogie that is the most accurate, effective, clean and impressive is the blow-gun spit. Gob is gathered in a ball to the tip of the tongue, the mouth forms a tight circle, and the saliva is fired by the lungs at the destination. That was our go-to spit style. We practised and perfected it as marksmen. The fourth option was limited to a very few experts who had to have the right dental structure. Spitting through your teeth was impossible for most and difficult to master. The thin spit came out in two sharp lines from the front teeth like a cobra. Its execution was fast, slight and remarkable. Those who were able to control it seemed to belong to a fraternity because they never made a show of it as though it was something they picked up yesterday, as easy as stepping on a crack.

The Raiders were all expert at drifting long, accurate saliva bursts at any time, place or target with the blow-gun approach but only Whaley could spit skillfully and easily from between his teeth. Sometimes spitting competitions were planned involving watermelon and sunflower seeds, which were usually for distance. More often, we would recognize an object that presented itself and the saliva squirting began. Anything was fair game to us: a huge spider web along a roadside, a swirl in a stream, an inner tube swing attached to a rope or a no-trespassing sign. Spitting opportunities popped up like targets at a shooting range. These contests were not only about accuracy and distance, but if no one had hit the mark after the first round you had to reload. This meant creating new mucous in your mouth as fast as possible by drawing in your cheeks and sucking saliva from the walls of your mouth like water seeping inside a cave. Breathing hard, we would be bent over working up new glutinous gob reserves to win the battle.

During one of these spontaneous competitions Skeese had the idea to just keep working up his spit to see how much he could create and still hold it in. Hands on knees in concentration, his cheeks swelled and his eyes bulged like Louis Armstrong hitting high saliva. We gathered 'round, sensing something important was happening. Then the levy broke and the foam began gushing out of his mouth. We stood back. Skeeser was shaking and he began to emit gurgling cries like a drowning man.

We reached to help him as though he was experiencing a saliva seizure until we realized he was laughing as he continued to spew white cotton candy pillows of gob-froth.

He sank to the ground, wiping his mouth and crying in convulsions of joy and shouted, "Check that out, you doofuses."

"Pretty cool man, how'd you do that?"

"I don't know. I just kept making more spit. The trick is to hold it in and not laugh. I'm going to call it the foam-gobber."

"Man, we gotta use that somehow."

"Yeah, maybe in front of my mum or some girls or a teacher on the schoolyard?"

"No, your dad would kick your ass."

"We don't want to be disgusting to girls."

"And in the schoolyard, once they find out you're faking, that's a one-way ticket to the principal's office."

"Taker' slack, Jack, we'll come up with something."

Eventually, we decided to go for the old lady. The Raiders spent the rest of the afternoon drinking a lot of water and practising our foam-gobbers, but Skeese always won. He seemed to have buckets in his belly of the repulsive saliva suds.

Our natural obsession with spitting took us into a new zone one day when we met Bobby the Dog. We were hacking around the old Navy Yard by the river by skipping stones, waving at boaters like we knew them to see if they would wave back, pretending to push one another into the water, ambling over the bank and jumping along the gabion baskets that fortified the land against the constant erosion of the water. Our attention was suddenly drawn to the chirping and singing of cicadas like tambourines in the trees.

"Those things creep me out," Rogie announced.

"I know, they sound like insect electricity," I replied.

"And they're weird looking, too," Skeese added.

"Yeah, like loud cockroaches," said Sticks.

"You've got cockroaches at your house?" Wiry wanted to know.

"Yeah, right. We ain't got not stinking cockroaches, but I've seen them before, you know in alleys and stuff."

"Oh so, what you hang out in alleys at night with the cock-a-roaches?" Skeese chided him.

Our cicada-cockroach discussion was interrupted by the appearance of a short and scruffy, two-toned mutt with oval eyes, scraggly hair and a long, panting tongue.

Who's this?" I asked aloud.

He ran over to us, wagging his tail like a bolo bat and whimpering. We petted him and searched our pockets for something to feed the poor little beast. He shook some as we patted the little pooch.

"Doesn't look like anyone owns him," Wiry said. "No collar."

"He's so skinny, you can feel his ribs," Rogan told us.

"Let's take him back to my place." I suggested. "I can get some dog food."

We trooped back to get him some grub, and he followed like he was one of our gang. It was when dogs ran free. They barked at whatever came along, chased squirrels and birds, and rolled in puddles and mud.

The mangey little pooch ate like a dog on death row. Maybe he was sent up the river for killing a cat? From then on, he would show up and the same thing would happen—we'd feed him dog treats, give him water and he'd follow us around like the Rankin Street Raiders' mascot. He'd jump up at our knees, get tangled in our feet, run ahead and beside us, barking excitedly and happily. We chose to call him Bobby the Dog, not just Bobby, it was always Bobby the Dog. He was an unnoticeable little mixed breed, but he ran with us so the elevation to three names seemed more suitable.

But what solidified him as the only honorary canine to be inducted into the Raiders' troop, happened a few weeks later. It was a busy Friday afternoon and the 'Burg was buzzing. The main intersection of Sandwich and Richmond was humming with life, full of kids spilling out of school to get fries and burgers, muscle cars cruising for chicks, new mums with strollers, youngsters roller-skating, guys getting Brylcreemed at the barber shop on the corner and teenagers smoking, slumped on the steps of the old stone library across the street—all to the sound of cars honking, radios blaring Motown, Romeos whistling, Juliets giggling, shouting and laughter.

The Rankin Street Raiders were out in full force, open to opportunities. We barked some banter with some of the guys we knew as they passed in hot cars, on tricked out bicycles or on skateboards.

"How you sound, big cat?"

"You know, just doin' my homework as soon as I get outta school."

"You just a cool breeze, you know that?"

"I know, I got four on the floor and a lot more."

"I'm gonna catch some Zs, man. I gotta gear up for tonight."

"I gotta take a whiz, I'll catch you on the flipside."

"Yeah, why don't you just put an egg in your shoe and beat it?"

As we strolled along, pooling our money to try to buy some hotdogs and pops, Rogie spit randomly on the sidewalk. Bobby the Dog scampered over and licked it up. No one really noticed but us.

We all stopped. I took a spit. Bobby was on it like a rat terrier on… well, a rat. *"Whoa!"* some of us thought and some of us said. Sounding like an old man accustomed to spitting at will, Skeese made that rattling, guttural sound down in his throat before he horked a phlegm-bomb the size of a snow-cone. Bobby fell upon it, paws on each side slathering it up, tail twisting in delight. It didn't take us long to realize that our spittle was like Milk Bones to Bobby the Dog. To him, they were mucous manna from the gods.

And it was too easy. All we had to do was wait for some unsuspecting victim: a child, a kid, a teenager, a tough guy, even someone else's parents, fling out an innocent spit and let Bobby take over. The reaction was always somewhere in the neighbourhood of, "Oh, that's completely disgusting." Then we would shrug our shoulders and shake our heads, miming that he wasn't our pet and walk away only to break into peels of hilarity around the next block. Sometimes tears would run down our cheeks, but the Bobster was a confirmed spit-dog.

Now we had both sides of the street covered: Skeeser the champion foam-gobber for old and especially cranky folks and Bobby the little spit-licker for the rest.

But we learned that you can only ride waves for so long before they crash into the surf and sand. Many spits 'n licks later he stopped showing up. We had kept him well-fed with dog food and treats and even brushed his hide on occasion, but a couple of weeks passed and no Bobby the Dog. We were up Spit's Creek without a paddle. Each of us watched for him when we were out and about, calling and horking into the distance for the wee saliva-seeking pooch.

We got the news from a friend. A dog that looked like our Bob was run over by a car on Alma Street. Our buddy said he saw it happen. The little pup was trying to lick a piece of chewing gum off the street. That removed any doubt, Bobby the Dog was gone. The Raiders hung our heads. At least he died in the trenches licking for what he believed in. We sighed a silent rest in peace for him.

His epitaph might have read:
Bobby the Dog
All spit and no polish.

Chapter 11

Rankin Street Bombers

We were running faster than ever, faster than forever. From Rankin we ran along the river past staid brick homes with sprawling porches and enclosed verandas, their lawns immaculate. Our feet flew through and out of town, taking us past the bank and the bakery, the dime store and Duffy's Tavern, Seaway Marine and the Coast Guard. Most were closed, nodding off in the warm night air. Like the view from a speeding train, the scenery seemed to be moving as we bolted by. Skeese was ahead of me, panting. There was no wasted movement, just elbows in, heads down and legs digging and driving. It wasn't a race. Fear was chasing us, an invisible mad dog. We were trying to get as far away as we could before we lost our energy and our breath. At the edge of A'burg, near the Blue Haven Motel, we had to give up. We slipped behind two cars in the motor court, out of sight and light. Sucking air like we had chest wounds, trying not to drown in our exhaustion we looked fish-eyed at each other, hunched over, bodies heaving, still unable to speak. In the darkness, illuminated periodically by the neon vacancy sign, a ghost named Panic sat between us.

Our one-summer obsession with water bombs ended that evening. Filling balloons with the backyard hose may have seemed an easy enough task, but the Raiders took it to new levels. Through trial and error, including many a burst bomb, we were able to gauge what size and weight the balloon should be, depending on whether it was to be dropped or thrown. For tossing, they had to be no bigger than a softball, otherwise they were too hard to pitch for any distance and, even more important, they would break in the release as the arm snapped forward. There was no point in lobbing a water bomb—it had to be fired accurately at the target. When dropping a water bomb, we felt it best to keep it under three or four pounds. The idea was to have it land beside the target, not so close that we would risk hitting the target but near enough to get he, she or it nice and wet. The result was a triple whammy: the initial sound and impact of the explosion, the tidal wave of water and finally, the realization on the victim's part of what had actually happened.

The balloon's skin had to be as thick as possible or it would break from the weighted pressure. Cheap, thin balloons were pointless for our purposes. Finally, they should be green or black so that when they blew up the shrapnel shreds of rubber would be less noticeable.

The objects of our water-bombing raids ranged from vicious backyard dogs and kids we didn't like, to mean neighbours and people who had wronged us. Our bombing blitzes became increasingly complex and unusual, employing stealth and cunning.

One day, we were out for revenge. The objects of our liquid bombing desires were some kids who had ratted us out for some minor escapade. We stationed ourselves one afternoon behind a neighbour's squared off boxwood hedge after seeing the parents leave in the family station wagon. We knew the kids we were plotting on often rode home from a nearby store, trying to steer their bikes with one hand, eating popsicles with the other. We were like duck hunters, our ears straining to hear the first quacks. When the two weasels cycled within range, responding to a silent signal, we stood up as one, water balloons held high. The kids gripped their frozen treats and tried to pedal out of danger. "Fire!" came the command. *Sploosh, sploosh, sploosh, sploosh* and *sploosh*. In an instant, our quarry was soaked, their popsicles scattered among the shattered balloon rubber. Half-crying and half-swearing at us, they stopped at the same time. Our arms were raised high again. "Fire!" Another volley of splooshes saturated them.

"That's what happens when you squeal," Sticks shouted.

"Next time it'll be worse," Wiry added.

We laughed and pushed one another about, soaking up our success. Then we fled the scene of our onslaught.

Lounging one summer morning in the empty schoolyard, reading and trading comic books, we hit upon another plan that would expand our water-bombing assaults beyond the horizon. We were discussing which comics were better: Marvel or DC. We never tired of that subject. I was Marvel and so was Rogan, while Wiry and Skeese were DC. Stickwood didn't go in much for reading comics so he was neutral. It was the Silver age of these 20-cent little books with lurid covers, cute dames, ads for everything from x-ray glasses to Sea Monkeys and, of course, superheroes. At first it was kind of close, as DC had Superman and Batman on their team. Marvel had Captain America and Iron Man. That's a fair fight.

But then something galactic happened. Instead of wooden figures with cartoon-style art fighting the bad guys and being too good to be true, Marvel began producing characters that were flawed. They struggled with their gift or curse of saving humankind, questioning themselves and their roles. Mutants, radioactive spiders, Norse gods and underwater kingdoms began appearing. At the helm were writer Stan The Man Lee and artist Jack King Kirby. A new stable of strangers, aliens who were from Earth, seemed to rise from the comic pages and boldly grab our imaginations with all the power they could muster. With the arrival of the Fantastic Four and Thor to Spider-man and the Sub-Mariner, a new universe was becoming possible. From the skies, the earth's core, other dimensions and your own neighbourhood, undreamt of champions were emerging. Superheroes, yes, but invincible, no. Wolverine with adamantium claws, Dr. Strange the sorcerer of inner space, the Silver Surfer, the herald for a world-eater, the Incredible Hulk, a Jekyll and Hyde creature of unbounded power, and Daredevil the first blind protector of the people, overtook DC's stars with the force, speed and brilliance of a nova.

Even the bad guys became three-dimensional, often wrestling with good and evil, helping the cause at times and thwarting it at others. Batman's foes like the Riddler, the Joker, Poison Ivy and Two-Face were no match for Spider-man's adversaries, Dr. Octopus, the Green Goblin, Mysterio and the Sandman.

Many of these heroes and villains had only one or limited powers, so they weren't unstoppable. They were superheroes but they were human, too. They had emotions and we shared them. It gave our young hopes promise that we had a chance despite our weaknesses. We could gaze with some confidence into the future, past the horizon and into the cosmos.

The long-standing DC vs Marvel feud was finally being settled. The winners were Lee and Kirby. No one could come close to matching them.

So, it was Marvel leading the charge that afternoon. We were all huddled under the iron fire escape, out of the wind, surrounded by our boxes of comics, which many of our parents threatened to throw out every few weeks. Our backs were warm against the red bricks. The school fronted onto Richmond Street, but it backed onto Rankin, so it was a regular haunt on weekends and after hours.

"How high do you think that fire escape is?" I wondered aloud.

"It's two tall storeys, so I guess seventy feet or more," Rogie replied.

"Anybody ever climb it?" I asked.

"Only during fire drills," Sticks said. "It's pretty strong."

"Let's go up for a minute or two, but we have to keep lookouts front and back," I suggested.

"I'll go with you," Rogan said.

"Me too," Sticks added.

Whaley and Thatcher stayed below at each end of the metal staircase with clear views of the two entrances while we three scampered up. The old red schoolhouse had two floors of marble staircases and hallways. The classrooms were cavernous with high ceilings, attics off the top rooms, windows like mini billboards and chalkboards the size of a station wagon. The fire escape, bolted to the outside of the building, descended from doors off the top floor. It looked rickety, but it was as solid as most of our Principal's decisions.

Amherstburg rose to meet us like it was popping out of the ground. We were seeing it from above—for the first time and all at once, it seemed: the filling station, men's clothing shop, hardware store, laundry flapping on clotheslines and vegetable gardens in backyards, red, blue and grey roof shingles, webs of telephone lines, trees sprouting at us, birds flitting from leafy branches and squirrels darting along fence tops, cone-shaped shrubs pointing up, people walking and kids riding bikes way down below us as we gazed from the skies. It all looked new and different, almost upside down. The fact that we were outside and could change our point of view made a major difference. Everything seemed to be unique, almost in motion. There was a secure, orderly connection to what we were taking in. Streets connected, sidewalks joined, the river and the main street were boundaries, community buildings like churches and the town hall, the fire department and the library stood out bold and solid. A photo would have told us that everything isn't random. There was a certain comfort in that.

"Wow," said Rogie. "You can see everything from here. There's the top of my house."

"I've never noticed all this before," Sticks said. "During fire drills you have to follow the person in front of you and get down as quickly and safely as possible."

"Yeah, this is something," I said. "It's like looking into an aquarium or an ant farm."

"Now that we've had the sight-seeing tour of our own town and visited your aunt's farm, you wanna tell us why we climbed up here, Matty?" Rogie snickered at me.

"Ok, here's the deal, ladies. What if we were to haul some water bombs up here at night and see what kind of cool splash they would make in the schoolyard?" I asked.

"Or even better, after some target practice, we could wait for someone to come along, aim not to hit but to splash and see how that goes?" Sticks replied.

"With all the streetlights around we would be able to see people coming from a fair way off," I said.

We hustled down the fire escape and explained the plan to Skeese and Wiry. It didn't take long to grab some balloons from our stash and fill them up at Rogie's place across the street. We took turns posting guards and releasing bomb after blasting bomb. They couldn't have blown up better. We would hoist the beasts up and tumble them over the railing, waiting for two seconds for the sound of splatter. It sounded like a surfacing, airborne whale returning to the sea.

The mark it left was a meteor crater without depth, surrounded by spray. The only thing we had ever seen like it was during the fad for throwing octopuses on the ice at the Detroit Red Wings' Olympia arena. They always landed head in the centre surrounded by splayed tentacles.

A couple of weekends passed, and we were ready for a live operation. We had heard our parents talking about some kids who had been breaking into neighbours' sheds and stealing stuff like shears, spades, watering cans and flashlights. It was petty thievery, so we figured they were guys our age or younger. Chances were, they would cut through the schoolyard from the other part of town rather than risk going through people's backyards or being out in the open on Richmond or Rankin. No point in getting caught before you had anything to show for it. It was a summer Saturday night so some parents would be out, no car in the driveway and the house lights would either be off, or the babysitter would be watching television in the family room. Easy pickins', if you knew what to look for. Setting up our checkpoints and wearing dark clothing we lugged three hefty bombs up to the fire escape platform. I was on the ground with Sticks, crouching between the light from the streets and the darkness, the shadow bars from the fire escape splayed across our faces. A quick whistle would signal anyone approaching. We brought some pops and Hickory Sticks for the stake-out.

After about an hour, a dog-walker and a couple holding hands and giggling passed through. Then, we heard a Raider whistle from above. We looked up, and Rogie pointed to the gate. Sure enough, two sketchy looking kids, whispering with ball caps pulled low, scuffled toward us. Sticks and I slunk back into the safety of the blackness behind us. Looking up we could see twin water bombs catching a glint from the streetlights as they balanced on the railing. Then we watched open mouthed as the first one did a jelly-tumble toward earth. We were prepared for the shock, but the junior burglars weren't. The fall was silent, but the landing must have seemed like the pavement was either erupting or giving out beside them. They were stunned and began to scream when the second phase, the water wave, hit them, almost knocking them off their feet, and drowning them in their own fear. Soaked and scared, the two-bit bunglers scrambled to their feet and took off like they were being shot at. Running crazy, they were zig-zagging to avoid the tentacles of the liquid beast that had attacked them.

Not wanting to blow our cover, the Raiders huddled together, whistling and whispering.

"Man, that was wicked."

"The way they peeled outta here, those dipsticks must be in Detroit by now."

"Those guys must have thought the sky was falling, pouring just on them."

"Stealing ladies' garden supplies may be off their cheesy little dance cards now."

"Nothing like scaring the whiz outta some dorks to set them straight."

""The Rankin Street Raiders were radical tonight, man!"

As we turned to leave, continuing to quietly congratulate ourselves like we had just won the Stanley Cup, a flashlight beamed on us. It was a cannonball of brightness. The Raiders froze and stopped breathing. Standing between two black puddles, surrounded by spray and balloon pieces with Rogie holding the last water balloon like a pumpkin in front of him, we couldn't have looked guiltier than a convict caught in the searchlight shinnying down the prison wall on a knotted bedsheet ladder.

A smoothly familiar and authoritative voice said, "Well now, what have you girls been up to tonight?"

It all came over us in a wave of recognition and understanding. Peering confidently and happily at us through his thick, black, horned-rimmed glasses was one of our teachers, Mr. Fleibs. He had a big head with a small patch of blonde hair on top and ornate eye-glasses. He was clever and funny so we were keen on him but wary. We all knew he lived nearby, he must have heard the commotion and rushed over to investigate. He was pointing his flashlight at us like it was a handgun, and it might as well have been. We weren't going anywhere.

The five of us had no response to his question. He motioned us to come down.

"It's obvious what you bunch have been doing, so I won't encourage you to begin lying," he said through a smirk. "You do know that being up on the fire escape at night is illegal and dangerous."

As a group we craned our necks back up to consider the fire escape then looked back at him and then at the ground as we nodded grimly.

"And you must know that dropping balloons filled with water on other kids could have seriously injured them?"

We inspected the ground and kicked a couple of pieces of rubber away, nodding wordlessly.

"Well then, all of you, bring that thing here. Let's have a look at it." We shuffled like a ten-legged creature over to him. As we gathered 'round, he shone his light on it, and as we all studied our handy work, he pulled some keys out of his pocket, stepped back and punctured it, saturating some of us. We managed to keep a soggy silence.

As though nothing had happened, he said firmly, "I don't want to hear or see of this again or I will contact your parents and perhaps the police, depending on the severity of your actions. I want all of you to think of the harm you could cause others when you pull these stunts. You can be doing better things with your time and mine for that matter."

Relieved, we greeted him with a chorus of "Yes sirs."

"And I want this mess cleaned up before noon tomorrow."

Another round of "Yes sirs."

"Have a good night," he said with a snarky laugh and waved us off.

We clammed up until we were out of the schoolyard and his earshot.

"Have a good night too Mr. Flea-bbers."

"Yeah, good night, Goggles."

"Sweet dreams, Mr. Egghead."

"Don't forget to buy your ticket for the nerd convention."

"Everything copacetic, Raiders?"

"Cooler than cool, you fool."

"Rankin rakes and garden tools are safe thanks to us!"

"We rule! We got the raid made in the shade."

But the recreational sport of water ballooning for pleasure had not quite been done with us yet. It turned sour in a hurry.

Another day, we were circling our bikes around what we considered to be our own park, half-racing, cutting one another off, popping wheelies, riding no hands, laying rubber on the asphalt by speeding up and then breaking for long skids, jumping curbs and playing chicken. Some of us had Mustangs with banana seats and high ram-horn handlebars; others had tricked out rides with flashy mud guards, streamers waving outta the hand grips and red reflectors front and back. Rogan even had a three-speed with power to spare. Sticks, to his shame, had to ride his sister's clunky cast-off with no cross bar so it was obvious that it was a girl's bike. In protest he rode it demolition-style all the time, hammering it into the ground every chance he got. It always looked fresh from the junkyard. I had a basic cherry red CCM one speed, but I had talked my dad into changing the handlebars so the grips would face upwards. I loved that bike and put more mileage on it than my dad did on his car.

"Our park" became known as Toddy Jones Park, but we always thought of it as ours because it was one street over from Rankin, near the high school, not far from the river and the Fort Malden museum. It featured Pucky's rink in the winter, a pool that was drained and refilled every day in the summer, due, no doubt, to the amount of human sludge that had accumulated at the bottom, the usual swings, teeter-totters and merry-go-round, as well as a completely dangerous and wonderful contraption known as the maypole. Attached by metal chains to a solid steel pole were six two-rung grips that kids would hang on to. Everyone would run as fast as they could in the same direction until the centrifugal force lifted all of us off the ground, swinging with power and speed around the pole.

But that wasn't the best part. As the weight of the miniature bodies added to the strength of the swing, the last kid would be propelled above and past the others like a whip being cracked. At this point you had no choice but to hang on or die. It was a combination of flying, trapeze work and body surfing, and it was out there way beyond scary. The Raiders, of course, worshipped and mastered that playground masterpiece of skill, energy and fear. We could soar one-handed like flying squirrels. Even we were amazed by what circus acts we could perform on that unparalleled apparatus. But after several bruises, broken teeth and bones, it was dismantled. All that was left was the pole. No swings swung from the metal maple's stripped branches. May had become December.

"Ya know, we gotta get back into water-bombing only for bigger game," Wiry said as we cycled wistfully by our old, lonely maypole.

"Like what, for instance?" I asked, swerving by.

"I dunno… moving targets. Something to test our skills," he said.

"We've already done bikes, not exactly a safari hunt," Sticks chimed in.

"I'm not talking about going to the Detroit Zoo for elephants, although that isn't all that bad an idea," Wiry said with a raised eyebrow.

"Forget it, they've got security guards everywhere and besides, an elephant wouldn't even notice a water balloon, no matter how big it was," Rogie replied.

"What about buses? Easy targets, nice and big?" Skeese suggested.

"Nah, we still need the cover of night," Rogeman said. "We gotta be able to split in a hurry, and the town buses don't run past six."

"Alright, Pips. What about cars? We haven't bombed any of those. We can aim for the ones that are going too fast down Rankin?" Wiry said confidently.

"Low-five on that, one Whaley," Sticks said happily. "That's what we do, hit some cars where we live then disappear into the backyards and alleys we know so well."

"And, I been workin' on another idea," Skeeser yelled. "Why not fill the balloons with Kool-Aid instead of water with extra sugar so they leave a sticky mess?"

We came to a dusty halt, grinding our bikes into the gravel. A new frigate had been spotted on the horizon. The pirate plotting began. We would field-test different flavours, sugar levels, throwing weights based on the distance from Rankin to our launching area behind trees and gardens and the impact results. Collecting the supplies we needed from our parents' pantries and kitchens, we practised on an abandoned shack down by the river. After a series of experiments, grape left the biggest stain spread and about a half a cup of sugar seemed to be the right gluey dosage. The result was a combination of a thud and a smack upon impact followed by a purple splatter that sprayed about five feet in diameter in all directions and it stuck to the shack wall like quick-drying cement. A new weapon was instantly added to the Raiders' arsenal.

Once again, a Saturday night was chosen to unleash our gooey grenades as there would be lotsa Fast Eddies out cruisin', flashin' their rides, blarin' tunes, lookin' for chicks and interrupting the sleepy neighbourhoods of A'burg. We decided to give some showboats a break: ragtops, really, really boss muscle machines, mum and pop sedans and guys with gals. That left the low-life crowd who couldn't afford or take the time to acquire or customize classy chassis—the greasers with more attitude than cool. They were the ones who lived to rev their B-grade engines and squeal their tires as they passed by old ladies knitting on their porches and kids playing in their front yards.

We picked the side of the Nevitt's house as it was quiet and covered with leaves and bushes and the neighbour was rarely outside. It also provided an endless series of hiding places among the parking lots, store sheds, backyards, waste bins, fences and gates strung out behind the houses that faced Rankin Street. We acquired Donny "the Hat" and his brother Ray

"Chompers" Nevitts' help, partially due to the location for the mission and because they had heard about it and wanted in. Ray was up for anything. He was short but tough, wiry and sassy. He could loudly tell anybody why they were wrong, and which was the best way to go about leaving. And he could eat more soda crackers than any buccaneer who ever swashed a buckle at sea or on land. That's how he earned his nickname. His younger brother Donny was funny, had a great singing voice, was a good hockey player and loved to wear hats all kinds, styles and colours. He also kept one eye out for the gals.

Across the street were two dark houses that shared unfenced yards. That natural alley led to our town park on the other side, so it had no lights and a lot of cover. One of the houses was the Jackson place. Mick Jackson had also heard about the operation, so he was in too. Mick was tall, lanky, lotsa freckles and laughs; real easy going. But he was a good guy to have on an assignment like this with smarts and speed when there was need. And for good measure, we added the services of our pal Jeremy High-Rise Thatcher, a distant cousin of Skeese's and a periodic Raider. He was tall and athletic, so he looked older than his years. He had thick, sandy hair, a square jaw, a long reach and a ready laugh. He could also pound the paint just like his idol the Piston's great Bob Lanier and sink swishes with ease. He used his torso and his elongated elbows to work his way into position to hit the hoops. It was a pleasure to watch him work the round-ball court. A talented, all-around athlete, we used to play tennis doubles in slow motion to pick up chicks. Sometimes it worked but slowly.

Our escape routes were not only prearranged but perfect. And the plan was simple: once the bombs were launched, we would watch them blow up, check the reaction and then dissolve into our dark network of concealment, holing up until the potentially stormy coast was clear. We arranged to meet back at the schoolyard in the far corner.

It was the Nevitt boys, me, High-Rise and Skeese on one side and Wiry, Rogan, Stickwood and Mick on the other. We wore dark clothes, sneakers and ball caps and cupped two Kool-Aid bombs in our nervous palms. The night was clear and the streetlights provided bright spots in the skirts that shone below them. That's what we were aiming for: a car revealed by the nightlights so we could shoot from the shadows. A few souped-up cars rumbled past, but they didn't suit our needs. We waved each side off in silence.

The Raiders and their associates were getting jumpy. We were all kind of walking in one spot, keeping our feet fresh for the run and our legs loose. A dog barked, and Jackson nervously squished one of his balloons. "Rookie," Wiry whispered. "Shut up, man. This gig is making me nervous," Mick said.

Then, an old, beat-up black Chevy came toward us, driving too fast and swerving. The guys inside were shouting over the radio blasting. Rogie gave us the high sign, finger pointing up and circling. We held our breath till they rolled into the cone of light under the streetlamp. Everyone pitched their water bombs at once. Some were lost in the release, some landed wide or short but a few exploded on the trunk and a couple struck the roof of the ride. The car lurched sideways like it had been hit with machine gun fire, tires screeching and smoke bursting from the tires. It skidded about twenty feet and we could hear the inmates inside the car cursing like demons.

And so, they were. Almost ripping the doors off, we watched as four grubby giants struggled out of the still-vibrating and blaring Chevy, roaring and pumping their fists. They looked like rhinoceroses being born, battling their way out of a metal womb. Illuminated by the streetlight were the blood red words Satan's Choice splayed on the backs of their vests. It felt as if our eyes had just touched an electric fence. It was a biker gang, *the* biker gang, sporting colours. They turned and lumbered at us, swearing monsters, two on one side of Rankin, two on the other. We didn't even take time to freeze. No one looked back. All I could see were my feet kicking out in front of me. I thought I would have to stop and shove my heart back into my chest. That's when I saw Skeester ahead of me, his legs whipsawing under him.

Crouched behind and between the cars in the motel lot, we finally stopped suffocating enough to speak, feet sore, lungs aching and sweating like desert rats.

"Who knew they drove cars?"

"Who knew they could run?"

"What do ya think they would have done to us?"

"Oh, nothing much. Maybe just burn us with cigarettes or make us walk on broken glass."

"When do you think it'll be safe to go back?"

"In about a year."

We heard all about it the next day. The Satan's Choice crew didn't catch anyone, but they sure as hell woke up the neighbourhood. Mr. and Mrs. Nevitt took turns yelling back and forth with them and threatened to call the police. Other parents joined in. Some brought out their dogs and had them bark at the bikers until they finally left, swearing at everyone and everything, smashing half-full beer bottles on sidewalks, flicking their butts on lawns, honking their horn, roaring their engine through their Thrush pipes.

Every parent knew what happened. Most of us received thirty days in the hole: stuck in our rooms, no TV, no radio, no phone calls, no outside privileges and no visitors. The water had been drained from our bombs for good.

Chapter 12

Have Guns – Willing to Travel

Lenny Stickwood lay prone on his backyard lawn, arms in the triangle position, hands tightened on a small air rifle aimed at a box target 40 feet away. His breathing was steady, but his face tightened into a grimace as his eyes squinted.

"Keep the bead at the end of the barrel levelled at the centre of the target," his father directed as he paced in measured steps behind him. "Take a deep breath and as you are letting it out, slowly squeeze the trigger while maintaining a firm grip on your weapon," he continued. "Don't flinch or move anything but your index finger."

Geoffrey Stickwood was lanky, bespectacled and proudly wore a goatee and a beret. He was a public-school teacher but on the firing range of his own design, he was Sargent-Major Stickwood of the 1st A'burg Cavaliers. He had purchased some regulation targets and set up a cardboard box stuffed with sawdust and old carpeting. His son was learning the ropes about marksmanship and he was damned if he would let him fire a gun without his austere guidance. He was a stern dad but fair and not without a sense of humour which appeared periodically and then disappeared like a will-o'-the-wisp.

"When do I get to shoot?" Stanks asked, not daring to move from his position.

"Let's go over the top five safety rules once more," his father replied, striding and about-facing behind the line of fire, swatting his bony leg with an imaginary swagger stick.

His son sighed, chancing a scratch of his ass.

"Ok, first never keep a gun loaded unless it is in use."

"Good, go on, son," his officer-father said.

"Second, never aim at a person or animal. Third, always be certain of the surroundings behind your target. Fourthly, ensure that your weapon is in perfect working order."

"Excellent, now what's the final precautionary rule when employing firearms?"

"Ah, I don't remember," Sticks hoarsely whispered, listing to one side on the grass to alleviate a cramp and brush off some ants.

"Think, boy, this is crucial. We can't begin until you get this right," his dad barked.

Squinting and sighing Sticks pleaded, "I don't know, can't we just start?"

"Safety first, you dolt, safety first," Sergeant Sticks thundered from above.

"Shouldn't that be the first rule instead of the last?" his son ventured.

"No, safety first is always important, but it is the fifth rule as well as a reminder. I've told you that."

"But doesn't safety first really include all the other rules?"

"Shall I pack up the target, the ammunition and your yet-to-be-used gun now and be done with it or do you want to get this right?" his commanding officer said, stamping his foot and slapping his thigh.

"Ok, ok, safety first and fifth, whatever."

"Right then, let us begin. Keep the bead at the end of the barrel levelled at the centre of the target."

Lenny's father's weapon of choice was a Daisy Cub BB gun, one step above a pop gun that fired a cork attached to a string. Its FPS (feet per second) has never been measured because it was too slow to register. The shooter can actually watch the copper BB leave the barrel as it sinks in an arc toward the ground. It would bounce off a good-sized beetle. A kid with a good arm could probably throw a BB faster than the Cub spat it out. The shot looked like an old geezer floating a lazy spit on to the sidewalk at the end of the park bench.

We were all lobbying our parental units for guns. It was a sign that the Rankin Street Raiders were coming of age. Never mind that none of us had one—according to the information each of us told our fathers (no point in going to Mum for permission to fire) their kid was the only unarmed youth in the group.

We started at the top asking for a pellet gun and the top of that line was the Sheridan Blue Streak Pump Action 5 mm with up to 675 FPS. It was a doozy. Wood stock, cool sights, nice and heavy, around six pounds and the best part was that it looked and felt like an actual rifle instead of an air gun. But getting a dad with any weaponry knowledge to sign off on this sharp-shooter was difficult, largely because pellets generally travelled a lot further and faster than BBs. And they were made of lead, which meant that they somewhat imploded upon impact. Also, they weren't reusable like BBs, which was a factor for parents who took the cheap skate on the pond every time. We were really shootin' the moon when we requested that prime piece of hardware.

Second on the list with a bullet was the Winchester 1894 Model 4.5 mm lever action BB gun. This was, by far, the coolest gun potentially within our reach. It held a magazine of about thirty little round balls of ammo, had a hardwood stock and you cocked it under the trigger to shoot. It was what the rifleman used on TV, and it was the Chevy Camaro of BB guns to us. The Winchester 1894 didn't have the power of a pellet gun, but you felt like you were riding the range hunting down desperadoes whenever you gripped one in your hands.

Here's how we netted out in the coveted carbine acquisition department.

Sticks, of course, had to put up with his glorified pop gun and the hours and days of weary instruction. Wiry got the only pellet gun and it was the Blue Streak, which he let us all take turns with occasionally. Thatch and I scored Winchester 1894s, possibly because we had the steadiest incomes from paper routes and grass cutting. We both employed the "It's our money, we earned it right?" approach, and eventually it worked.

Unfortunately, Rogan got burned. No way he was gonna get a gun. He might as well have been asking for a motorcycle. Instead, as compensation, he received the best slingshot available, the WHAM-O 170 featuring a solid wood frame, adjustable tension for the tubular elastic bands and a soft leather pouch from which to release the steel ball bearings, the WHAM-O ammo. He kept it polished and wrapped in cloth like an amulet. Within weeks he was a better shot with that catapult than we were with our air rifles.

After a certain training period for all of us (nothing as rigorous as Stanks had to endure) we were allowed armed, into the wild. The first place we headed was our hallowed Arch, our sanctuary of adventure. Along the way, after shooting anything that didn't move: mailboxes, signs, abandoned house windows and weathervanes, apples dangling from branches, rusted cans and muddy bottles fished outta ditches then balanced on fence posts, light bulbs in front of derelict shacks, goofy lawn ornaments, cucumbers in one field, tomatoes in another, birdbaths, sundials, abandoned cars and any manner of growth that attracted our attention from milkweed pods and puffy flowers to thorny husks housing chestnuts, the Raiders began to seek bigger game. We had been able to pick off whatever we wanted and now it was time to move on. Of course, we were all warned not to aim at any living creature let alone shoot it but stopping something dead in its tracks was almost impossible to ignore. It was in our noggins like a fever.

Entering the heavy bush that protected the Arch, that yearning was enflamed by the tweets and twitters, chirrups and cheeps and warbles and whistles of so many birds in the trees, bushes, thickets and glades. Early autumn, the birdsong and birdcalls were everywhere, whisking through the chameleon leaves waving and changing as the Raiders marched happily into its familiar embrace. It was no more than two abreast for each path, and we knew better than to shoot sideways, only forward. Under the leafy cover, the piping of wrens, nuthatches and chickadees mixed with the rarer music of indigo buntings or blue canaries, the *kaw-kaw* of the yellow-billed cuckoo as well as the shrill *klee-klee* of the merlin falcon filled us with energy as we listened like bird-dogs to every sound, noise and echo. But no shots were fired.

When we sat down in the shadow of the temple of the Arch, it was obvious that some Raiders were beginning to have reservations about blasting these winged jewels to smithereens.

"Guys, I don't know if shooting birds is such a great idea?"

"What if it's a partridge or a grouse? Then we could bring it home to eat?"

"Yeah, who's going to pluck it, chop its head off and gut it?"

"Besides, a pellet or a BB or even a mini ball bearing isn't gonna kill a pheasant. It might just fly away to bleed to death."

"Plus, you need a hunting licence for game birds. We aren't old enough."

"And what would be the purpose—proving we can shoot straight by knocking a bird off a branch only to have to pick it up and feel it die?"

"Why kill anything unless it's for food anyway?"

"Or a varmint or if it's diseased."

"Like a rat with rabies."

"Yeah, and how would shooting a cat or dog be any different than a bird?"

"I wouldn't want some kid shooting my dog for fun."

By then, we had talked ourselves so far out of Slayerville, we were no longer in Essex County.

For the first time in our lives, we had been given the opportunity to take lives. In that realization these birds that surrounded us had become precious, glowing in the woods, illuminated by their song and beauty. Perching and flitting with serene pride through the Arch's glen, the Raiders' secret hideout, were these harmonious, delicate gems essential to nature's ornamental cloak. A kaleidoscope of fowl, they filled us with a new appreciation and awe. It seemed that we were seeing, hearing and feeling their presence for the first time.

Suddenly, a tiny flock of unusual birds landed in a tree right above us. Later, after looking them up at the library, we found out they were Cedar Waxwings. Tawny with tufts at the back of their heads, grey wings with red markings and yellow-tipped tails, they wore thin black masks. None of us had seen anything like those radiant creatures huddled together. They began passing red berries with their beaks among one another like bandit friends having lunch.

Kind of like us sharing lunch.

Chapter 13

Saints Preserve the Rankin Street Raiders

The train whistle sounded sharp, weaving its way into the ears of elated visitors who were picnicking, roller-skating, flirting and winning Kewpie dolls and teddy bears. It reached people who were swaying to the music, flying high and speeding low on mechanical monsters designed for fun and fear and disembarking from giant riverboat ferries full of excitement and expectation.

A train ride is popular because it offers an ultimate comfort: travelling and sight-seeing without concern. There's no threat of crashing from the skies, plowing into an automobile, springing a leak and sinking or having the carriage horse pull up lame. It's just lean back and watch the world swim smoothly by and your cares float dreamily out of the coach.

Boblo, of course—to add to its allure—had a train, small but essential. There were no tracks. The open-air bus ran on tires, not steel wheels, but no one cared. It looked and sounded like the real thing. The Boblo train escorted guests on a long, circular tour of the isle: here were the Midway and the arcades, Kiddie Land and the zoo, there were the mini-putt, cafeteria and souvenir shop, then the huge Palisade dance hall, concession stands and first aid station, all under and among the shadows of the aerial rides. It chugged its way past the baseball diamonds and makeshift badminton courts, the lawns full of families roasting wieners and grilling hamburgers and groups celebrating reunions, birthdays and company outings. The old lighthouse appeared out of the crowd of birches and poplars. The little locomotive made its steady way among the whispering willows, bent sturdily over the banks, their bark rough from the wind and water and their leaves-on-strings providing a veil for the bays they protected. Canada geese honked and flapped along the riverbanks, wood ducks clacked and splashed in the inlets, seagulls and terns squawked and dove near the point. Around a bend, the old block house sat solid in the shadows of time.

There was something for every visitor, providing passengers with postcard vistas, unusual scenes and cherished memories.

"Alright you lot, get the hell offa my train. The ride's over. You're not getting a free trip."

The voice was coming from the conductor, who considered himself the Emperor of Boblo and it was aimed directly at us. George Chemsky was shouting through his nicotine-stained, gnarled-roots of a moustache, complimented by his twisted spokes of ear hairs and his burley cy-brow, from under his wobbly hat box of a conductor's cap. He looked like a bowling ball painted with a drab uniform and wedged behind the engine. We called him Conductor Chumpsky.

Steaming and wheezing like a broken-down human train, he bellowed at us again, "And next time, no standing, arms and legs inside the car, no profanity and no spitting gum."

We eased ourselves out of the caboose like we were deaf.

"You won't be allowed on my train again if you don't toe my rail line," he added, as if by decree, chuckling to himself.

Chumpsky stayed in our conniving thoughts as we sauntered toward the Moon Rocket for a no-charge ride from the operator.

"We gotta do something about that bum. He's becoming a drag."

"And I ain't payin' a plug nickel to sit in his stupid train ever again."

"There's gotta be a way to get that guy's goat and ride for free."

"Hang loose, lads. The Raiders will come up with something."

It took us a while to find the answer. I got the phone call from Skeese one night. He was all excited and giddy.

"Hey, Mighty Mouse. You know our problem with Chumpsky and his dinky toy train?"

"Yeah, I got nothin'."

"Well, I think I have the answer and it's in the Raider cool zone."

"Lay it on me, man."

"Ok, check this out. It's a trackless train, but it has to take the same route every trip. Sure, it goes by the centre of the amusement park, but it also drives passengers around the woods and stuff. There's a buncha' places where it passes under over-hanging trees. The middle of the train is covered by a canopy, but the last few seats are open, you know, where we always sit," Thatch said, giggling as he talked.

"What if we found some branches that were low enough to reach and sturdy enough to hold our weight? Chumpsky usually slows down a bit going under them. If the last seats are empty, we could either drop in or pull ourselves up and out," he said like he was being tickled.

"I get it! We could land in the back bench on one side of the island and lift ourselves out before Chucklehead conductor pulls into the station. And he's not allowed to stop until he gets there unless there's an emergency. Plus, what could he do anyway? He can't run, he can barely walk."

"Free boarding and detraining, Matty," he chortled, "and the trees will hide us."

"It'll drive him nuts."

"And dig this, we could employ some of our usual covert ops and do some advance field work by finding the right spots with the best tree limbs, one on the east and one on the west side of the train route. Then we could clip off some of the twigs and sucker branches and smooth out the places where we would swing from for good grips."

"Outta sight, man! First you see us then you don't."

"Another classic Mandrake the Magician act courtesy of the Rankin Street Raiders."

A few days later, some of the Raiders, Terry, Rogie and me, along with D'nell, made the river passage with some specific tools hidden in our pockets. We had two pairs of garden shears, a coupla files and some sandpaper. Rogie was sporting his customary white t-shirt and jeans, D'nell had cut the arms off a sweatshirt and wore it inside out, Skeese wore a paisley shirt with a button-down collar, corduroy shorts and desert boots, while I was in clam-diggers, a striped t-shirt and bright red Keds sneakers. We were also topped off by an assortment of ball caps and Skeese had a straw fedora with a green, artificial grass band and a golf ball nestled in the crown.

The plan was to split into pairs and head to the two different sides of the island, find along the route the ideal branches for swinging down or up and give them a manicure.

One guy watched and listened for the train to come huffing and puffing along while the other kid clipped away twigs and suckers, filed the bumps down and then sanded the branch smooth for easy gripping and release. The trick was to remove as few leaves as possible for maximum cover. We worked fast and hard, laughing and sniggering all the while. Then we heard the tiny train's horn tooting.

"Stay in the tree and see if he notices you, then we'll know if it's gonna work," D'nell said to me, as he jumped into the bushes above the riverbank.

Sure enough, our grumpy conductor passed within three feet of me and didn't notice a thing. I might as well have been the invisible boy. When it passed, we cut across the island to the tree Rogan and Skeese were preparing. D'nell gave Thatch the same instructions and the rest of us hid behind the block house. Same deal, sleepy Chumpsky, it seemed, couldn't see an elephant if it was clinging to a branch in that leafy tree. He was too busy being the conductor/engineer/tour-guide, pointing out all the sights and items of interest along the route, all the while blowing his own horn for special affect. Our camouflage was complete. We proved that the hiding part was aces, now it was time to test the dropping in and out of the miniature choo-choo. The heat of the day gave us an edge for our early practices because most riders were in the shade under the canopy, which left the last few cars open for us.

It was Terry's idea, so he went first. The scheme was to lower himself into the train on the east side of the island and then lift himself out on the other side before the fake locomotive reached the station. One of us spotted him for the drop and the other two hid and watched for the lift-off. Despite half-flopping and landing sideways in the seat like a jellyfish washed up on a beach, Thatch pulled it off. On the home stretch he wished he had done a few more push-ups in preparation because he dangled over the tracks, struggling to pull himself up. The conductor blathered away and chugged on oblivious to the skinny kid behind him, hanging out of a tree. In a moment, his strength gave way and Skeese crumpled to the ground, but quickly rolled behind the tree. We were on our knees screaming with laughter, but he had pulled it off, proving our efforts were not in vain. The rest of the afternoon we took turns, riding the invisible rails for free.

For our last successful run, we decided to fall into the train at both junctures then disembark at the station. What did we have to lose? We'd save more train stowaway tactics for another day and include our missing comrades, Whaley and Stickers. Strike-Force and I took the first shift, timing our jump so we tumbled into the last car like gymnasts. It was a quiet, unseen and successful drop. A couple of passengers ahead turned around, but they just seemed to think they hadn't seen us there before. They shrugged and we looked comfortably out at the scenery. Then it was up to Thatch and Rogie. We made room for them and gave them the thumbs up. Rogan landed like he'd been sitting there for an hour, perfectly still and smiling at his accomplishment. Skeese wasn't quite so lucky. He managed to land with his torso inside the train and his ass and legs hanging out the side. We stared straight ahead like nothing was happening, covering the actions of Rogan who was struggling to drag Skeeser in before Chumpsky saw anything. No one noticed and we settled in to enjoy the rest of the ride, flush with victory, unable to control our glee. We slipped one another five and beamed out at the island countryside.

After entering the station to disembark, we ambled out of the train like we owned the place. I turned around just in time to see our flabby conductor, scratching his wrinkled skull, sopping the sweat from his face with his grimy handkerchief and staring hard at us. We fought down the temptation to wave or flip him the bird. Might as well let him wonder.

Rogan and Skeeser had to head home to do some chores, but Strike-Force and I decided to stay and get in a few more rides. It had already been a peachy day, why not add some ice cream on top? One of our favourite haunts was the Dodge 'em Cars at the back of the park near Kiddie Land. They were housed in their own dark building on a concrete platform. The Bumper Cars operated like pint-sized street cars. There was an electrified wire-mesh suspended from the ceiling. The vehicles were outfitted with steel poles that ran up to the grid and made contact using thin, pliable, metal connectors attached to the top of each car's shaft. At the start of the ride, the operator threw the switch with satisfaction like he was animating Frankenstein's monster.

Suddenly, the cars came to life and as they moved, the current crackled overhead. It was scary at first, driving these things around in that dim cave with mini bolts of lightning dancing above us, but we didn't care. We got to ram other drivers for a full four minutes, so danger wasn't much of a concern. The small, round cabs were outfitted with heavy-duty rubber cushions, as was the entire bumping lot. Also, around the walls, just off the floor were reinforced rubber pads backed by steel springs so when we hit the wall, or were driven into it, we were not only protected but bounced backwards. There was a kind of reverse sling-shotting effect that we never tired of and not everyone understood. Sometimes we would pile into the wall just to get propelled away from an adversary.

Each year, at the start of the season, we field-tested all of the cars to find the two or three that had the highest speed and greatest mobility. We marked them with a small 007 on the back below the electric stem. Covert ops, baby. And we were experts behind those wheels. They had to be cranked quickly for sharp turns and spun completely around for reverse. It usually took newcomers most of the ride to figure out how to drive backwards, while we slammed into them again and again in their learning frustration. Ramming speed all down the line. When we slipped into those seats, we were Stirling Moss and Jackie Stewart at their best.

Flush from our recent train triumph, we strode up to the gate to see our pal Dale Yips York, the operator, or electrician, as he liked to call himself. D'nell and I shared some Vernors with him and asked how the fleet was running. Yips told us that there were a coupla duds that he hadn't had a chance to fix but they weren't our two favourites. He knew which carts we wanted to drive and let us know that they were fine and "dandruff".

We always let a full house in the line-up on before us so we could be first on the circular track when the next ride started. That way, we could dart to the cars we wanted and hop in before anyone else tried to take them. While we waited and shot the breeze with the Yipper, two nuns in full habits came up behind us. It was a stunner. We had seen the odd nun eating ice cream or even cotton candy and sitting on the carousel or the train but never behind the wheel of a Dodge 'em Car. Two aliens with fangs and four heads might as well have been standing in line. Even Yip was startled.

"Excuse me, ladies," he cautioned. "This ride can be pretty rough, you know. Lotsa banging into one another."

"That's alright, young man. We can take it," one of them replied with a slight wink.

"Ok, but if you have any problems, I can shut the system down in a second. You just lemme me know."

"We'll be fine, but thanks for your concern," the other Sister of Mercy said.

D'nell and I looked at each with some alarm.

"Hey, we might want to think about helping those two out if they get into trouble," he whispered.

"Let's see how they do. Just hang loose and stay together in case they need us," I said quietly.

When the gate opened, we pretended to give our tickets to Yips and then leapt into our special rides. The whole lot of them were usually bunched up so we swirled the wheels all the way around to ensure that we could back out of the traffic jam as soon as the juice got turned on. We also kept an eye on the nuns. When the place started humming with electricity, we wove over to the other side of the enclosure. Sure enough, the nuns were struggling to get the hang of driving the unusual little cub-cars. We took a few runs at each other, bounced off the walls a couple of times and then drove beside the sisters and explained how reverse worked.

"You have to spin the wheel all the way to the left to go backwards."

"Thank you and bless you boys."

People were zooming around, screaming and shouting. Then I saw two older greasers ram into one of the nuns at the same time. Her white wimple almost flew off her head, but she grabbed it in time and jammed it back on. The other nun looked ticked off. The Fast Eddies with the slick ducktails began to back up for another hit. Before that, without a word, D'nell and I took action. Slamming our accelerators down, we shot in between the nuns and their attackers, taking full T-bones on our flanks but before they could react to our running interference, we backtracked and hit the first guy together and then plowed into the other loser. As they tried to back away, we spun around and hit them again, hammering them away from their penguin targets. We got one turned around and crashed into him from behind and watched as his head snapped back and hit the metal pole. Just as we were re-grouping, D'nell and I looked up to see the hapless hot shots out in the open, trying to swerve out of the way of both sisters bearing down upon them.

The nuns might as well have been smacking those guys' fingers with a ruler at the piano. Now it was four to two and not a fair fight at all. Our team circled our quarry and hit them front, side and back, blindsiding them and bashing them into the boards. It became a derby of destruction. The pounding went on for a long time, and I looked up to see why. The Yipster was smiling like the master of the Midway, hands on hips, arms akimbo, watching the whole massacre. We were well past our four minutes but that didn't matter. He was enjoying it too much, so he let us run, have our fun. When it was finally over, the two tough guys slipped out the gate as fast as they could, yellow humiliation streaks almost visible down their backs. We wouldn't be having any further trouble from them. Not too many people were interested in taking on Strike-Force anyway. They skulked away like they had just seen two ghosts dressed as nuns.

"Man, that was weird, but I loved it," I said to D'nell and Yip when we were leaving.

"Never seen anything like it on my watch," Yips said, thanking us.

"Kinda makes you wonder if there is a God," D'nell said.

"There is for some folks, that's for sure," I replied, and we slapped each other on the shoulders and sides like boxers.

The nuns were waiting for us, suddenly younger and giggling like they just finished winning at hopscotch in the schoolyard.

"Boy we showed those two bullies, didn't we?" one said, shaking our hands.

"They weren't so tough after all."

"I can't wait to tell the sisters back at the convent about this."

"Thanks again, boys. Don't forget to say your prayers."

We didn't forget.

Chapter 14

The Raiders Hit the High Seas

We darted in and out of the waves, hurtling through and over their crests, riding them sideways like surfers shooting the curl. All the while, we were being saturated by the river and broiled by the summer sun. Joyously waving our imaginary Jolly Roger, we cut and ran, lunged back into the fray, shaking our fists at the unrelenting swells, attacking them again and again like hawks flying into the wind only to be buffeted backwards. Our little motor churned, the propeller sometimes exposed by a big dip, whined up and out of the water. Sometimes we were vertical, pointing skyward, clinging to the gunwales and gasping for the air that had been suddenly sucked out of the little launch. Then we would dive, stern-up into a momentary trough that threatened to swallow us whole. First airborne, then smashing and crashing, we had turned our boat ride into a trapeze act without a net. We were daredevils of the waterways, speed merchants without limits, dangerous cruisers taking no prisoners.

It wasn't easy getting out on the Detroit River that placid summer day to bounce around like ragdolls in a windstorm. It began with the christening of the *S.S. Lady Stickwood* a few weeks earlier, at the end of the school year. Sticks' father had purchased a "yacht" as he called it, but it was really just a wooden runabout with a thirty-horsepower in-board motor, bench seating, forward steering and a maple-framed windshield. It was an eighteen-footer that almost sat five comfortably. Senior Sticks had been lovingly preparing it for the maiden voyage and once his teaching duties had been fulfilled for another year, the time was right and ripe. We knew it was almost ready for launching when even on a visit to the grocery store, he began sporting a black and white Captain's hat with gold brocade trim. The prized vessel was named after Lenny's mum, a quiet and kind woman. But we all knew she wore the breeks in the family.

Christening it with cups of tea down at the Waterworks boat launch at the end of Rankin Street, the Stickwoods motored their stiff upper lips and straight backs out on a voyage that might as well have been designed to yield the discovery of a new world.

After that, the pleading began. Lenny had talked his dad into allowing him to steer periodically, being the first mate in the family. But what he really wanted was the golden permission to take it out by his lonesome, without parental supervision. As soon as his father bought the craft, Sticks had signed up for water safety courses and began studying everything from right of ways, types of buoys and launch and docking procedures to legal regulations, speed restrictions and emergency measures. Of course, if he ever wanted to wave adieu to his dad on any dock, he knew he would have to learn every boating safety precaution ever invented.

Eventually, part-way through the summer, Captain Stickwood gave in.

"I've got some gardening to do today, but I might take the boat out in the early afternoon," he began, staunchly.

Sticks was all eyes, ears, nose and throat.

"I thought you might like to invite your friends out for an excursion, with you at the helm, my young sir," Captain Stickwood continued.

"That's great, Dad," Sticks Jr. squeaked.

"Only you will be allowed to steer the vessel, as you are well aware," he reminded his son, "and it is certainly and always safety first. First and foremost, son, first and foremost."

Sticks was nodding like a baseball bobble-head doll.

"I, of course, will escort you to the river and assist you in setting our ship afloat."

And so, that calm morning we clamoured into the *Lady Stickwood* with pops and chips and a boatload of excitement. Sticks invited me, The Hat Nevitt and Scotty Whaley for his first tour as the helmsman. We hunkered down in our seats, life jackets secured and waved to Senior Stickers on shore.

"Enjoy your nautical tour, young chaps, and don't do anything that will force me to throw you in the brig," he shouted with a self-satisfied chortle.

The second he put the car in gear, Sticks gunned the engine.

"Raise the Black Flag, mates," he shouted above the din of the motor.

"Aye-Aye, Captain Bluebeard," we screamed like chimpanzees swinging into Tarzan-land.

"Let's rip some doughnuts," Nevitt hollered from the back bench.

"Your Skipper will grant your wishes," Sticks said, bombing along at full throttle.

Out in the channel between the 'Burg and Boblo Island, Lenny wrenched the wheel hard right, pitching us to one side of the boat like we were on one of the amusement park's thrill rides. He cut a full circle and then looped a figure eight to pull the craft into the opposite direction for another, reverse circle. We were colliding and clapping behind him.

"Circle the buoy," Wiry shouted.

Sticks stood up for this one and burned three ever-tightening doughnuts around the closest marker in the shipping lane, a red for return. A few other pleasure craft operators looked on in obvious disapproval. We all waved triumphantly to them and sped on. We cut under big wharfs, threatened to swamp canoeists, sprayed sunbathers close to shore with sharp turns, pulled up beside two guys painting a boat house in the heat of the morning and yelled at them, "Work harder, ya bastards!" All the while, we took turns using the Senior Stickwood-supplied binoculars to keep a watchful eye for the Coast Guard, Provincial and State Police who regularly patrolled those waters. This wasn't our first mission of mayhem.

Our gleeful pandemonium tour continued until we heard a long, big blast that shivered our timbers. It was a Great Lakes freighter bearing down on us like Goliath on David. The towering, volcanic smokestack was panting black above us. Then the same warning horn bellowed again.

"We must be in his shipping lane, let's get outta here," The Hat warned.

Sticks hung a sharp right and zoomed out of the way of the humungous tanker. It wasn't an unfamiliar sight on the Detroit River, but they can run almost silently by, especially with the engine and the propeller at the back, about a mile and a half behind us.

Shaken but safe, we stood up and saluted as the colossal vessel passed. A few deckhands waved back to us. Still standing, we watched the ship churn by, an entire parade consisting of one float.

Most of these monsters, proudly plowing through the Great Lakes and the St. Lawrence Seaway, were built after the Second World War between 1952 and 1968. Their average length is over 700 feet, almost twice the distance from home plate to the left-field wall at Tiger Stadium. Originally steam-driven steel ships, they eventually converted to diesel. The freighters could carry up to 25 tons of cargo—twice that of earlier vessels built 30 or 40 years before. Iron ore, coal, grain, salt, limestone, cement, salt, potash and gypsum could be found in their holds.

Lakers were constructed specifically to traverse the Great Lakes in shipyards from River Rouge and Detroit, Michigan, Cleveland and Toledo, Ohio, Sturgeon Bay and Manitowoc, Wisconsin, Chicago, Illinois in the United States to Collingwood, Midland, and Port Weller, Ontario and Montreal and Lauzon, Quebec in Canada.

They were issued stately names after people and places, like most great works of engineering and ingenuity. The people were usually owners and builders while the places were often mythical, denoting a proud heritage on both shores of those international waters. When a mountain moves down a river or lake, it had better have a lofty and lasting moniker.

Watching the freighter continue to part the river on its way to Detroit, between countries, we felt its power, sucking the water from the twin shores and returning it with great washes of wakes. That's when Sticks had the idea.

"Hey, why don't we ride some of those waves?" he suggested. "It would be like fighting a storm."

"That's cool, we could roll with the punches. That'd give the *SS Lady Stickwood* a real work out," Wiry agreed.

"We could slice in between the breakers, steer around and into them because we could see them all coming," Sticker Junior said, brimming with command.

"Yeah, we could follow the Laker and pick our spots," I added.

That's when our yachting circus act began. It went on for some time, none of us knew for how long, we were having too much pirate sport to notice.

Then, like a cloud obscuring the sun, a roller rose out of what seemed to be the bottom of the channel and loomed over our heads like an aquatic monster full of fury and foam, twice the size of any whitecap we had witnessed from the hulking hull of the ship that afternoon. In an instant, it plunged into us like a bull with its horns down, busting into our boat, swamping the small deck. The wheel spun uselessly out of Sticks' grip, spinning wildly in the onslaught. He managed to turn it before we hit the side of the freighter but not before the windshield was blasted apart, the wood frame in splinters. It was like being in a car accident that kept happening; the wave just kept ripping into us. We hung on to each other and anything that was bolted to the floorboards. Choking in the drenching, we watched as our little boat almost capsized, and then turned limply toward shore, the motor still sputtering alive. Thirty feet from where we had been, the river was flat, beyond the reach of the deadly wake of the Laker.

"Everyone ok? Anybody hurt?" Sticks shouted.

But he didn't have to raise his voice, all was calm. The rest of us were slumped in our seats like drowned river rats. Fear was finally giving way to disbelief and then shame. It had happened so quickly and with such ferocity. We just nodded and groaned, realizing that we were foolhardy junior sailors who had just about shipwrecked their own craft.

"We're good, Lenny. Let's just try to clean up and fix whatever we can and then head back," The Hat Nevitt said.

"Yeah, and you guys check and see if there's anything floating that we can fish out of the water before it sinks," Sticks said with a bit of a stammer.

There was no rest for the Raiders of the high seas. Sticks steered and scouted for any of our own debris, which Wiry netted while Donny and I were busy bailing, sweeping up glass shards and wood slivers from what was left of the windshield. The good *Lady Stickwood* was otherwise sound. Our short-term skipper turned her homeward. We were lucky, depending on who was deciding.

After much silence, broken by sighs, I asked Sticks what he was gonna tell his dad.

"I know exactly what I'm gonna do. I'm going to ask him not to trust me with his boat ever again. I might as well because that's what he's going to do no matter what I say."

We all knew he was right, pretty hard to almost scuttle a boat on a smooth river. Moses might have been able to help us, but he wasn't around. There was no lie big enough or deep enough to get us out of this disaster. We were marooned on our own lifeboat.

The plan had been to drop one of us off at the dock and walk up Rankin Street to get his dad. Then Admiral Stickwood would bring down the trailer to crank the boat out of the water. No one wanted that assignment. We did Rock, Paper, Scissors for the disagreeable task, except Lenny, as the former Captain, had to stay with what was left of his ship. My scissors were broken by a rock, which is pretty much what I felt like.

Dragging my drenched self along Rankin, I tried to shake my clothes dry as best I could. It was like walking to both the gallows and the guillotine.

Luckily enough, Senior Stickers was in high spirits. He didn't notice the gloom I was wearing over my soggy shorts.

"You know, I finished all my gardening, so I'm going to take her out for a spin. This is such a perfect day for it."

I nodded.

Inside the car, towing the boat trailer, El Capitano continued to enjoy his soon-to-be-devastated day.

"Little wind but some clouds to keep me in and out of the sun. I even packed a lunch and a beer. I'm having my own yachting picnic just for a treat."

Nod, nod, from me. It was getting unbearable.

"Well, let's just get you young blokes sorted and then I'll head out. I might even cruise around Boblo once or twice."

Then he stopped talking and started staring. I knew he could see the broken windscreen, but I was already out of the car, zipping down to the dock.

Senior Stickwood caught up with me, yelling like a cop at a crook.

"What the hell happened? Why didn't you say anything? What's wrong with you, you, you little blighter?"

I held my open hands up looking at him, eyes wide, eyebrows raised like I had never been issued the power of speech.

"It's ok, Dad, it's my fault. I'll tell you all about it once the boat is out of the water and we can get it home," Lenny said, peering down at the sorry little launch that had been his charge.

The elder Stickwood glowered at us above his goatee and began to say something more but there was no one there. We were well-practised at fleeing the scene of a crime, especially one we had perpetrated. His raspy words hung in the air like a swarm of cranky wasps.

Lenny did get to climb behind the wheel of the family boat again, but it took him a year in dry dock to do it. We were never asked aboard again, nor would we have accepted the invitation. As a result of the Raiders' code of secrecy, no other parents were alerted to our near sinking of the good ship *Lady Stickwood*. It was ahoy and then bon voyage.

But that Laker wasn't our enemy. We had been reckless, underestimating its unintentional might. A lesson learned, the surprise and power in a wake on river, lake and sea, nature or man-made. We admired the dignified Great Lakes freighters, cruising the shipping lanes, keepers of a singular, shared legacy; outliving the generations of ship mates who had roved their decks and ran them. We had a new appreciation for their supremacy and took more than a small measure of pride in that. And from our wave crash on, we viewed them with new respect for their colossal might, always accompanied by involuntary shudders.

Strangely quiet for creatures so gargantuan, we always loved to watch them glide up the channel at night, their lights blinking at us as though the stars had delightedly descended to take a ride on the river when no one was watching. They also seemed to be drifting by us from the past when they were built, like noble dinosaurs appearing from nowhere, out of a mist of yesterday and into a future that was uncertain and foreign, their bows held high, still driven by purpose and promise.

Chapter 15

Black Water Raid

We thought we were Acapulco cliff divers, arcing up and out into the air, arms spread like eagles' wings, floating in a fall then suddenly contracting into torpedoes, hands clasped above our heads to pierce the water with minimal splash. Practising for that eventual moment when we would be hired to test Timex watches down on Mexico's Pacific Coast; the precision of the timepieces and our dives uniting for television audiences the world over. Pulling ourselves from the churning surf, our tanned bodies and gold watches glistening in the Aztec sun, we would wave to our fans, mums and soon-to-be legion of girlfriends.

Our high-diving internship took place, oddly enough, at a local golf and country club, a few miles out of the 'Burg. It featured a huge swimming pool that boasted an extremely deep end with a springboard just off the water, a middle board that was about fifteen feet above the surface and a top, rigid board over thirty feet up.

It was a blissful recreational refuge designed for adults and children alike. In the summer, non-working mothers, who were numerous, could drop their kids and their friends off at the pool, under the serious supervision of the ultimate babysitter, a lifeguard, and then amble off to the fairways to play golf with the gals. Rare for the times, and due in part to the local population and the closeness of Detroit, the club accepted Black families, so we could bring D'nell and some of our other pals.

None of the Raiders' parental units had memberships but we knew all our friends who did. Often, we would promise to take some of the kids on plundering missions with us in exchange for an afternoon on the triple diving boards.

The boards provided a graduated system of diving know-how. The springboard taught us the basic art of diving: propelling ourselves upward, curling our bodies in half and then straightening out before landing in the pool. It was learning how to achieve the Jackknife Dive. If we did everything right, we hit the water like an otter. That was the one the girls loved. And we knew when we nailed it because the chicks were looking up and smiling. Part acrobat, part swimmer and part show-off, the Jackknife was hitting the note, the cool deal. But its archenemy was the belly flop. One slip-up on the launch, the bend or the entry and the worst could happen: a loud smack on the surface that made everyone stop and stare, and then a red stomach for an hour. If that happened, we knew what to do: stay underwater and swim to the shallow end, or otherwise, the single-most humiliating procedure at the club would take place. The lifeguard would blow the whistle and order everyone out of the pool, then swim over to see if the diver was alright. That was a bad scene. It resulted in a red face to match the rouge solar plexus.

The second board gave us more room to manoeuvre above the deep end, so we practised routine plunges but also made up all kinds of dives: the Front Flip, a gymnast's tumble; the Back Dive, facing away from the pool; the Can Opener, holding one knee and cutting through the surface with the out-stretched leg; the Polar Bear, a head-first lunge, hands at the sides; the Bummer, pretending to dive and then landing on the board with your butt and projecting yourself in with posterior propulsion; the Reverse Cannon Ball, a head-first plunge arms holding legs; the Corkscrew, one or more twists before hitting the water; the Motown Meander, performing one of your favourite group's dance moves while entering the pool; the Octopus, flailing arms and legs and then coming together for a smooth entry; the Walking the Plank, warming up on the board for what looked to be a difficult dive and then simply strolling off the board and into the water; the Barracuda, leaping strait out with hands clasped together to cut the surface; or the Cyclist, running off the board and still pedalling into the pool. We came up with new ones every summer.

But the high board really demanded only one type of dive discipline into what suddenly seemed a much smaller and unreachable body of water far below. It was the classic Swan Dive and nothing else mattered. All of us had attempted and completed it with some measures of success except for Thatcher. He had jumped once and that scared the liver, kidneys and pancreas out of him. Jumping off the top board didn't count because it was nowhere near the majestic swoop of the Swan Dive. Plus, it was more dangerous. Everyone who had climbed unsteadily to the pinnacle of the platforms and left the high board with a bathing suit full of fear had heard the legend of some kid who jumped and landed wrong, real wrong. He had hit the surface doing the splits and cleaved his cajones apart.

It was a horrible vision with wailing and blood circulating in the water followed by some tender stitching taking place in the emergency ward and no cycling for some time. It always scratched at the back of our necks as we stood in line on the ladder, waiting for our turn to leap into space. We started by taking a simple dive just to make sure we could survive a drop from that height without ripping our scalps off. Each successive attempt was to add, teaspoon by teaspoon, the ingredients for the ultimate Swan Dive.

That included kicking out from the board as far as possible, free falling, arms outstretched and horizontal with the pool for about three endlessly long seconds and then tucking vertically and torpedoing into the centre of the deep end. It was like springing out of an airplane; riding the crest of the surf; flying alone without mechanical support. We were frozen for a few moments between the earth and sun, the sky and water and the past and future, holding Time's breath.

We five Rankin Street Raiders, on this day, were reclining on beach towels, ignoring the rough concrete underneath our backs and enjoying the snacks and sodas for sale. Tahiti Treat was popular as part of our imagined ocean setting. The speakers above the swimming pool were playing pop hits and, of course, our beloved Motown.

The Motown magic spell was cast when an ingenious record producer named Barry Gordy Jr. formed the Motown Record Corporation with an initial $800 as start-up capital. A former professional boxer, he also loved music and had produced singles and albums by Smokey Robinson and Jackie Wilson but then, with his own company, he started to look for new artists to sign to his label.

The architect of Motown Manor began constructing a solid foundation for the Motown monolith by hiring two essentials for his soon-to-be greatest hit factory in history: three progressive songwriters with a penchant for punchy verses and melodies and a sturdy stable of hard-working and inventive musicians. The tunesmiths and lyricists were Lamont Dozier and Brian and Eddie Holland. The back-up band, consisting of thirteen or more members over the years, was loosely called the Funk Brothers.

Setting the Motown wheels in motion, he began attracting flashy groups with great voices and arresting stage appeal. The list ranged from Little Stevie Wonder, Marvin Gaye and the Temptations to the Supremes, Gladys Knight and the Pips, Martha and the Vandellas and everything in between. The stage was set. In just over a decade Motown had about 100 hits that were not only chart-toppers but destined to be endearing classics.

The sound involved parts of rhythm and blues, gospel, rock 'n roll, jazz and the soulful crooning of the 1940s and 50s. But it was different than all the rest and instantly became its own genre. The songs were almost always about love, lost or found, everlasting and even unrequited love could later be met around the corner by requited love, waiting in the shadows. They reached out to new, young, existing and old lovers, male and female, and set them adrift on a starry Detroit River of heartfelt emotions and memories. They took us through all the twists and turns on Love Street, sent us down Despair Alley and up Sweetheart Road with never a dead end. They were happy, upbeat and rarely without hope. Motown made us dance, sing and revel in life.

To add to the enchantment, to keep them in our ears long after the music stopped, the lyricists used single, powerful hook-lines that the rest of the words were built around. Often, they were the titles of the tunes.

The individuals and groups that delivered these affectionate love bombs were talented, tight and as entertaining as possible. Their stage presence was electric with cool clothes, smart dance moves in unison and most of all, a direct connection to their audience. The back-up singers would croon the harmonies and choruses, with moves like mercury, fluid and shiny. In sync, they pantomimed what the singer was professing to the listeners. When it rained, their fingers rippled the drops down from above. When it was time to beg for another chance, they were on their knees, and when the heartache was too much to bear, they held their fists to their chests and bowed their heads, all as one.

The music was funky, snappy, soulful, righteous and precise. Using layers of sounds and tight beats to fuel the desire and passion in the lyrics and the vocals, the musicians drove that black Motown Cadillac all day and night long.

For us, it was hit after hit, day after day, rippin' it up with a smooth elegance. We followed Motown around like puppies lapping up every note, harmony and lovely lyric. We made those songs part of us, lived them, sang them and opened our hearts to them. We were just kids, but Motown carried us into a new world of enchanting tenderness, revealing to us the face of love, giving us glimpses of what could be and teaching us to wait and watch for those precious experiences.

The Motown ship sailed around the world with its crew singing harmonies to the stratosphere, snapping their fingers at the sun, winking and jiving from cloud to cloud—their melodies of the heart lifting forever into the future.

All those miraculous songs, number one in the nation, were being generated just down the road from the 'Burg. Motown was a powerful tidal wave of music and it was ours.

Lying there listening to the cool ripples of sound flow through our ears, Sticks announced, "I don't care what any of ya'll say, the Four Tops are the best group to ever come outta Detroit, and Levi Stubbs has the best badass name for a singer."

"Don't be a dipstick, man. The Temptations got two lead singers, David Ruffin and Eddie Kendricks, and they're both better than Stubbie," Skeese said.

"Hey, the Supremes' name says it all. They rule, and Diana Ross is singing to me, not you rubbies," Wiry spoke up.

"I got dibs on Smokey Robinson and his Miracles," Rogie claimed. "He's so smooth he makes glare ice seem bumpy."

"Forget it, dorks. Marvin Gaye is the man," I said. "He's the Emperor of Cool and his Kingdom is Motown."

"Ok, ladies, why don't we have a draw?" Rogan suggested. "Each of us puts up four songs from their faves and then we all pick our top five from that list, but you can't vote for your own."

"Man, that ain't right, not picking from your own group," Sticks complained.

"It's the only way to settle the top best Motown songs. We'll see who has the most on the list," Rogie maintained. "I'll get a pen and napkins from the snack bar."

The vote was on. Wiry was rootin' for the Supremes' "You Can't Hurry Love," "Stop in the Name of Love," "Back in My Arms" and "Someday We'll be Together." Skeese picked the Temptations' "My Girl," "Ain't too Proud to Beg," "Just My Imagination" and "I Wish it Would Rain." I took Marvin Gaye's "How Sweet it Is," "Ain't No Mountain High Enough" (with Tammi Terrell), "Mercy, Mercy Me" and "I Heard it Through the Grapevine." The Rogester went with Smokey Robinson and the Miracles' "Tears of a Clown," "I Second that Emotion," "You Really Got a Hold on Me" and "Gotta Shop Around." Sticky chose the Four Tops' "Baby I Need Your Lovin'," "Bernadette," "Sugar Pie Honey Bunch" and "The Same Old Song." Then we made our selections and gave them to Rogie to tally. It involved a fair amount of arithmetic on his part, but heck, it was his idea.

The official Rankin Street Raiders' top five Motown songs, those timeless classics were: "You Can't Hurry Love," "My Girl," "Sugar Pie Honey Bunch," "You Really Got a Hold on Me" and… wait for it, "Heard it Through the Grapevine." They were entered into our logbook. It was settled, a done deal, so we could get on with our renegade pillaging plans.

"I got an idea about Skeese finally diving off that high board," Sticks said looking up. "It's Wednesday in the summer so no one will be around. Let's ride out here after dark to swim and dive for a while."

"After dark, won't that be too late for us to be out?"

"We can be back before curfew."

"Yeah, we can tell our parents that we are some other kid's house watching 'The Twilight Zone'."

"Cool, but are you up for diving from that high, Thatch?"

"I guess," he hesitated. "I might as well get it over with."

"That's righteous man, atta go."

Hours later, as we swam below, all in our t-shirts and bathing suits, Terrence was frozen at the edge of the high board. Rogie waited behind him on the platform, as a spotter. Shaking with fear, Skeese peered from the sky into an even darker night. The black pool below seemed to be calling him into its warm, watery embrace from which he would never be released. A night-bird whistled right at him. The chilling breeze at his back nudged him inch by inch, closer to the edge.

"C'mon, Skeese. You can do it. Don't keep us hangin' on," Sticks called to him in a hush.

"Yeah, man, you'll be on cloud nine after this dive," I whispered up at him.

"I second that emotion," Wiry said.

"Just don't jump, anyone can do that, and it won't count. You gotta dive and remember to break the water with your hands," Rogie said quietly. "I got your back, Thatch."

Shivering, hugging himself with both arms, perched like a frightened animal on a ledge, his feet were creeping toward the end of the board, grating on the rough sandpaper surface. Caught between fright and pride, he bent closer, realizing that climbing back down in shame would be worse than hitting the hard surface below. Open mouthed, we waited and watched, our friend, barely visible, was teetering above us, gripped by dread. A car went by and he hunkered down, the headlights displayed him turning white with a growing panic.

"I'll come and get you, Skeese. We can do this another time. It's cool," Rogan suggested calmly.

Then a dog barked, a big bark. It was coming from the clubhouse. The animal began to howl. We stood more than stock still, especially Thatcher. A light blared on, then another, like searchlights at a prison.

"Who's out there? What's going on?" someone shouted in a traffic cop's voice, above the now closer, snarling and panting dog.

"You gotta dive, Skeese. There ain't any time. You won't make it otherwise," Rogie yelled as he bounded down the stairs. "We gotta get gone now, man."

Our Raider on the high board was figuring that he was down to only two options: mauled to death by a dog or diving into the uncertain depths below. We heard a shriek and turned to see him enter the swimming pool like a slightly bent arrow. He surfaced in a second but was still screaming as he pulled himself out.

"What's wrong, are you hurt?" I yelled.

"No, I lost my bathing suit when I hit the water! I can't find it."

"Forget that, the dog will tear you to bits," Rogie hollered.

"Ok, ok, I'm coming," Skeese cried as he struggled quickly but carefully over the fence.

The night watchman and his canine from hell were on the other side of the compound but we could hear them running hard, cursing and growling.

We had mounted our getaway bikes, raring to go when Skeese came staggering up to us. He was wearing his t-shirt upside down with his legs through the arm holes. It looked like a huge, striped diaper. We were in too much of a hurry and too scared to laugh. And we didn't get the chance anyway because in an instant he was way ahead of us, peddling out of sight like a comet, then disappearing into the dark.

He wasn't seen again that night. We never did know what arrangements Skeese made with the open neck of his t-shirt, his boys and the bicycle seat on the way home. Our guess was that he rode standing up without looking back, making no stops.

Another Raider quest bested, barely.

Chapter 16

Of Marsh Hares and More

There was raw life everywhere. Dragonflies flitted about us like miniature biplanes, their wings performing prisms in the sun. A mother catfish wriggled cautiously by, her baby brood following like a cloud of spilled ink in the river. Venus fly traps, miniature horror plants, waited for their insect meat on decaying, moss-coated logs lying against the shore. A shiny, black water snake with a sickly white underbelly slid past, leaving a current of Ss in its wake. A kingfisher with a Watusi Warrior headdress of feathers speared into the stream and emerged with a wriggling fish in its beak. Water striders skated in droves making mosaics along the surface. Leopard, tree, green, pickerel and bullfrogs croaked and burped like unblinking statues from the water's edge. The bullfrogs commanded lily pads like potentates, their floral aquatic chairs designed for their comfort and ease to compete for passing flies. Two snapping turtles, sun-bathing their jagged backs, with menacing calm, rolled off a flat rock like alligators. Crayfish scuttled backwards from their underwater hideouts, spooked by our shadows.

Somewhere up ahead a beaver tail spanked the water in warning. A spotted, slimy, mudpuppy with gills like flowerets, snatched an insect from the surface, then retreated to its cave under the bank. An otter, perched proudly atop its mudslide, sat munching a fish gripped in his paws, whiskers twitching with delight. Sawgrass, reeds, bullrushes and thistles hemmed us in, making the paddling difficult, the air hotter. Gliding slowly, silently, Whaley and I took this all in, amazed by what this little tributary was displaying for what seemed to be for our enjoyment alone.

We felt like the first humans in a prehistoric place. We might as well have been floating in a dug-out canoe down the Zambezi River before time had given it a name.

Our adventure was the result of the annual family tradition of booking a cottage for one week for fishing, relaxing, stargazing, card-playing, hiking, snoozing in hammocks, picking blueberries, grilling hot dogs and hamburgers, swimming and sitting around campfires burning marshmallows. We used an outhouse, bathed in the lake, picked flowers for Mum, identified animal scat and went boating. For a few too-short days each summer, we lived like our ancestors, having a holiday in yesteryear. No phones, cars, TV, streetlights, supermarkets or air conditioning. It was during those vacations that my dad taught me how to chop wood and make kindling, catch and clean fish, start and steer a boat, use a compass, make flapjacks, build and stoke fires, sharpen knives with a wet stone, identify constellations, bird species, snakes and other critters, tell directions by the sun and shade and, on that day, catch bullfrogs.

Most of the Raiders' families did the same—some went on sight-seeing trips and others stayed home and took 'er slack. After a time, we were allowed to bring along a friend for companionship and to keep us out of our parents' hair so they could unwind. Sometimes, this was in return for having been away with another family the previous year. This time 'round it was Wiry who got to come with us.

The two of us took out an old rowboat just to oar ourselves around the lake. My mum made us sandwiches with meat from a tin that was unlocked with a key, which we would normally not touch but found them somehow tasty when eaten outdoors in a boat, surrounded by a shoreline of thick woods. Cruising at low speed, each of us on an oar, we spied the mouth of a creek, full of lily pads with lotus-like bright white flowers. The stream was almost hidden, shaded on the sides by thick undergrowth. We headed right for it, quietly paddling into a wild display of plants, animals and bugs. We felt like its first visitors: Wiry and Matty, famous explorers, sailors into the unknown, the uncharted. The breeze rustled in the reeds and among the birch trees, wafting the fragrance of pine trees and wildflowers at us.

Birds chirped and trilled, the stream gurgled in small riffles around corners and the frogs splashed into the shadows to escape us. There were bullfrogs on almost every lily pad. Big and plump with bronze backs, their legs looked to be two feet long when they leapt away from our rowboat. We began to sneak up on them and then startle the chunky monsters into flight with our oars. Eventually it was time to leave our new world. We picked a few lily pads blossoms for my mother and rowed for the cottage. We couldn't wait to tell everyone about the cool stuff we had seen and heard. My dad was particularly keen on the bullfrogs.

"How many do you think there were?" he asked us.

"Hundreds, Mr. McKendrick, maybe more," Wiry replied.

"That's right, Dad, there might have been a thousand," I added.

"Okay, okay, seems like there were a lot, boys. Now, how big were they?"

"Huge, sir. Big as basketballs," Wiry said.

"And when they jumped, they were this long," I told my dad, and we held our hands apart like we were showing the size of a big northern pike.

"Well, how about you take me there tomorrow and I'll show you how to catch them? What do you say to that?"

Wiry and I were all for it. We couldn't wait for the sun to come up the next day. We dreamt of giant bullfrog pets: racing them against each other, getting them to thrash around in a water-filled washtub, feeding them flies and watching their sticky tongues dart out, keeping them in little wooden cages with bars that we'd whittled ourselves and giving them majestic names like Brutus, Kongman or Lothar.

Our second expedition left the dock early on a bright morning, the air full of the promise of adventure. My mum had packed more tinned meat sammies and canteens of ice water. My dad brought a large fishing net and a sack. As we pushed off, my mother told my father to take it easy on the frogs. He winked and puffed on his pipe.

The secret stream was as beautiful as before. A slight mist rose and the sunbeams sparkled through it. A few broad bullfrogs had already claimed their lily pads for the day, like the first lounge chairs on a beach.

"Let's go a little further in boys. Keep the oars quiet and no splashing," my dad whispered to us.

We nodded, rowing carefully. Suddenly, we floated around a bend and the little river opened into a long pool, lit up by the rising sun and chock full of bullfrogs squatting like sultans on their lily pad thrones. It took our breath away, there were so many of them and all lined up down the stream.

"Here's what we'll do," my pa said in a hush. "You two keep the boat steady and I'm going to dip the net in the water, slide it under the lily pad and then lift it fast and high. The frog will try to jump up and away not dive into the water. He'll be leaping right into a wall of netting. Get it?"

Our heads bobbed yes, and we tightened our grips. Sure enough, as we eased up to the first pudgy frog, my dad quietly and quickly performed the manoeuvre and in an instant the frog was wriggling and kicking in the net at the bottom of the boat. It worked like magic and it happened so fast. We were about to shout and clap when my father put his finger to his lips to keep us from saying anything.

"There's more up yonder where this guy came from," he said, motioning upstream.

We settled into our positions, giggling to one another. Then, without a word, my father grabbed the tubby bullfrog by his legs, pulled him out of the net and with an axe-like movement bashed his head against the side of the boat. Blood spattered. Frog innards dribbled. The slimy body gurgled once. It was one swing and then one dead amphibian. Wiry and I stared in horror. We tried not to ralph, fall into the water or pass out. We went horribly quickly from delightful daydream to a bloody nightmare with way too much reality.

Things got worse. After stuffing the frog's remains in the sack, Dad waved us along like nothing had happened. I think he was whistling. Numbly we rowed on, oarsman of death. We looked away as one bullfrog after another was bludgeoned into the afterlife. We could feel their heads hit the hull, rattling through us like a whiplash. But my father, suddenly the supreme assassin of frogs, might as well have been picking the black-eyed Susan's that grew along the woodland paths. By the time the brutal massacre came to an end, the rowboat was awash with blood, entrails, eyeballs and bits of gore. Chewing happily on his sandwich while our guts churned, my dad told us that we would be having a big frog legs fry that night.

"They taste like chicken only better, especially with garlic and butter, boys, especially with garlic and butter," he said smiling and humming. "We'll cook them over the campfire. It's a rare treat, just you wait."

On the checkerboard tablecloth for dinner sat a salad bowl chock full of frog legs, the fried skin stretched tight over mostly membranes, ligaments, bony knees and long feet. My dad was chomping into the little meat that was available like he hadn't eaten in a week. My mother, Wiry and I sat in unmoving silence, trying not to look at the revolting procedure while my pa swiped his mouth with a tea towel and dug in for more. We weren't sure we would be able to eat for a week.

Wiry did not accompany us on vacation again. His croaking nightmares remained his own affair.

But this was just one of the frightful food experiences our fathers seemed to delight in terrorizing us with. Rogie's dad took a few of the Raiders to the Windsor Farmer's Market early one Saturday. He was a big, jovial guy, with a hearty laugh and a ready pat on the back for Rogie and his friends. He loved good food. They had arrived just past dawn when the marketplace was coming to life. The drafty, old two-storey concrete building that housed the weekly shopping adventure was just waking up but in a hurry. The Raiders seemed to be pushed along by a tide of bustling vendors setting up their wares and an increasing swarm of shoppers. There were flower stalls brimming with fresh cut arrangements, each a different rainbow of colour and scent. Vegetable stands teemed with the fresh Essex County tomatoes, still warm from the morning fields, redder inside than out and delicious as a dessert. Goose and duck eggs the size of baseballs at one counter, and corn, as gold as the sun and sweeter than candy floss, at the next. Baked goods fresh from the oven to the vendors' stalls got in the Raiders' noses. From pies and pigs' ears to breads and bagels, their warm smell drew customers like flies. Preserved meats, pickled veggies, home-made butter, honey and jams were scattered about the market like edible jewels. The lads munched on goody samples as they were swept about the market, trying to keep pace with the long strides of Mr. Rogan.

"Well, boys, you've seen the open market. Now it's time for the specialty shops, fresh meat, cheeses and fish," he announced.

"Yes, sir, we're ready for that, alright," Wiry said.

"Yeah, I've never been in a place like this before," Stickwood added.

"Ok, let's start with the butcher's shop," Mr. Rogan said as he ushered them into a bright, white and red store off to the side.

The blood-stained aprons of the proprietors were their first clue that this room might not be as delightful as the general marketplace. Rogie's dad marched them up to the open counter where the skinned and plucked bodies of freshly dead animals were stretched out in rows. There were chickens and pheasants with their heads still attached, pork and beef ribs, the bones protruding from the gristle and membranes, and baby lambs on the hoof, skinned and shiny. Rogie, Sticks and Wiry were still digesting their Red River Cereal, Count Chocula and Lucky Charms but that process suddenly wasn't going so well.

Saving the worst for last, Mr. Rogan pushed the three boys down the counter and stopped in front of what looked like a bunch of artifacts in a meat museum.

"Look at all of these delicacies. What a treat, eh boys?" he said, beaming like he had slaughtered everything himself.

"What are those, sir?" Whaley asked pointing to some clotted, chunks of goo.

"Those are calf's brains, son, and they're great fried on toast."

"What's that stuff, Dad?" Rogie asked, pointing to a trough of chocolate-red, rubbery and smooth chunks of meat.

"Those are all organ meats lads: hearts, kidneys and livers. Kidneys can be stewed and made into meat pies. The beef hearts are also perfect in stews and the livers are good fried with onions," he explained proudly. The butcher looked over nodding in agreement as he swung a monstrous cleaver to delightedly hack away at some big animal's corpse.

He went on to show them the greasy pigs' knuckles and heads, thick beef shanks clotted with bright red meat and glistening pork bellies. The Raiders were imagining every part of the animal, still attached, as Mr. Rogan identified them: the palpitating organs, cows' leg bones, the skulls of tame, innocent, barnyard livestock. The boys were swooning like seasick voyagers with no land in sight. They rushed to the door as one with Rogie's dad's last butcher shop comment ringing in their ears.

"Here's my favourite, blood sausage!"

The three of them slumped on a bench, inhaling the fresh market air in gulps, fighting like young soldiers in their war against the vomit hordes.

Mr. Rogan appeared with some thick packets of butchers' paper, smiling like he had just won the fresh meat lottery.

"Now, off to the fish market. You kids are gonna love this place," he said, striding past us.

The Raiders groaned and followed, as best they could, after him.

That shop was similar, and the lack of blood everywhere was more than compensated for by the smell. It was so thick; the boys could taste it and smell it on their clothes like a drizzle of stink. Sure, they had inhaled the pungent odor of dead fish before, even cleaned some freshwater species like pike, bass, pickerel and perch but this was an exotic stench, foreign to their nostrils. It made their stomachs perform acrobatics on the trapeze without a net.

"Breathe through your mouth," Rogie cautioned his pals. "It helps."

"You've been here before?" Sticks asked angrily.

"Uh, yeah, once or twice. It ain't that bad, really," Rogie said.

"What a rat-fink. You should have warned us, man," Wiry said quietly.

Mr. Rogan introduced them to the fish monger who looked like a grinning, Asian Dracula welcoming some fresh young blood into his aquatic castle of gore. Once again, the dead were displayed in artfully arranged columns. The vampire-like proprietor and Mr. Rogan took turns pointing out and discussing their favourites in terms of flavour, texture and cooking options. Breathing like they were scuba-diving, the Raiders were introduced to: sticky pink octopi, floating in their own saliva; flat flounders staring up at them with two glazed eyes from one side of their heads; bloated carp with scales like dull silver dollars, long-neck clams, oozing like slugs out of their shells; oysters encrusted with barnacles; salmon steaks like florid horseshoes, lobsters and crabs trying to pinch them through glass-walled tanks; slimy and slick eels, twisted around one another; red snappers, mottled like leper fish; and swordfish capable of gutting them.

After the mini tour, the Raiders re-enacted their ritual of slouching on a bench outside until Mr. Rogan appeared with more parcels full of dead creatures.

"One final stop, boys, and then we can be on our way," he told them. "It's the cheese shop and there you can taste some of the wares."

They followed his lead, feet dragging, heads bowed.

"How bad can this one be after what we've been through today?" Wiry asked Rogie.

"It's not as bad as the butcher's shop," Rogie replied.

"Let's just get it over with and then head to the car," Sticks said.

"I just hope I don't ralph before we make it to the parking lot," Wiry said grimly.

Clean and full of colourful cheeses, the shop was a welcome change from what they had endured to that point. There were wedges of all sizes, cheese in buckets of brine, blocks the size of breadboxes, marbled, runny, smoked, aged and mold-covered. The shopkeeper was a young blonde woman with a bright smile, pigtails and a white surgical apron.

"Would these young gentlemen like to taste some of our cheeses from around the world?" she asked Mr. Rogan. "I have some crackers to go with the samples."

"I am sure they would, right boys?" Rogie's father nodded at us and waited until the Raiders all nodded back.

"Maybe some light cheese snacks will sooth our stomachs," Rogie whispered.

The three of them bellied up to the counter. The cute cheese girl beamed down upon them.

"Let's start with a crisp apple-cheddar?"

Using a slotted spatula, she shaved off a few pieces for each of them on crackers. It was a new taste for the Raiders. Cheddar and apples, they were used to, especially with pie, but never together as one cheese. They munched gaily, mostly in relief.

"Now, this is a chalkier cheese, which means it is a little drier and flaky," she said singing to herself and carving them off three more bites. "It's a Wensleydale with cranberries."

More crunching from the Raiders.

"This stuff's great, eh guys?" Rogie said, trying to redeem himself from the horrors that had come before.

Wiry and Sticks agreed, wiping their mouths and looking up expectantly at the increasingly attractive cheese maid.

"Here's one of my favourites, I'm sure you'll like it," she said. "They're cheese curds and they're fun to eat because they squeak."

She handed those down on three napkins. The Raiders squeaked, squeaked and squeaked like three excited Mouseketeers.

"Now this is a stronger variety, with lots of rich flavour. Are you ready for a Limburger cheese that is going to wake up your taste buds?"

The Raiders kind of knew what she meant.

"Oh, we're ready. These cheeses have been great," Rogie said proudly.

Each of them ate the cracker and cheese in one bite, chomping with glee. Then the rank smell and taste exploded into their mouths and noses and even their ears began to hum. Sticks shoved his napkin down his throat, Wiry started to cough and Rogie's eyes bugged out like he'd seen the ghost of cheeses past.

"Water, water," he managed.

They rushed out into the hallway and took turns at the water fountain, rinsing their throats and gasping. Then they sprinted to the public bathroom and made simultaneous use of the sink, urinal and toilet. There was no speaking but plenty of noise.

"Anyone want to stop for a pizza?" Mr. Rogan asked cheerfully on the way home. From the back seat there were no takers, just scowling and the growling of angry stomachs.

The Raiders thought they were off the meat hook after that, but for some diabolical reason, the dads decided to get together to dish out a new form of edible torture for their boys. Maybe it was in return for all the trouble and anguish their sons had caused them with their Raider capers.

One of the local service clubs held an annual father and son banquet. There were about 400 service clubs in the 'Burg: The Kinsmen, Lions, Rotary, Kiwanis, Oddfellows and Rebekah's, Optimists, Elks, Knights of Columbus, Orangemen, Bisons, Loyal Order of the Goose, Temple of Tempermentalists, Banana Boaters, Comfortable Shoeists, Screechers, Dog-Walking Dads, Bad Behaviourists, Steaks and Jokes for Us, Button Pressers Unite, The Ancient Order of Froth Blowers, Muscle Car Revvers, Fraternity of Fun and Games, Getting Away from the Wives Club and so on.

One of these elite organizations held its Marsh Hare feast every spring. For some unknown reason, Mr. Whaley, Mr. Thatcher and Mr. McKendrick decided to band together and drag their sons along to this event. Their sons talked about it, considering the implications and the importance.

"You ever eat rabbit before?"

"Yeah, my dad hunts them and they're not so bad."

"They're supposed to be all dark meat and kinda tough, right?"

"My mum stews them with a brown sauce. It softens them up."

"Why do you think they call them marsh hares?"

"Well, obviously, dolt, they hang out near the cricks and cattails and stuff."

"They must be young, getting them in the spring, and all."

"Yeah, like lamb and veal."

"They cook 'em up special for this big deal. I bet they taste great, not gamey."

We three Raiders had to take baths, put on our Sunday suits, comb our hair, brush our teeth and shine our shoes. Since Dad was taking me to this big dinner, I shined his shoes, too. I used his kit with the different colours of polish, buffing brush and smooth finishing cloth. Terry's dad had volunteered to drive instead of taking two cars, since they lived just down the street. That was always a pleasure because he was such a good driver that it felt like being in a limo with a chauffeur. Sitting in the back, there could have been volcanic eruptions, trees falling across the road and lightning striking the hood and no one would have noticed. He was so smooth, he seemed to put the car in only one gear called glide.

Mrs. Thatcher met my father and me at the door. She was a Raider mum to be reckoned with: pretty, blonde and blue-eyed as well as tall and imposing. With enough children for a hockey team, she had to be strict or there would be chaos. She had a big heart, especially if you were on her sunny side, where we all wanted to be. If you found yourself on her shady side, you had better be on the move. And could she ever make desserts. Every pie, cake or cookie she touched with her magic baking wand turned into a delicious dream that looked, smelled and tasted heavenly. Mrs. Thatcher could transform a pumpkin into a royal carriage of a dessert with the blink of an eye.

"My, don't you gentlemen look spiffy tonight," she said to us, "and Matty, you with that handsome red vest and hair all combed perfect."

I could feel the Brylcreem crinkle when I looked shyly up at her. My dad thanked her and shook her hand.

"Yes, this is a special night for us and the boys, a real guys' night out, right Matty?"

"Nes is just warming up the car out back. He'll be out in a minute," she said. "You boys have fun and stay out of trouble now."

"Yess'm, that's for sure," I said, as polite as one of her cherry pies, "and we'll mind our manners."

When we arrived at the Anderdon Tavern, we were welcomed by the president or the Grand Poohbah and he escorted us to our table where Whaley Senior and Junior were already seated. It was six to a table but we were with our dads so there was no way it was going to be three kids on one side. It was dad, son, dad, son, dad, son all the way 'round. The fathers shook hands and began to chat. We three Raiders gazed around at the fancy lights, ribbons at the doorways, linen tablecloths and napkins, crystal water and wine glasses.

Everything sparkled and the place smelled like new leather and roasting meat. Waiters were bustling about with drinks orders and seating new arrivals. For us it was a Hollywood movie about a grand dinner out and we were the junior cinema stars. Our dads ordered a scotch neat, a dry martini and a Heineken. We ordered Coke, Dr. Pepper and Sprite, on the rocks. As we sipped our drinks like we were in Buckingham Palace, a big bowl of breadsticks was placed in the centre of the table with chilled tabs of butter on the side. We waited for a dad to take one first and then we dove in, chomping away and tipping them like cigars at the side of the table. It was hard not to put one in our ears or up our noses, but this was too high-end an affair to pull something like that. Then the three dads solemnly addressed us.

"I'll always remember my first Marsh Hare dinner. It's a turning point in your lives, lads."

"Yes, you're young gentlemen now, there's no turning back."

"They'll serve the main course, the hares at the same time and then you can order side dishes. It's part of the tradition."

"No cold hares at this banquet. Not sporting, eh boys?"

"And fresh from the banks of our rivers and streams—young, tender and tasty."

"Nothing like it anywhere, you kids are in for a rare treat."

"Here's to the Hare of the Marsh, may he return to our plates every year."

"The March of the Spring Hare!"

"Hear, hear and cheers!"

We three Raiders clinked glasses like we had just won the Kentucky Derby.

Suddenly the lights were lowered, and the servers lit candles at each table. The music changed to some classical march and the curtains opened to the kitchen. Out rolled trolley after trolley of silver-covered serving dishes. They were positioned delicately at the centre of the dining tables, a large carving knife on one side and an oversized fork on the other. The waiters stood at attention, a sharp bell was sounded and the shiny silver lids were removed from the platters to reveal the specialty of the night, of the year. Chins just above the tablecloth, we Raiders squinted at the thing in front of us. It was the whole animal, and it didn't look like any rabbit we had ever seen. Its fur had been shaved but the ears were tiny, its teeth looked menacing and it had a long, leathery, skinny tail.

We gulped.

"Shall I carve?" our waiter asked the dads.

"Please do and serve the young men first," Mr. Thatcher said. "This is their first time."

"Oh, well, in that case, it is my pleasure," the server said. "Would the young masters prefer an outside or an inside cut?"

Skeese squeaked out, "Outside cut, please."

The menacingly sharp, slicing knife revealed a dark, gnarled meat. It was placed with care on his plate, followed by a similar portion for each of us. When we had all received our allotment our dads raised their knives and forks and dug in. We sawed off a morsel and began to nibble it like we were eating cat food. I couldn't remember the flavour, just the gritty sand in between the membranes. I'm not sure any of the Raiders had swallowed when Wiry piped up.

"What is this, Dad?"

"Why, it's a delicacy Scotty. Marsh Hare. You know, muskrat."

"And, even better news," my father added with a wide grin. "One of the side dishes is frog legs!"

Chapter 17

Black Sun Rise

The heavens were thick with a billowing, black smoke that rose and prowled like a demon of destruction. Its ugly wings wafted from the fires beneath it, fuelled by fear, hatred and anger. Early on, no one knew what it was or would become but it would grow more beastly and hideous: choking us, watering our eyes and stinging our nostrils. It gripped our minds with its twin talons of horror and terror. The rising clouds of ash on that hot and horrible day in July eclipsed the sun and rained rage, spreading the soot of dread and panic wherever it smeared the sky.

The Detroit riots were cooked up in a cauldron that boiled over with racism: unlegislated but used in full and open force and segregation was at the centre of it all. Much of the Black community was shown the back of the bus, denied housing outside of the poorest neighbourhoods and refused entry to all-white clubs, schools, stores and restaurants. If they couldn't find the lowest-end work in the car plants, they were either unemployed or handed brooms, dishcloths, shoeshine brushes or shovels. To make matters worse, every day, they could wake up and look across the river to Windsor where their friends and relatives had moved and were treated humanely. It wasn't one hundred per cent, but it was far above what they were receiving stateside.

It was the fires that ravaged the city, burning a path for killings, chaos and brutality. Over the course of a few days, the riots ballooned from battles to a full-scale war. The first match that sparked the atrocities to follow was lit by the Detroit City Police when they raided an after-hours club in the 12th Street district. The community was celebrating two Black soldiers who had completed their tours of duty in Vietnam. Everyone there was arrested, more than eighty people, shoved into paddy wagons and carted off like cattle to jail. The commotion woke people up, got them out of their beds and in the darkest hours before sunrise, they retaliated by throwing bottles and bricks. And then the fires began to blaze. Over the next five days, there would be 1,500, not counting those that went unreported. Detroit became an inferno, engulfed in rage and searing smoke. As more flames were kindled, firefighters were attacked by the rioters, forced to retreat and watch helplessly as parts of the city dissolved like burning cellophane. Everything escalated. Within a few hours after the raid, the mob swelled, more police were sent in and additional firemen arrived as the funeral pyres rampaged throughout Detroit.

On day two, there were 600 more fires. State police were sent in with the National Guard's support to stop the volcanic violence. President Lyndon Johnson finally deployed U.S. troops and paratroopers to the ravaged city. More than 12,000 armed forces combined to stop the riots and arson.

Forty-three people died. Thirty-three were Black. Only one white person was dead—a policeman.

As kids, we didn't really understand what it was or why it was happening, but during that week, some of our Black friends and baseball buddies looked at us differently, as though we had changed somehow. They turned to themselves, showing us their backs or looked grimly away as they passed us on the sidewalk. We learned quickly that there were only two kinds of Black families in the 'Burg: those who condoned and supported the riots with fists held high and those who were largely Baptist and viewed protests that took the form of cutting fire hoses as a heinous crime.

But we didn't know what to think. Our world was upside down, inside out. It was an uncertain summer. The heat and rage lingered, smouldering above the Motor City like a spectre, mourning the lost lives and the destruction. People wondered, were hope and truth burned in the bargain?

Laine Howard was the best athlete in our school, the county, maybe the province. He could hit a baseball, left or right-handed, further than any of his instructors, clearing fence after fence. Laine could kick a soccer ball through a net and into the next block. He could crank footballs in torpedo spirals for sixty yards and run like a cheetah with a sore tooth.

And those were on his bad days. He claimed he could race the hundred-yard dash one second off the national mark and that was only because he smoked cigarettes. No one disputed it. And Fast-Laine learned to box from his older brother, a Golden Gloves fighter who trained in Detroit at the famous Kronk Gym. Laine was smart, confidently calm and received respect without demanding it. He could sing like Smokey Robinson and whistle a bird out of a tree. He spoke smoothly and assuredly like what he was telling you was exactly what was happening. Long, muscled and angular, he oiled his dark skin and kept his hair slicked like the wind was blowing it back. He wore silk socks, muscle shirts, tight jeans and a necklace that sparkled off his chest. He had one eye on the ladies and the other on the sky, his limit in anything he chose to do. The son of a Black preacher and a teacher, he knew right from wrong as well as an eye for an eye. He carried himself like he was in charge: no question, no discussion, no misunderstanding.

One clear and crisp Monday morning early in the school year, seven or eight weeks after what became known as the Detroit Rebellion, a few of the older kids discovered that bees had nested in a hollow tree at the back entrance of the school. One of them got the idea that by pounding baseball bats against the trunk, they could encourage the insects to swarm out of it, scaring and stinging students who were just arriving at the gates. The ringleader was a new kid named Reggie Cochrane, but his nickname was Coconuts because he was a wild, brutish guy who picked on anyone younger and smaller than himself. He had greasy, blonde hair, a red face and scars on his knuckles from fighting. Coconuts Cochrane had only been at the school for a few weeks but was quickly labelled an A-1 Jerk. He was also considered, by the three Raiders who attended that school, dumber than road apples and just about as appealing. Batting the bee-stinging machine soon turned into a day-marish frenzy, sending young and older boys and girls screaming and swatting throughout the playground.

Then a teacher, who was also new to the school, Mr. Green, appeared, shouting as he strode toward the frenzied scene with kids scattering everywhere like pinballs. He was tall with white streaks on the sides of his black hair. Mr. Green wore little wiry spectacles and cheap, un-ironed shirts. He was also colour blind, which some of us found funny. By the time he showed up, the instigators had dropped their bats and had escaped into the crowd.

"Who did this?" Mr. Green whined, his skinny Adam's Apple bobbing. "I want the kids responsible for this, now!"

Some children sobbed and sniffled, but no one spoke.

"I want whoever did this to speak up or I'll have all of the older students strapped for hiding the real culprits."

"It was Reggie Cochrane. He started it," a small voice sounded from among the kids who had settled down a little and gathered around.

Reggie stepped forward; arms folded across his chest. "It wasn't me. I was over here with these guys," he said, looking at his partners in bee-bashing who were nodding.

"If it wasn't you, then who was it?" Mr. Green demanded, his eyes bulging, the size of golf balls through his glasses, his face turning greyer.

Cochrane gazed around and stopped. "It was him," he said, pointing to Laine Howard who had just walked up to see what was going on.

The schoolyard went quiet, the birds swallowed their chirps, the kids stopped crying, the wind died around us, muffling us like snow. Laine looked up and didn't say a word.

"Was it you or not, Howard?" the new teacher asked.

"No," Laine said staring at Cochrane.

"Don't you have anything to say for yourself?" Mr. Green demanded.

Laine kept glaring at Coconuts, who was looking away while his bee-buddies eased away from him.

"It wasn't Laine. He wasn't even here," Wiry spoke up.

"Yeah," Sticks agreed, "It was Cochrane, the new kid."

"Laine wouldn't even do that," another student piped up.

Some other kids chimed in, supporting Fast-Laine, including all the Black students who were there.

But Mr. Green wasn't having a bit of anything we said in Laine's defence.

"Alright, that's it. You're not getting away with anything this time," the sub-principal said as he reached to grab Laine's arm. Howard pulled back before the teacher could touch him, stepping smoothly away, his eyes boring deep into Cochrane's neck.

"I know your kind, lying, cheating and stealing. You come with me. We have an appointment with the strap," Green said shoving Howard toward the school.

The boy shrugged him off and marched toward the door, head high, making long strides ahead of the teacher.

"It wasn't Laine! It wasn't him!" students shouted as they disappeared inside the school.

Then, most of us shuffled over and grouped below the open office window. The principal was away that day, attending a meeting at the schoolboard. The Raiders knew what the strap looked and felt like. It was a smooth, well-worn length of leather about two inches across, fifteen inches long and a little less than half an inch thick. No one said a word, then we heard the strap come down—five times, a pause and then five times more on the other hand. Still no words were spoken. We scurried around like ants to the rear school door. Laine Howard stepped out smiling and rubbing his hands together like he was warming them by a fire.

"Where's that cockroach Cochrane?" he asked to nobody in particular.

"He ran home, real fast," someone answered.

Laine's grin grew wider and he nodded to himself.

"I can wait," he said, his words smoother than a sail ruffling in a warm breeze. "I can wait."

During the afternoon recess, a kid shouted, "Dwayne Howard's coming, Dwayne's coming! He's just up the street!"

That was Laine's older brother, the boxer. The crowd of us arrived at the front gate to see him marching toward the school like he was walking through walls. He was over six feet tall but with his muscles and his grim scowl, he seemed seven feet six. He wore a pork-pie hat, tilted sideways, real tight black slacks, polished Florsheim shoes and a white, short-sleeved button-down shirt through which his guns were bursting.

"Where's this here Mr. Green?" he thundered at all of us.

Almost everyone pointed to the front door. Dwayne's huge hands curled into cannonballs. He tipped his hat back and hurtled the stairs, like a bull heading for a wavy, crimson cape. Once again, we hurried over under the office window where Mr. Green was about to meet his worst nightmare in the flesh and bone. First, we heard the door crash open and then a chair hit a wall.

"You Mr. Green?" Dwayne demanded like a foghorn on a black night.

"Now see here, whoever you are. This is the principal's office in a public school, you can't just…" Mr. Green started and then stopped, his words strangled behind his bony Adam's Apple. Looking up, we saw Dwayne's head peak out of the window, it was wearing a big smirk with his gold front tooth beaming in the soft afternoon sun. He put one meaty finger to his mouth to shush us. Then he winked and slowly closed the window. All we could hear was muffled shouting and more furniture being re-arranged. The teacher on yard duty hustled us away to the playground.

A few minutes later, the back door was flung open and Dwayne stepped into the sunshine. He looked around until he saw Laine. He stretched out one of his telephone pole arms and pointed at his brother. Then he raised his fist in the air. Fast-Laine did the same. Dwayne pushed his hands into his pockets, turned sharply and strolled, nice and easy, out of the schoolyard, a toothpick in his teeth and a swagger in his step. He looked like he had just eaten the blue plate special and finished it off with apple pie and ice cream.

Mr. Green left school later with a hat pulled over his face. The next day, after a lot of yelling by the principal, with the window once again closed, Mr. Green took Laine aside, out of our sight, to apologize. Word was that Laine didn't accept it or say anything at all. He just stared through Mr. Green like he wasn't there. That teacher was never acting principal again.

The following Monday morning, just before the bell rang, the whole schoolyard went suddenly quiet. Reggie Coconuts Cochrane was slipping in the back gate, slouching and squint-eyed like a rat in the rain. He must have used up all his sick days. Everyone froze: every student, teacher and every stray dog. Across the yard, Laine looked up and stared, a razor-sharp smile on his mouth. It was as if there was no one there except for Reggie and Laine. Coconuts turned and tried to run but that was foolish and without hope, like a souped-up Chevy Camaro chasing a Volkswagen Bug—not a race at all. Laine caught the weasel before he could take but a few steps and dragged him whining and pleading off school property to a nearby park. There, he methodically issued Reggie his whuppin'.

Eventually, the exterminators arrived to get rid of the bees and cut the hollow, dead tree down. Fists clenched on his hips, Fast-Laine Howard stood and watched with most of the kids in the schoolyard and a few of the teachers standing behind him in his straight and rigid shadow.

Chapter 18

The Albino Ox Incident

He was a big, blurred kid, out of focus inside and out. His hair was like fresh cut straw, all prickly and stiff, pointing in different directions. He had blue, squinty and slightly crossed eyes and always seemed to be peeking out from behind a rock or a tree. His face was misshapen like he had been beaten before he was born. Built like a white marble statue, he was almost as slow to move. And, he only had a few full fingers. Slow to respond, he had the tips pinched off when he was mooring boats down at the docks for quarters, his hands caught between the barges and yachts and the piers. It didn't seem to bother him, though. They say he could lift the ass end of a pickup truck or throw a donkey. He crushed cans, wrestled with dogs, swam in swamps and climbed to the top of traffic lights.

His name was Chester Mallet, and there was something of the hammer head about him but we called him the Albino Ox. He wasn't a bully by choice, he just happened into it once in a while. Not fully formed or completely human and nowhere close to being rational, his deck was ablaze so we Raiders steered our ships clear of him. But it wasn't always easy.

Chester was from the poor side of the 'Burg. He wore other people's clothes—mostly men's hand-me downs because he was so large—given to him by his pa when he was home or his uncle when he was drunk. He also ripped them off clotheslines or stole them from laundromats. In fact, his chief love beyond Windsor-style pizza from Fargies, was stealing. It didn't matter what it was, it was shinier, prettier and tastier if he had lifted it from someone or somewhere else. If it wasn't nailed or cemented down, it became fair game for him, but all the shopkeepers knew his traits, so he wasn't allowed in stores. Whenever anything weird went missing from out-of-doors, folks blamed Chester. Cat's dishes, flower planters and light bulbs: Chester. Sun dials, drain-spouts, tires, rakes and garden hoses: Chester. Signs, mailboxes and birdfeeders: Chester. Kids' toys, barbeques and ropes, he loved ropes: all Chester. He even tried lassoing stray dogs while riding stolen bicycles: Chester, the cowboy rodeo star.

He pawned part of the pilfered goods, but the rest of the stuff he must have stashed somewhere out in the countryside because he was a one-boy filching fleet. As he grew bigger and braver, he began to come out of his crude shell: taking more chances, thieving more often and seeking bigger treasures. Lumberyards, service stations, grocery stores, restaurants and stores had to be careful what they left out back or within easy access.

That was also about the time that he graduated to kidnapping kids' bicycles. It wasn't really abduction because he didn't keep them and there were no ransom notes. He just rode them wherever he wanted to roam and left them there. That drove Corporal Tice, our Bone Rack Bobby, nutsoid. The 'Burg police would get a report of a stolen bike and then a day or two later it would turn up on someone's front lawn, in a parking lot, down by the river or in a bike rack in front of a store. It was like he was taking a book out of the public library and not bothering to return it. The Albino Ox was still just a youngster at heart.

Riding to our two schools one morning, the five of us were chatting and bantering about the National Hockey League playoffs, trying to decide what bets to make based on which of our individual teams were matched up against one another. It was the usual wager, the loser would have to take the winner to Lydia's, the local luncheon capital. Those burgers or clubhouse sandwiches with coleslaw and a pickle on the side, accompanied by chocolate or strawberry milkshakes poured from sweating, steel containers always tasted a whole lot sweeter when your team had won the series and another Raider was forkin' over the doubloons.

"Hey, where do you punks think you're going?" a hoarse voice called out.

We all stopped and looked around, one foot on the road and the other on the pedal.

Chester Mallet lumbered out from behind a parked car. He blew a big green gob toward us and said, "Get off yer bikes, babies."

"We're going to school," Wiry said, mildly. "It's a school day."

The Albino Ox heavy-footed it slowly toward us.

"Well, yer gonna be late and one of you will be really late."

It was five against one, but we knew the Ox's style: he would grab one guy, beat him up while ignoring the others pounding on his thick back. We dismounted.

"Whaddya want, Chester?" Rogie said, almost sternly.

"I want one of yer bikes, and I want a good look at all of them. Maybe even take a couple for a spin to see which one I'll be riding today."

We sighed, knowing there was so little we could do. Even if we let him have one, we knew we couldn't rat him out. We were all thinking about what happened to Bennie Orsini. Mallet-head took his bike from him, so Bennie told his parents who called Corporal Mice, who tracked down the perpetrator and dragged him to the station to chill his worn-out Keds until a parent, an uncle or even his sister showed up. The next day, Chester went to Orsini's school, took his bike again and rode in circles around the building, yelling Bennie's name and knocking on his classroom window with a baseball bat. When the cops arrived, Chester rode away laughing and waving the bat. Then he waited for Bennie to walk home and proceeded to give him the nickname of Bennie the Bleeder. We shuddered as one.

"Here, take mine," Rogie said, stepping forward almost in defiance. We followed his lead and offered our bicycles.

"Mighty generous of you girls," he said smiling through broken, brown teeth. "I'll take one and then you can go back to yer dollies."

He took the newest one. It belonged to Whaley. We watched him wrenching it back and forth down the street, trying to wreck it as he rode.

This went on every week or so until the Raiders had had enough.

"We gotta do something about that guy. I can't keep being late for school," Wiry said. "I'm getting the business from my homeroom teacher, Mrs. Chicken Legs Lavine."

"Yeah, and my principal called my parents," I said. "I couldn't tell them the truth, or I'd end up Mashed Matt McKendrick."

"I got an idea," Stickly said. "It may not be much, but it might be better than what we got."

He told us and we agreed. A few days later our Ox stalked out in front of us, grubby paw held high like a deranged traffic cop.

"Hand over a bike, you little chumps," he shouted in between phlegm hacks.

We climbed down and Lenny eased his ride over to him.

"Hey man, I can't keep showing up late. I'm already in trouble."

"I couldn't give one little piece of worm shit about that."

"Well, I thought that maybe I could be your taxi only you get to drive?"

"What the hell is that supposed to mean?"

"You take my bike, but I'll sit on the handlebars and then you can ride me to school. If you want to use my bike for the rest of the day fine, but maybe you can drop it back off or pick me up at the end of the day?"

Chester scratched his thick noggin' and tried to think about that. It sounded like a concrete block being dragged across the sidewalk.

"Ok, but no tricks, Sticks."

The plan worked out fine for a few weeks with Stickwood balancing atop his own bicycle like a basket of apples and Mallet pedalling merrily along like he was off to the market. When Chester saw him, he would shout out, "Hey Sssssssticks," and Lenny knew it was Ox-ride time. Until one morning their taxi tandem was pulled over by the law. Out stepped Officer Mice, cap pushed forward and rubbing his hands with excitement.

"Stay where you are, you two," he barked. "You know that riding double is against the law."

"Sorry, sir. It won't happen again," Sticks said quietly.

"Who does this vehicle belong to?" Tice demanded.

"Me, sir. Chester's bike has a flat, so I was helping him on his way to school," Lenny replied polite as a choir boy.

"Don't give me that. If this guy has his own bicycle, I'm Captain Kangaroo," the Corporal squawked, "and the next time he attends classes, it'll be a blue moon in Timbuktu."

"Where's Timbukwho?" Chester asked gruffly.

"Never mind. I catch you riding double again, and I'll confiscate the bike and write you a citation," Tice roared, his bony finger rattling and pointing at them.

"What's a citration?" the Ox wanted to know, with furrowed, prickly cy-brow.

"Get out of here this second and one of you had better be walking."

They watched the squad car pull away and Chester said, "What'll we do now?"

"Oh, don't worry about that chucklehead," Sticks said. "I know his routes and where and when he gets his coffee and doughnuts. We'll just take side streets from now on."

And so, the taxi service continued without incident, despite the efforts of the riding-double detective.

Our Saturday mornings were usually reserved for sports, the Arch or cartoon watching, depending on the season. This time we were combining two of the three. With our hot brekkies of Weetabix or Shredded Wheat covered with boiled water and then drained and floated in milk under our belts, we converged for our convoy to the Arch at the schoolyard. It would be an afternoon run, so by pleading with our mums, we had packed our favourite sammies. It was late September so the leaves hadn't started falling, but they were beginning to turn colour and some of the smaller ones were crisping up.

But the mid-day was warm, and everyone was outside grabbing as much fresh air and fun as was left in the late-summer season. We cruised past kids playing marbles and skateboarding, girls jumping rope and playing hopscotch, mothers pushing babies in strollers or having coffee on their verandas, dads' dog-walking or packing their golf clubs into the trunk, grandmothers knitting on porches beside grandfathers puffing on pipes. Wolves whistled from top-down and waxed hot rods at girls giggling on street corners, their hair bobbed and their barrettes glinting in the sun. Restaurants still had their patios open where people were gobbling pizzas, fried chicken, clubhouse sandwiches, fries and gravy and double-decker burgers, downing them with soft drinks and shakes. It was a slow-motion movie of contentment.

We rode on past it all, the sacred Arch hideaway in our heads. Just past the edge of town, beyond the water tower, streetlights, fireplugs and the last convenience store, we raised the invisible Raider flag by riding faster, snaking down the country road like we were straddling Harleys, making the wind rush over our backwards ball caps, crisscrossing each other, yelling, riding no hands, pumping our fists in the air.

Around the first bend we came upon an older guy we knew by reputation to be a mean bastard. Without a word, the Raiders swerved past him and picked up even more speed. He shouted something that was lost in the breeze, but it made us pedal harder. At the crest of the hill in front of us, two of his buddies stepped up out of the ditch and blocked our way. There they stood: arms crossed and feet spread in ragged running shoes, wearing torn jeans and stained t-shirts, cigarettes dangling from their dirty mouths. They were zit-faced, foul smelling and ragged. For us, they were the front-page photo on the Bad News paper. We ground to a halt, knowing the third member of the deadbeat club was coming up behind us so we were trapped.

These were the scruffy losers who were too filthy, stupid and ill-mannered to get dates or even dream of girlfriends, so they took their low-lives out on their pet dogs and younger kids like us. Their idea of a good time was to knock over garbage cans, beat up rural mailboxes with baseball bats, smash windows with bottles and cut up old ladies' prize rose gardens. We also knew that one of their specialties was to cook marbles.

They would heat them in a frying pan then drop them into a bowl of cold water where they would crack but not break. They could then be used to throw on streets and sidewalks to shatter upon impact, causing flat tires and cut feet. These skuzz-buckets were also known to trap house cats in cages with sardines as bait, then take them out of town to torture, set on fire or shoot them with air guns. We were also well aware that they loved to trash kids' bikes.

That's about where we rode in on that previously happy morning.

"Get off yer bikes, you little puke heads," one of them growled.

We slowly stepped off, looking at each other for an idea about what to do. They stood on all sides, so we felt like we had just rolled into Box Canyon and were surrounded by Comanches with war paint, feathered spears and repeater rifles.

"First, we're gonna give you all wedgies so you can wear your gotchies over your shoulders like diapers. Then we're gonna take your little kiddie wheels for a ride, and then we're gonna bust 'em up real good," one of them snarled.

"Yeah, like they were run over by a train," the third chump added.

There were only three of them, but they were two feet taller than us and a few years older. The Comanches were closing in.

"Push yer bikes into the ditch and then line up over there behind those trees for wedgie duty," one of them ordered, laughing.

Heads down, feet dragging, we eased over to the side of the road.

"Hey, you guys want some sandwiches?" Skeese asked them. "You take it easy on us and we can give you lunches. We've got five."

"Yeah," Wiry added, "there's plenty of food and pops."

"Cool. Gee, thanks for letting us know, guys," one of the creeps said. "We'll just take it all and you still get the business."

"The full treatment for the mama's boys," another one chuckled.

Just then Sticks, all in one movement, jumped on his bike and rode back toward town like someone had set him on fire.

"Hey, let's get that little dope."

"Naw, we still got four bikes, one extra and lotsa food so forget him."

"But the rest of you dolts ain't goin' nowhere."

The loser patrol was right. Stickwood's escape didn't really improve our lousy situation although it was great for him. Plus, it was three against four, even worse odds. They plunked us down by the side of the road and began rummaging through our bags, drinking, eating and slobbering like hyenas on a goat carcass. When they finished every last crumb and drop, they hoisted us up and began to march us toward the bush.

"Time for a visit to wedgie world," one of them guffawed.

Accepting our fate, we trudged like condemned men, our underwear soon to be our gallows.

"Hold on over there!" we heard a gravelly, familiar voice holler from behind. "Where you guys going?"

Everyone turned around to see Chester Mallet riding right at us with Sticks perched on the handlebars and waving. We ran toward them while the bullies froze.

"You three armpits get over here," the Albino Ox yelled at them.

The goons knew Chester could wipe the ditch with all three of them with one short-fingered hand tied behind his beefy back. The sun had just set on their evil day. They rabbited out of there in three different directions.

We would have hugged the Albino Ox but none of us wanted to get cooties.

Chapter 19

Demolition Derby Part Two – the Darkside

As far as the Rankin Street Raiders were concerned, Queen Victoria never had a birthday. She never opened presents, blew out the candles, received funny birthday cards or was served breakfast in bed. In fact, according to us, she was never even Queen of the Commonwealth: from Australia to British Honduras to Canada. That's because Victoria Day was Firecracker Day, and it was held in our honour not hers. During that painstaking but exciting dawn-to-dark day we roamed free, dispensing explosions wherever we felt necessary or fun or both. Everything was fair game (well, except for pets, seniors, birds' nests, babies and actual muscle cars, not our painted, plastic models).

The ritual was the same every year. We saved as much money as we could and then lined up waiting for our variety store, the Green Lantern, to open at 7 a.m. Then we spent every cent we had from our piggy banks to our pants pockets on row upon tidy little row of firecrackers. We had learned that our march of mayhem about A'burg went much smoother if we sat and carefully unravelled the entwined wicks first. The brands were strange: Black Cat, Atomic, Blue Dragon, Red Devil, Zip Bang, Lotus, Cobra, Mandarin, Mad Rat and Firebomb. They were all made in China with flashy labels glued to red see-through cellophane wrappers. The Chinese just lit each pack whole and threw them in the street to go off with a series of bangs, roars and crackles. We had more varied uses, so we had to separate each of them, trying not to break any wicks as they were always short with fast fuses. Then we'd throw our precious blasters into a paper bag with the small corndog style punks that the Green Lantern lady gave us to smoulder for lighting our fireworks. Why play with matches when you are handling explosives? Safety first.

Our parade of explosive plunder would begin with us wandering along, looking up, down and around corners for anything that needed blowing up. Tulips had their heads blasted into colourful confetti. Sewers echoed with cannon fire. Through the end of a tin can or pop bottle we could direct the sound of the bursts, *krack-a-towa-ing* at each other with hand-held rockets. A few veggies snuck out of our parents' pantries would die honourably at our hands. Zucchini and eggplant worked best with soft flesh that tore apart easily when stuffed with our small gunpowder sticks.

We would arrive at our park for detonations in the hollow handles of the teeter-totter, railings and in the maypole rungs. Firecrackers were taped to swings with one of us pushing and another lighting, so the concussive bursts would take place high in the sky. Erupting in drainpipes they sounded like howitzers. Knotholes in trees backfired.

We twisted the tops off signs releasing firecrackers to the bottom of the hollow posts to wait for the resounding booms. We threw them around with abandon and bounced, rolled and kicked them. We shot them at far-off targets with slingshots. Empty garbage cans rocked with our echoing thunder. We taped our burning punks to long sticks to detonate from a distance. Our crackers of fire found their way into everything from back alleys and avenues to roads and right of ways. You could map our trail of detonation and destruction from one end of Amherst to the other end of the Burg.

Outside of town, where our explosive travels took us, we bombed old milkweed pods, every hole in the ground and anything that held rainwater. We lashed thistles together with elastic bands and exploded them. Abandoned muskrat dens were ripped open by thrown and planted firecrackers. Fungi on dead trees were blown apart, spitting spores and rubbery, alien-like flesh everywhere. We made mud-castles on creek banks then sent them skyward and back again in a rain of wet dirt.

Not unlike the Mayans, we too made sacrifices to the gods in our temples of boom. Each of us had to pick a plastic model, usually cars or horror stars, to offer up to explosive maiming and wreckage. These were often older creations that we had lovingly assembled with airplane glue, then added the finished flourishes with tiny brushes and mini pots of paint like junior artisans. But those had been replaced by newer models that were more intricate and expertly completed as our talents grew. Our earlier efforts began to collect dust on their shoulders and hoods. Rather than give them to our little brothers or cousins, what better send-off could there be than blasting them into next month? So, after a lunch break on Firecracker Day, we would gather in the schoolyard to blow the roofs and wire rims off T-Birds and the neck bolts and boots from Frankenstein's monster.

In the afternoon, we Raiders would make our way to the water with whatever ammo we had left. We had discovered that you could turn firecrackers into depth charges. It wasn't easy, but when perfectly executed, the minute bombs would sink below the surface with the wick still burning inside, resulting in a muffled underwater burst followed by a tiny volcanic eruption of water spray and blast. The whole beautiful operation was concluded with a mist of yellowish-green sulphur smoke rising from the depths like Satan's breath. Coveting our last little blasts, we took turns, trying to be as accurate as possible. The trick was holding on until the last possible moment and then throwing the firecracker into the river before it exploded. Any errors were greeted with a useless air explosion or a dud floating in the water. Which, of course was followed by much name-calling, jeering, sniggering and sarcastic taunting.

"Gee, that was fun, lighting a firecracker and drowning it in the river. I don't think that has ever been done before."

"Wow, you scared the water with that one."

"I think my baby sister is at home, I can get her to give you some tips."

"Yeah, my grandmother could come along, too, you could learn a lot."

"Why not just divvy the rest of your firecrackers up with us then they would at least be in the hands of professionals?"

"Hey, here's a better idea… why even bother to light them? Just throw them into the river and watch nothing happen?"

"Yeah, it would be like re-arranging your sock drawer only less exciting."

Then more water-bombing and depth-charging would ensue. Conversely, successful immersion-explosions would be met with rare but much-appreciated Rankin Raider praise.

"Whoa, I think you might've blown Moby's Dick off with that one, Sticks."

"We should call the Coast Guard and teach them your technique, Jarvis Whimple."

"That one waited until the water gave up on it, M&M."

"What a wet blast from the past and the future, Rogie."

"I expect some dead sucker fish to float to the surface any second now, Wiry."

"We rule the Waterworks with sound and fire, lads."

But sometimes the Rankin Street Raiders, due to their lack of respect for risk, their craving for adventure and their capability of peering over and teetering on the edge, resulted in them strolling happily into their own misfortune, one they had created, admired and bowed to in previously cheerful service.

It was a perfect May 24 holiday, a morning glowing with warming sunshine, softly removing the crispness in the air. Soon-to-be-silenced birds tweeted and flitted from elm to maple to walnut branches. Cats yawned and stretched on windowsills. Few cars eased on down the drowsy streets. Adults were sleeping in, snuggled in the embrace of a day off from punching the clock, setting up shop, changing tires and oil, writing reports, washing, cooking and being chased by necessity.

The five Rankin Street Raiders had gathered in the empty schoolyard along with a sixth occasional member John, Johnny, Johnfwee, Bandi. He was a sturdy lad, serious first and funny second with straight, well-trimmed hair, conscious about his clothing and a set of big, proud ears that must have enhanced sound. He was up for most anything, including some of our more daring and dangerous schemes.

We were separating our firecrackers and inspecting how many we could each afford based on our savings, paper routes, grass cutting and garden work. We looked like a knitting circle, only our steady work was unravelling. We had been the first customers when the Green Lantern lady unlocked the front door. Like swimmers waiting for the lifeguard to blow the whistle on a bake-oven hot day at the Lions' Pool, we couldn't wait to dive, jump or tumble in.

"I got fifteen packs of Red Devils."

"I like the Cobras and I got eighteen."

"Forget it, guys. I had extra tips setting pins at the bowling alley this week, so I got twenty packs of Black Cats. Deal with it, ladies," Wiry announced.

We sighed but kept up our finicky splitting up of each precious stick of mini dynamite. Soon we were off to blow up the day, meandering like gypsies from one bombing invasion to another. Whaley was the most boisterous with a large paper bag bulging with his artillery. He was flipping his tiny grenades here and there, leading our group with a variety of ideas for mayhem: attacks on ant hills, the open ends of handlebars on children's tricycles left out in the yard and keyholes in shed doors where no cars were in the driveway. He used unattended garden hoses that allowed him to echo the firecrackers bursts from a distance. He was on his game and he knew it, a general in a minefield under his command.

Just as he was about to put on another display, the lit firecracker slipped out of his hands and fell into his open bag of gunpowder rolls. We all leapt sideways, as bangs and blams roared from his precious stash. Whales was jumping from one foot to the other trying to stomp out the exploding horde of firecrackers. Then he started kicking dirt on them, but they were like fire-snakes, whizzing slithering in burst after burst. There was no use, his day had been detonated and he had no one to blame but himself. The Black Cats were out of the bag. He slumped to the ground and stared at the charred remnants all about him in silent sadness. Watching, startled from a distance, we kind of enjoyed the display but knew it was bad news for our former General. He was being issued a twenty-pack salute. His Firecracker day was over, taking his annual fun with it. We offered him some of ours, but he wouldn't have any of it. He made the mistake and a few firecrackers from each of us wasn't really going to help at all. We patted him on the back and watched Whaley slink away with just a few victories under his belt in a lost war.

Of course, we soldiered on with smoking punks and new resolve to complete our missions. Soon after, Sticks got cocky, as was his want. The hockey goalie in him rose to the surface of our roar of a day!

"Hey guys, I brought an empty medicine capsule and I'm going to light one in it and hold it in my hand," he said, like he was a superhero about to stand in front of a moving car.

We pleaded with him not to. We were already down one Raider.

"C'mon, Stanks, that's crazy. The plastic will blast apart."

"Yeah, you're gonna blow your hand off."

"I can take it, just watch."

He put the firecracker in the little container, lit it and held it up like he was lighting the Olympic Flame, teeth clenched and eyes squinted. In one instant the medicine container ripped apart in a fiery flash. Sticks fell to his knees clutching his wrist below an already swelling hand.

"Part of it is numb and the rest still stings like hell! Help me, you guys!"

I grabbed the garden hose that Whaley had been sending cannon fire out of earlier and sprayed his hand.

"Holy crap that hurts!" he screamed.

I kept spraying but I told him he had to go home. Everyone else nodded staring in terror at his scorched fingers. They were turning colour and seemed to be throbbing.

Running fast, he shouted over his shoulder, "You can have the rest of my firecrackers, guys!"

We trudged on, sadder, shaken and worried about our fallen comrade. This was proving to be a tough and dangerous outing. But we were the Raiders, and we knew no slowing or stopping when we were on a quest. We regrouped in the schoolyard and counted what we had left. Sauntering about we hit our usual haunts and then found ourselves at the river again for more depth-charging operations. Things went well until Rogan tossed one near Johnfwee, either by mistake or to scare him.

"Hey man, that almost hit me. You think that's funny?"

"Whattya yellow? Yer little chicken heart can't take it?"

"The heck with you, jerk bait."

In retaliation, Big Ears lit one and tossed it at Rogie. Boldly, he tried to kick it away, but the firecracker exploded when it hit his foot. Rogan screamed and fell, rolling sideways. Then he started swearing but the pain was obviously too much, so he tore his running shoe and sock off and plunged his foot into the water. When he removed it to look, there was a red circle, singed and raw. Rogie sunk it back in the river, panting in pain.

"Sorry, man," Bandi pleaded. "I didn't mean to hurt you. I was just throwing one back at you."

We gathered around asking our burnt buddy how he felt and if there was anything we could do.

"Naw, thanks guys. I better go home and put something on this before it gets worse."

Limping home on one bare foot and a dripping sock and shoe in hand, that was the last we saw of him that increasingly not-so-great day.

We were down to three. Gloomily, we decided to head home ourselves. Walking in silence like we were heading to Queen Victoria's funeral we clutched what few fireworks we had left and tried not to think about what was quickly becoming our worst May 24.

In the park, we met up with some older guys, including one of Bandi's cousins.

"You squirts got any firecrackers left?" one tall red-headed kid with acne and an attitude to go with it wanted to know.

"Yeah, but you're not getting any," Johnfwee piped up, suddenly bold because of his cousin connection.

"We can take them all if we want, you little sissies."

"No, you can't cuz' I'll tell Aunt Cheryl," Bandi stated, standing his and our ground.

His cousin said, "Ok, how about this… we got a few cherry bombs left, how's about we trade them for what you have?"

Now, cherry bombs, those were something completely different. We'd never even been close to one, but we had heard about how loud, destructive and powerful they were, like TNT golf balls. Huddling together we considered it. No one said so, but we had already had it for one day, so we were all three secretly willing to finish it with some cherry bomb blasts and head home.

"Ok, how many you got?" Johnfwee wanted to know. We dickered and the deal was done.

We made the trade, but as they were leaving the big guy sneered at us, "You tell anyone where you got these and we'll drag you down to the river at night and wash you out."

Left alone in our park we looked about for a proper igniting of the highly cherished and illegal explosives. We agreed that an empty trash can would make the concussion much louder so why not?

We had three of the beauties, one each. This was gonna be great. Johnfwee automatically went first because he had brokered the exchange. The sound was amplified as a fire-breathing loudspeaker. And the can erupted like all four tires blowing out on an old jalopy. Suddenly, everything seemed deafened and still. We could feel our hearts pounding but couldn't hear a thing. We stepped back, dazed but delighted.

"Ok, me next," I shouted in woozy excitement.

"Fine but make it quick. Two more and we are outta here!" Johnfwee cautioned us.

This time we all stood back, and I tossed it into the bin. Once again, the whole park seemed to shake. We could feel it in the ground. Flame, smoke and a bellowing burst tore into the air, shattering the surroundings.

"Now mine. Look out guys," Skeeser said, waving us back.

Just as he threw the cherry bomb, before it exploded, we heard another, more fearful sound, that of a police siren. After the bombshell went off and while the siren kept roaring, tires suddenly squealed on the pavement at the edge of the park. They seemed like pipsqueaks after what we had just experienced but they were going through us like long knives.

Out jumped a tall, skeleton of a man in a flapping, ill-fitting uniform. He was screaming, adding his high-pitched finger-nails-on-a-blackboard voice to the cacophony that enveloped us. We were well-acquainted with him. He escorted us to the back of the cop cruiser and drove us to the station.

Our old enemy Corporal Tice towered over us like a beanstalk giant, hands on hips, shouting at we three marauders trying not to quiver in our seats. We had all had a stark look at the cold and empty jail cell on the way in.

"I want to know where you got those cherry bombs, and I want to know the young men's names and where they live," he barked.

We sat solid, three kids as one, not responding. He was threatening us to make us squeal. The Raiders didn't go there, no ratting out; that wasn't the street we marched down.

"Tell me or I'll charge you right now!" he said stamping his wide, flat foot.

"We didn't know the kids, they were older," I mumbled.

"Yeah, we just traded some firecrackers for the cherry bombs," Skeester said.

"How were we to know they were illegal?" Johnfwee added.

It was a strategy that had worked before, mixing a lie with the truth.

"I'm going to give you one more chance or I'll throw all of you in the cell to let you think about who it was," he screamed.

We weren't taking the bait. We were going to pass on his invitation to join Corporal Mice's rodent club.

"I'm serious, gawd damnit!"

A seriously big weasel with bad teeth and an oversize police cap, I thought but didn't say.

The Raiders had learned to deal with bullies: just stone-wall 'em. Don't let them think they're getting to you. We stared and glared; arms folded on our chests.

"Alright that's it," Tice blared. "I'm taking you to each of your homes, telling your parents what you've done and I'll make sure you check in with me once a week for a month."

First stop was my house because it was the closest. My mother answered the door and looked like she had just seen the ghost of Queen Victoria. Eyes glazed, fixed on Officer Scarecrow Tice, I thought she was going to pass out. Whiter than a snowbank, she looked like a paper doll in a sudden gust of wind. Then I remembered that my dad wasn't home. He was on his annual May 24 weekend fishing trip with some buddies. At least there was that.

Later my father returned and heard all about it from my still-weepy mum. Some of his pals had caught fish but he got skunked so that didn't help my case one jot.

"Why do I always have to come home to your mother in tears?" he hollered uncontrollably. "And it doesn't help that she has to worry about you all the time."

I was going to say something, but I quickly decided against throwing any further kerosene on his burning temper.

"I don't want to have this sort of thing happen ever again. Do you understand me?!"

I nodded in agreement with understanding his request but not to being able to make it happen. When his rage reduced, he probably realized, too, that he was asking the impossible.

"Go clean your room until it is fit for human use," he said, gnashing at me between vice-like gritted teeth.

Over at the Thatcher household, the result of the police visit went something like this.

Senior Bowl Cutter was also yelling, "How do you think it looks to the neighbours when a squad car pulls into our driveway?"

Skeeser had no answer. The floor swallowed his stare.

"Is this how we raised you, to be a criminal, a juvenile delinquent?" his dad stammer-shouted.

Skeese thought that one over. It was news to him. He tried not to scratch his head but did so anyway, mulling it over.

"Has church taught you nothing about doing right, about obeying the law?"

That caused another scratch because being hauled home by the cops had never really come up in any religious lessons. These mute reactions of puzzlement only served to enrage S.B.C.

"Get up to your room and take your empty look with you. You'll eat your supper there and think about what you've done," he added.

Skeese scrambled upstairs happy to be away from the bellowing and knowing he was lucky he didn't get a swat or a boot to the rear.

At the Bandi home, Johnfwee's mother was pleading with his dad, who was stretched out comfortably on the sofa like a cat on a sunny couch.

"The police just dragged our son home. We're fortunate that he didn't get arrested or fined or I don't know what. Do something!"

Bandi Senior half-rolled over to get a look at his son, inspecting his hands and feet.

"Ok, clean the basement, the garage and wash my car," he said sternly and lay back down with a sigh.

Johnfwee was gone before his father said "car," delighted to be off the punishment hook so easily.

The swelling in Sticks' hand reduced after about a week and he had the feeling back in it within a few days. With some cleansing and ointment, Rogie healed but with a ruddy scar on the top of his foot that sometimes bothered him when he wore sandals. They weren't punished due to their injuries.

Alas, another Firecracker Day had come to an end. We would have to wait another year.

Happy birthday, Queen Victoria!

Chapter 20

The Silver Alligator with Whiskers

The line went tight, followed by a sharp tug and then the fish ran, making the reel hiss loudly as it unwound. Our Captain fed it some taught line, cranked it in some, but again let his prey have its way. Then he bore down and wrenched the fish in with just enough tension to ensure it didn't break the line or attempt another escape. In a moment, a big shiny pickerel reluctantly rose to the surface, twisting to avoid our ample net. About eighteen inches long and chunky, it squirmed on the bottom of the boat as Senior Thatcher calmly plied the hook out of its bony jaw and held it up for us all to marvel at its beauty: forest green-backed with a tinge of gold along the sides, white underneath, big auburn wall-eyes blazing in the sun and a wide, speckled tail tinted blood red. He had played it like a guitar, sure and sturdy, allowing the song to have its will and then with cool reserve, reeling in the notes, herding them toward the final, expected refrain. Every moment of the fight was executed with a perfect combination of precision and a love of angling.

We slumped on deck, in awe of a fishermen who was in control of everything: the boat's course, the depths at which we fished, the presentation, the fight, the netting and the respect for nature's brave nautical adversary.

"Terrence, get that fish into the cooler with plenty of water," Senior Thatcher said sharply, "and you, Matthew, rinse out the net and put it back in its holder."

"Yessir, yes, sir."

"Nevitt and I will re-set the lines," he added.

We sailors scurried about our business under direct command. It was fishing and it was fun, but it was also a mission to catch the tastiest freshwater fish on earth: the famous walleye (or pickerel as we called them). We attended to our duties until everything was once again ship shape and our lines were back in the water with one of us at the bow, one at the stern and one on the side. Senior Thatch fished standing straight-backed at the helm, sniffing the breeze, attentive to birds diving for bait fish, surveying the horizon for weather changes and steering steadily with the calm assurance of a man cutting his back lawn.

The powerful Detroit River with its dangerous undertows, jagged bottom, deep channels and unforgiving currents was also a rich habitat for waterfowl: Canada geese, ducks, terns, egrets, seagulls, herons and mergansers. It also harboured muskrats, snapping and painted turtles, big black water snakes with white bellies, leopard and bullfrogs and racoons and opossums. It was a purveyor of people on all types of ships and schooners and barks and boats from Lake St. Clair to Lake Erie. It also provided commerce for the gargantuan Great Lakes freighters and maintained a key link in the rich marine history of the largest freshwater shipping concourse in the world.

On that sunny summer day, we eased out into its languid centre, cutting through seaweed, blooming lily pads and elephant grass. Seagulls circled above us searching for small fry. Steam rose from its recesses as the sun slowly revealed the shoreline. The air was warm and embracing, but a fresh breeze kept the heat from smothering us. Everything was waking, beginning to stretch and move. On one side of the river Boblo was getting washed down and cleaned up for another day of merry-making and fun-seeking for Americans and Canadians alike. Its green shores shone, framed by white birches as the waterway began to nudge and rouse its edges.

On the other shore, it was an array of showcase landscaping and exterior design of tightly trimmed lawns stretched down from stately homes to the riverside, dotted with shrub sculptures, hammocks, screened-in gazebos, tidy fire pits and shiny barbeques, striped and dotted umbrellas and awnings, sophisticated boat slings to protect all manner of pleasure craft from the ravages of the river, carefully stained and treated docks and decks and rock and flower gardens presenting a myriad of floral images to the boaters who floated past.

But we weren't there as sightseers. We knew we were fortunate to be chosen to accompany our Captain on this fishing trip. It was the height of the pickerel season so there were many anglers out on the river. It was too easy to get lines caught or tangled with others, so we had to be sharp and attentive to his directions. He had worked the tugboats in his youth and had fished the river longer and more often than our ages put together. He ran a tight and bright white ship constructed specifically for fishing with a walk-around centre console, built-in rod holders, windshield, ship-to-shore radio, lights and a big engine that purred even when it was wide open. His pride and joy was named *Sophia*, and she had nice lines. Not everyone received an invitation to step aboard, and if we wanted to get asked again, we had to toe Senior Thatcher's line, swab the deck, haul the bailer and catch some fish in the bargain. We Raiders were good at delivering on a mission, but not knowing the difference between a dinghy and a downrigger, it wasn't going to be easy.

It was a June day out on the powerful river. We were trolling the depths between Boblo and the 'Burg, full of hope of catching some prize pickerel and later enjoying a fish fry of their light, sweet meat. Also, of course, each of us wanted to land the biggest fish.

"Now, I know you all want to catch the big one," Captain Nes Thatcher said, reading our thoughts as we motored out from shore just after dawn, "but this has got to be a team effort. We all have to help each other, especially when there's a fish on."

"Yes, Dad, I mean sir, I mean Captain," Skeese said looking up at his father's stiff silhouette against the brightening sky.

"Here's what should happen, if everyone mans their posts," he explained quietly.

"When you get a bite, bend the rod toward the fish to let him have some line to swallow the bait, count to three as you do so, then rip it back like you're hitting a reverse home run. That's to sink the hook. Savvy?"

We all nodded. We all savvied.

"If it's a big one, shout 'fish on' and start reeling, not too hard, just enough to keep the line tight and the fish moving toward you. Meanwhile, everyone else reels in and gets their rods and lures outta the way. Whoever is closest gets the net. I'll steer."

"What if you hook one?" Nevitt The Hat asked, reclining with his straw fedora tilted back.

"What do you mean if?" Captain Thatcher replied with a scowl.

"Oh, I meant when you catch a fish, you know, what do we do?" Nevitt responded quickly, to our relief.

"Ahem, 'when', I catch fish, follow the same procedure, but Terrence will take over the wheel as he's been out here before and you girls haven't."

"You'll probably have to do a lot of steering," Senior Thatcher said with a wink. "Just keep her straight and stay well clear of any other boats or buoys."

"When handling the net, try to keep it away from the fish until he is played out and ready for it and then scoop it up from underneath, so he doesn't see it coming and spook at the last second," he continued.

"Many a good pickerel is lost at the hands of the net man," he added solemnly.

We looked glumly down at our already inexperienced but suddenly weakened and small hands. No one wanted to screw up the netting responsibility.

"And, if you catch a garbage fish, you're on your own. You'll have to yank it out of the water or net it if it's a big one, but you do it yourself. The rest of us will keep fishing. Okay, kiddies?" he said with a grin.

"One more thing, boys. Don't snarl your lines. Keep your eyes on your rod tip for any action but always be aware of where your line and lure are. If you tangle, you untangle and I don't want to have to cut a bunch of bait, leaders and sinkers outta the propeller because somebody was daydreaming about fast cars or watching some chicks sunbathing on shore."

"I'll handle that part," he assured us with another wink. "Now let's get out there and haul in some keepers, ladies," he said, gunning the motor, throttling us out to the main channel.

"Aye, aye, Capitano," we shouted, bouncing backwards, worried and excited about the challenges that lay ahead.

Trolling with pickerel rigs, which Senior Thatcher had constructed himself, we were angling at sixteen to thirty feet, depending on where the river cut deeper or ran shallow closer to the shores. The riverbed was strewn with rocks and concrete, scrap metal and whatever else had been thrown overboard or dumped into its powerful jaws over decades of heavy marine traffic, manufacturing near its banks and a less-than-studious regard for the environment. But there were also weeds and dark nooks where the walleyes could hide while they stalked bait fish. The trick was to keep lures and bait as deep as possible without getting snagged or having your line sawed off on sharp objects.

The rigs our Captain outfitted us with were built to do just that. The line was attached first to a bottom-bouncer: a mini cigar-shaped sinker with a sturdy wire sticking out of its lower region. The wire would indicate when it touched the bottom, without miring or hanging up the sinker and the rest of the rig. For the presentation, a hook was attached on a leader to the juncture where the sinker was connected. It was light, designed to travel straight out about a foot and a half above the bottom-bouncer. The leader was adorned with a series of buoyant beads. Above those brightly coloured orbs was a tiny horseshoe clevis, hollow at the tips to allow the line to pass through it, while the clevis allowed the blade or spinner attractor to move freely. They, like the beads, were often chartreuse or orange to get the walleyes' attention. The clevis was the high bar, and the blade was an expert gymnast rotating around it. In short, the bottom-bouncer held the line straight down and indicated with its tell-tale bumps when it had run out of river while the bait, usually worms attached to the hook, and the spinning lure swam well above bottom, out of the snagging demon's grasp, to entice the pickerel. It looked like a submarine circus act and worked like a mini magician. The fish were silly for it. Not just our prized pickerel but a whole flotilla of aquatic species—all of which were secondary to our Capitano.

Nevertheless, he delighted in watching us hook something that he instinctively knew, by the way it hit the bait or tugged awkwardly or was dragged in like a wet rag, was not a walleye. The only time he would shout, "Reel in and get the net," was when he knew a pickerel was twisting and brawling at the end of a line out in the dark depths.

"Hey, Nevitt, what's that you got nibbling there?" he suddenly asked.

Unaware that anything was near his bait, The Hat began to reel.

"Paste him first lad, make sure you've got him before you start winding him in like grim death."

"Ok, ok, I'm trying," Nevitt muttered, straining at his task.

"And you, Terrence, what are you goggling at? You've got a fish on, too. Sink the hook and get him in here. What am I, the social convener at a church picnic?" he added.

"Matt, what are you playing at? Your rod is upside down. Are you suddenly left-handed, an ambidextrous angler? The rings face down boy, toward the water to act as shock absorbers in case you manage to catch an actual fish! Lord are you watching all this?" he pleaded to the skies.

No net was called for, Senior Thatcher didn't slacken speed and he grinned as he watched us struggle like our bait worms on a wet sidewalk after a sudden sun.

Nevitt hauled up some squirmy, slimy creature that looked like it would snake up his line and eat him.

"What is this thing, what should I do?" he pleaded.

"Get the pliers and save your hook from that. It's a mud puppy. They're harmless and they sure are cute, aren't they?"

"I got a big one over here, Dad," Skeese shouted. "Get the net."

"Hold the wedding son, you got a whopper but it ain't no keeper. It's a sheephead."

Emerging beside the boat was a flopping white mass that looked like a cross between a flounder and a clown. It was gurgling and the hook was embedded deep in it fleshy, mutton mouth.

"When the Hatted One over there finishes with the forceps, use them on your new little lamb," our Captain said, snickering.

"What are you girls going to catch next?" he asked us all. "A flying fish, an electric eel or a barracuda?"

"Are those things down there?" Skeese asked, eyes and mouth stretched wide.

Capitano Thatcher whistled through a smile into the breeze and fished on like he just sunk a 30-foot putt.

We did catch pickerel that bright morning, a lot of them, mostly at the hands of our skipper. We also caught underage bass and perch, tiny garbage fish, a coupla suckers, a channel catfish and a skinny gar pike with a sideways rake for a nose. Although we were busily occupied with hooking each other's lines, snagging the bottom with regularity, losing our tackle and spending what seemed like hours untangling birds' nests in our reels, we Raider representatives managed to hold our own, landing a few keeper pickerels each. There was more than enough for a grand fish fry. Cleaned, de-boned and filleted, dipped in flour, egg and rolled in crushed Rice Krispies then fried briefly in butter and oil, they were going to taste sweeter than the kisses of angels fluttering in the moonlight.

It was almost time to head back. "Last run so look sharp, you guys," our Capitano said happily, "I'm setting a course for home so let's make it count."

Although weary and weak, we let our lines out carefully and smoothly, watched our rod tips like hawks and settled into our last task with purpose. Most of the other boats had left the area or dispersed into bays and inlets looking to finish the day with some bass fishing in the shallows. We alone trolled right down the shipping lane in the centre of the Detroit River, our larder full of fish and our hearts as proud as though we had invented the sport. Suddenly, Senior Thach's line went taught and his rod began to bend in a powerful arc. He calmly hit reverse and asked us to pull all our tackle up.

This had happened to us so often in the past few hours that we hardly noticed. If he was hung up on a rock, then getting past it on the other side should free it but if it was a big log or a sunken tire, the whole rig might be lost. He reeled hard to pick up the slack but there wasn't any, the line stayed tight and the rod continued to bend like rubber. We motored well past where the snag took place. Whatever it was out there kept moving behind the boat.

"Mattie get the net and Terry you steer. Turn us around and just keep us in the channel," Captain Thrasher said in a firm voice we hadn't heard that day.

"What should I do?" Nevitt wanted to know.

"Keep your hat on," our skipper replied, with a grin.

His reel began to whine as the line paid out quickly. There was a fish on all right. He kept the fishing pole as high as he could, but the big sea monster kept tugging it down toward the river's surface. Captain Thatcher tried turning the thing but no dice. He attempted to bring it up from the depths, no way. He even tried to let it run for a while, but we all knew that he would eventually run out of fishing line once this beast got into the backing. He was running out of time and line.

"Throttle down a little," he said in desperation, "maybe we can tire him that way."

We suddenly found ourselves on a Nantucket Sleighride: the *Sophia* and all hands were being pulled slowly but without hesitation down the river, like a tugboat towing a barge.

"Wow, that has got to be some giant fish out there," I announced, gripping the gunwale.

"Thank you for your assistance, Matt, but I would much rather you concentrate on netting her if we get the chance rather than stating something that is obvious to all of us including the kitchen sink," Senior Thatch responded with a smirk.

Then the tide turned. In a long, out-stretched circle, the creature swooped over to the other side of our suddenly smaller fishing boat and started to head toward the opposite shoreline. Our Captain played it perfectly, shifting positions like he was walking in the dark, planting one foot at a time without looking down while keeping the line tight. He began to reel, like a hoist winching up a slab of steel.

"She's coming up," he barely breathed to us. "Get ready and keep the bow upstream."

Give and take eventually became take and give. Then the fight turned into pull up high then reel. Whatever it was swam closer. Like the pirates we copied, hauling up sunken treasure, our eyes strained into the depths.

When the brute broke water, it was like a plane landing upside down. It rolled once, angrily churning and crashing on the surface. The thing looked like a mongrel-fish, thrown together with God's leftovers: part alligator with an armoured, bony back, a shark-like pointed snout, a touch of catfish with the whiskers and part whale because it was so huge. It must have run to fifty or sixty pounds and was longer than the *Sophia's* stern.

"It's a sturgeon," our Capitano shouted. "I'll try to bring her around back, so cut the motor and Mattie fetch the net and keep it low in the water."

Mouths open, we watched as the great beast shook its head. Nothing on earth could have diverted our attention. Captain Ahab told us, in between tugs and reels, that sturgeon can live up to a hundred years and grow as long as fifteen feet.

"It's too big, so we'll have to try to get the head into the net first and then Nevitt and Terry, you two try to wrestle its body into the boat," he added curtly.

We sucked in our breath as we saw it seethe closer, convulsing as it came. Rod held flagpole-high; Senior Thatcher eased its horny head into the waiting net. I held on like my life depended on it, but just as Skeese and Nevitt tried to wrangle it up and out of the river, it broke through the net and dove deep, ripping what was left out of my hands.

"Try to grab the handle and pull the net up so it is out of the way," Thatcher said calmly.

This, two of us managed to accomplish.

"Give me the other net, Nevitt."

"Where is it?" he wanted to know, startled.

"Under your ass, boy, in the cargo hold."

The back-up net in hand, the tussle began afresh after our skipper expertly slipped his rod and reel through the gaping hole in the first net, freeing them for the work at hand.

The brute had run again but it soon tired and came to the net easily like an extremely large and gnarled puppy to a bone. For the second time in excruciating moments, we netted her head-first and tried to wrench her body into the *Sophia*. It almost worked until we heard a loud crack as the net snapped in two. I held the broken handle, and the fish swam serenely away, taunting us with its power and reserve, like the ancient entity it was, having seen and done more than all of us put together. Our skipper stood up straight to his full height and looked wistfully at his noble adversary still thrashing here and there.

"Nice work, lads. We've done what we could, but we were never going to keep her so it's time to give her back to the river. The hook will dissolve over a short time and she'll live to spawn and fight again," our skipper said, as he solemnly knelt and cut the line.

We Raiders sank as one to the deck exhausted. But we knew we had earned our stripes as fishermen, seamen and soldiers.

"Not a bad outing, wouldn't you say, lassies?" Senior Thatch said with a chortle.

Then, whistling once again, the Captain with his hat at a jaunty angle, jaw set and chest puffed, guided the *Sophia* triumphantly toward the dock like we were crusaders returning from the Holy Land. Finning its way silently behind us in our wake was the shadowy ghost of a giant, prehistoric, silver alligator with whiskers.

Chapter 21

Saturated Saturday

The elevator door creaked open and Rogie jumped inside, hitting the second-floor button as fast as he could. He counted out the time as he watched the floor needle swing down from top.

"One machine gun, two machine gun, three machine guns."

The cage clanked to a halt, and just as the doors began to open, Rogan darted outside.

"You're it!" he shouted triumphantly.

A deep voice from the corner said, "No, son, you're it."

Rogan looked up to see a huge cop in full uniform with a six-gun the size of a small cannon attached to his black leather belt. And there was another policeman as well as the building's security guard on the other side the parking platform. If ever a Raider felt like a rat caught in a trap, this was the time.

"Let's go, young man. We're taking you to the office," the second cop snarled.

"Yeah, you're in the kind of trouble you can't get out of," the guard added, a greasy, hand-rolled sawdust cigarette bent in his mouth.

On the way to the ground floor, the lead cop told Rogan that the security guy had called them in because we were causing havoc with elevator wait times, cars were stuck in line-ups and there were too many complaints for one guy to handle.

"Do you have any idea how many problems you've caused and what a dangerous game you were playing?" he growled.

They led Rogeman, the condemned prisoner, into the dingy office, a single lightbulb dangling like a sick plant from the ceiling. As he looked up, Rogie saw slumped in the shadows all the rest of the Raiders, heads down, pawing at the concrete with their runners. It was worse than he had worried. There was no exit, no magic door to freedom, no hope for salvation. We were cornered Raiders, disarmed of our cutlasses and flintlocks, like drowned men washed up on the salty shore of our misdeeds.

That Saturday had started with a rocket blast. It was early in the new cartoon season when animated series were introduced to joyful youth across the land. Sweetened cereal on our TV tables, we sat glued to the tube to see what the studios had come up with for us and us alone. Usually, the Raiders differed on personal favourites, but this year, down to the last Rankin buccaneer, *Jonny Quest* was our main guy. It was part horror and part futuristic science fiction, and the heroes were kids like us always seeking or creating their own adventures. Jonny's best pals were Hadji, a South Asian kid with a turban, which was rare for TV then, and his plucky pooch, Bandit. His father, Dr. Benton Quest, was a genius scientist and inventor. They faced stone gargoyles coming to life, mechanical spiders from outer space, Sasquatches, underwater spies bent on taking over the earth, menacing condors and lizard men. We never missed an episode.

We began to realize that we weren't just in the Golden or the Silver or even the Bronze Age of cartoons we were living through all three. Warner Brothers had begun the whole pageant many years before, creating characters that were to live forever: Bugs Bunny, Daffy Duck, Yosemite Sam, the Tasmanian Devil, Road Runner and Pepe Le Pew. That process began before television, so the action-soaked adventures were only available as entertainment shorts in movie theatres before the main feature. These were largely slapstick characters with some vaudevillian roots, with either strange or booming voices.

There were good guys and bad guys who were usually the same stars in each episode. The hero figured out how to foil the villain time and time again, usually with witty dialogue, ingenious traps and plans. Love interests cropped up here and there, usually to the strains of heart-sick, swooning classical music. We experienced the "William Tell Overture," "Barber of Seville," "Vienna Waltzes," "Flight of the Valkyries" and Hungarian dances with crazy characters leaping all over the screen. We were witnessing animators' imaginations come to life before our astonished eyes.

As televisions found their way into more homes everywhere, Warner Bros. adopted their cartoon mainstays for the small screen and began producing a whole bunch more of them.

While this was happening, Bill Hanna and Joe Barbera, two former MGM animators who had created *Tom and Jerry*, formed their own company and began to create, the Silver Age of cartoons. Their stable of characters and series were immense, ranging from Huckleberry Hound, Quick Draw McGraw, Yogi Bear and Snagglepuss to the Flintstones, the Jetsons, Magilla Gorilla and yes, Jonny Quest.

The team Hanna-Barbera adapted cartoons to the TV format with commercial breaks, fast action and punchy storylines. They invented a whole host of good and bad guys with unusual attributes that allowed for broadened storylines and wider-scoped adventures. They took over Saturday morning cartoons for kids across North America and abroad. Hanna-Barbera also gave rise to, out of imitation and admiration, many new cartoon companies largely in New York and California as well as some in Canada. Existing newspaper comic strips also came to life on the TV screen, a ready base for already popular characters to join the fun. Some of the smaller, independent studios produced more eclectic but imaginative cartoon characters, like Under Dog and Beany and Cecil.

The most outlandish of the independents, Jay Ward Productions, came up with *The Rocky and Bullwinkle Show*. There had been nothing quite like it, from its talking Moose and Flying Squirrel heroes to Captain Wrong-Way Peachfuzz, the nuttiest Captain on the seas, the always dastardly Snidely Whiplash and Dudley Do Right, the hapless Canadian Mountie. There was also Mr. Peabody, the time-travelling genius, and his young pal Sherman and the crafty Iron Cold War Curtain duo of Boris Badanov and Natasha Fatale. *Fractured Fairy Tales* rounded up the bizarre yet hilarious group with retellings of the famous stories from our childhoods. This was a cartoon country mile from *Tweetie Bird and Sylvester*. The Silver Age blossomed, unlike its predecessor, in little more than 10 or 12 years.

We were mesmerized. We couldn't wait until the next episodes burst into our living rooms. That was why it was so hard for us to cough up a Saturday morning for lawn mowing or snow shovelling, visiting ancient

Aunt Agnes for dry scones, a church social, a rummage sale, washing Dad's car or the dog.

Then, something near and dear to our Raider hearts happened. The comic book superheroes we had cherished since that day when we snuck them into our rooms to read and re-read until the covers and pages turned ragged and see-through began to appear on Saturday morning television. For the first time, we could hear Superman and Batman talk. We could watch the Fantastic Four fly on fire, stretch around the block, turn invisible and walk like a moving pile of rocks.

Aquaman controlled the seas, swimming alongside great white sharks and Spider-man dangled down on his webs to impress Mary Jane. This was the Bronze Age, and it took over before we could blink. Marvel, DC and independent small comic book companies had a vast parade of characters that could be brought to the little screen. And they were right in time with space travel, sci-fi, vast, unusual powers and intellects. There were ready-made plots, storylines and cute gals our superheroes were sweet on. Marvel and DC even had their own universes with characters who teamed up, interacted with one another from different times and dimensions. The pool of resources for cartoons was almost limitless. Being comics, they were already completely developed for animating into cartoons. And they were created in series with one issue leading to the next. Comics swarmed onto TV and took control of the cartoon ship. We couldn't have been more delighted.

"Look, dad, the comics you don't like to see me reading are on TV now!"

Through the increasing use of re-runs, we could watch characters from all three eras over and over again. Because they were pure imagination, invented characters, animals with human traits, huger-than-life beings, they fuelled our dreams, set our wishes ablaze and gave us an excitement that could be created. It was as though we were sitting with our TV tables on Cartoon Island, in the middle of three types, styles and timeframes of animation. They converged on us, washing over us with the tides of all that we loved: peril, feats of daring, cute girls, triumph, otherworldliness, dark secrets, the unknown and life experienced above the commonplace and beyond the present. It started with Bugs Bunny and was still raging with the X-Men, and we were there for the whole cartoon parade, saluting and applauding as each comics character marched, swam or flew into our living rooms.

Not just content to have a great morning in front of the tube, this Saturday was special for another reason: for the first time we had talked our parents into letting us go to the movies on the big screen in Windsor by ourselves. Of course, we had an ulterior motive. We told them we were going to see *The Sound of Music*, but we were really heading for *Muscle Beach Party* at another theatre. It featured more than a few things we were keen on: girls in bikinis, California beaches, girls in bikinis, muscle cars, girls in bikinis, surfing, girls in bikinis, rock 'n roll and girls in bikinis. Our anticipation was even more enjoyable as we knew that there was no way our parental units would have let us attend that film. It starred Frankie "the Crooner" Avalon and the girl he was always around but never could seem to get, Annette Funnyjello.

We rode the bus the eighteen miles to Windsor through LaSalle, sight-seeing along the way like we were heading to a private country club we had never visited. We grabbed some pizza at Cavello's and snuck it into the movie theatre. Our five heads bobbed to the beach dances: the Frug, the Monkey, the Boogaloo and the Twist, and the tunes by Jan and Dean, the Beach Boys, Dick Dale and the Del-Tones, the Safaris and the Ventures, as well as all the jiggling that was enhancing each song and dance. And when the guys surfed, we surfed. We hung ten, Eskimo-rolled, shot the curl, duck-dove, walked the plank and, of course, wiped out. That bus ticket from the 'Burg was like a free pass to Surf City.

When the waves slowed and the sun began to set on the movie, we kissed the girl, strapped our boards to the tops of our wood-panelled station wagons and headed out the theatre doors back into reality. It was a little chilly after all that California heat.

On the way back to the station we passed a big six-storey parking garage. We strolled in like we owned the biggest Caddie in the joint. It was solid concrete, dingy and dank with fetid water seeping down the walls. The place felt and looked like an asylum for cars. The deal was, people parked their automobiles and then got the heck outta there.

Spotting the decrepit elevators, Sticks suggested, "Let's take a ride up top."

We took in the matinee for *Muscle Beach Party* so we had plenty of time left and there would be more buses in the afternoon. Everyone climbed aboard, eager not to let our surfing adventures ride out with the tide for the day. Just off the sixth-floor ramp we could see the Motor City with its Penobscot Building's beacon some twenty-five storeys above us. It could be seen for miles and miles outside the flatlands of Essex County and deep into Detroit, a watchtower of pride, guarding the river and all those who lived and worked in the two border cities. We had seen it many times before but never at this height. We were only up to its shins, but it seemed even more colossal.

"I got an idea. Why don't we play elevator tag?" Wiry asked. "You know, with no tag-backs."

"There's nobody around, people just leave their cars and go shopping or take the bus to Detroit," I agreed.

"And the rule is you can't take the stairs, but you can step outside and wait for another elevator," Rogie said.

"I saw a watchman on the way in, but he looked like he was asleep," Skeese told us.

The game was on. We were like pinballs on a vertical table, bouncing from floor to floor and door to door. We played for what seemed like hours, scrambling, outta breath, figuring our next moves. Every once in a while, the security guard would spot one of us and yell, but nothing came of it so we elevator-raced on, getting craftier and more cunning. Sometimes, the Raider who was It would surprise two players in one elevator, press the button for another floor, touch one of them and then hit the door-close button. The second guy in the cage would be It by default. Another tactic was to hide behind a family, in the back of the elevator so the Raider who was It couldn't see us. Shuffling out behind them and pressing the down or up button on the way out would leave the Raider trying to catch us alone in the elevator car.

We were completely unaware that out in the six levels of parking lots a traffic jam had developed. There were line-ups at the elevators and some people's kids were getting lost in the chaos that was building and people started complaining and yelling. More and more impatient families were waiting outside the elevator doors, but we just figured it was rush hour at the parking garage. Besides, it made for a more interesting game with human obstacles thrown into the bargain.

Then the doors of the conveyors of human cargo opened and closed on us for the last time that previously glorious Saturday. The uniformed and furious authorities rounded us up one by one, catching us in our own cages. The dark shadow of the law was cast over our short-lived and to that point highly entertaining and successful sport of elevator tag.

In the security office we were told that there had been more than fifty complaints that afternoon about slow elevator service, kids running around pushing and bumping into people like they were in an amusement park, missing children and line-ups at the entrance and the exit, on the ramps, at the stairs and at the elevators.

"We've never been called here for anything other than a car break-in," the big cop thundered at us.

We shrugged, trying to look smaller and more innocent. According to Raider code, we didn't utter a word and barely breathed.

"In a few hours, you five hooligans have turned this place into a goldurn zoo," he blasted. "And the worst of it all is that someone, some child could have fallen down the shaft."

All ten of our eyes opened wide like we had never considered that sort of thing because we hadn't.

"Well, you should have thought of that before you started on your crime spree," he howled at us, his voice getting scratchier and hoarser.

"Now, I want your names and your home phone numbers," he said, heaving and sitting down, "and no one is going anywhere until we get in touch with your parents or guardians, even if it takes all day and night."

This guy was good. The home phone numbers, and the not-leaving parts scuppered our Raider ship. We knew we had to cough up the goods or else.

"And next Saturday, don't make any plans because you're gonna be right back here, cleaning this place from the top to the ground floor, every bloody inch, until it shines," he told us wearily. "So, bring your work gloves, girls."

After all our families had been contacted, they escorted us out the exit.

With his hands on his gun belt, the officer in charge said, smiling, "Don't worry, I've already contacted Corporal Tice. He told me he'll gladly meet you at the Amherstburg bus stop."

It turned out that because the misdemeanours had taken place outside of Mice's jurisdiction and he wasn't a party to the escapades, he was only able to issue us a warning. He had us line up in front of him, and he yelled at us for what seemed like hours. We refused to blink, scratch or cough, all the while fighting back the urge to smile or even laugh out loud. We were beating the rap and we all knew it. No matter how much hot air he hollered at us, we didn't twitch; just stared straight ahead like alien automatons on *Jonny Quest*.

On our way home, we rolled and tumbled against one another, leapt up and slapped the leaves in trees, skipped, stride-jumped, roundhouse kicked invisible attackers and laughed at the sky. It was like a get-out-of-jail-free pass until we turned the Rankin Street corner and remembered that we would have to face our parents who had all received the calls from the cops.

It was a Saturday saturated with daring Raider adventure and it was all worth it even if there wasn't a perfect ending. Full of plunder, our Raider ship had been scuttled before it could cruise into the sunset, but we knew we would raise its sails again.

Chapter 22

Not Just any Fort in a Storm

We were on manoeuvres: running low, rolling into bunkers, scrambling crablike up and over the other sides, dodging shafts of light, silently staying in touch with whistles and hand signals, timing ourselves, sucking wind and keeping nimble. Sometimes the Raiders had to prove themselves to themselves by testing their team skills. We had to depend on knowing where each of us would be on a mission, moving easily as one unit under a thick blanket of darkness. We were honing our sabres, keeping our powder dry and thwarting an invisible enemy. Stealthily barking up the tree of adventure, we were bringing our bravado to a boil and winning at our own invented conquests.

What better place to practise our brigand craft than at Historic Fort Malden, formerly Fort Amherstburg? A major player in the War of 1812 between British and American forces, it was a bastion outpost at a key juncture on the Detroit River before the river opened into Lake Erie. With its rolling earthworks, restored cannons, barracks, museum and waterfront, it provided the perfect grounds for rehearsing our covert activities.

This would be a multiple-stage operation that would take place over four weeks, culminating with some of us getting inside the museum after dark while avoiding detection by the night watchman. Then we would make some rearrangements, supposedly the work of ghosts or reanimated privates of the past. Phases one and two involved casing the joint first during the day and again at night.

The daytime operation we devised had two of us wander in trailing behind some parents with just one or two kids so our operatives looked like part of the family. Whaley and Stickers drew those short straws. The Raiders slicked their hair down, buffed their shoes and turned out in their Sunday best, looking as close to Mama's little angels as they would ever get. We other three strolled separately and innocently about the grounds searching for opportunities for our final plan while we pretended to read the various plaques and study some of the outdoor historic munitions and artifacts. During the day there was a guard on duty who walked about sternly and precisely, often stationing himself at the doorway to the main museum building known as Hough House. That guard was all by the book and conducted his routine with military regimen, so we stayed shy of him.

The museum was our target so the primary objective for our inside guys was to oil the front and back door handles, locks, and hinges so they didn't make a peep when opened or closed. It was a simple ploy, but it could sink the Raiders' pillaging ship if our comings and goings were announced by creaks. The raid would take place a few weeks later, so if the guards noticed anything, they would have just figured that the custodian had lubricated a door knob or hinge as part of his maintenance procedures and quickly forget about it. It was easily done as Skeese and Rogie were on the lookout to give the high sign when Captain Correct marched over to another part of the fort enclosure. Whaley greased first one door then the other with a sleight of hand that was faster than Mandrake the Magician. He also checked to see if they could be easily unlocked from the inside. No problemos. All aces.

Phase two was to look for places to hide. The upstairs was ruled out in case we were cornered on the second floor with no exit. The Raiders weren't about to become rats getting caught in their own trap. And finally, there would be little or no light, so the two made mental notes of where dangerous artifacts like a sword or a musket with a bayonet might be sticking out from a wall or in the hands of a dummy soldier. Bloodshed at our own hands by accidently running ourselves through was to be seriously avoided.

Hiding behind a uniform seemed to be suitable as did a couple of recesses in corners behind cabinets and a spinning wheel. With the first and second phases complete, we regrouped to confer about our findings at the Dairy Queen, which had recently opened in town.

The sparkling new frozen dessert palace was part of a lesser Raider ambition, which was to eat every single item they sold before the end of the summer. From each type of shake and sundae to pops and parfaits, blizzards and banana splits and drumsticks and dilly bars, it was ice cream all the way down the line, one at a time. So, our meeting served two purposes. Multi-tasking was a natural for us Rankin Street boys, like getting in and out of trouble.

We shared information about the inside and outside of the area and determined where each of us would be stationed for the mock, yet potentially dangerous, raid. If caught inside the closed museum at night, we could be in more trouble than the first American ship that tried to glide past Fort Malden at the start of the War of 1812.

Part three of our siege of the Fort was an evening visit to the garrison to monitor the activity of the night watchman, most importantly his customary comings and goings, so we could decide on our own timing for the raid. His name was Jerry Pitkowski, but he was known as Cherry Pit. He was skinny and sketchy, usually unshaven and slovenly. He looked like a boiled possum. Everything about him was sleepy: from his slit eyes and slow gait to his oafish lack of attention and his unmade bed of a uniform. A grizzled, porcupine-like creature with fewer movements, he didn't exactly pose much of an obstacle to our plans. Both the evening casing of the Fort and the actual raid were set for Friday nights when we could be on sleepovers at one of our houses and we knew Pitts would probably be un-performing his derelict duties.

We were conspiring to invade an historically important command post. After the United States' independence, Fort Amherstburg was constructed in 1795 to defend British North America's border that flowed invisibly down the centre of the Detroit River. With a glorious but unusual past, the palisade had endured for more than a century and a half, when the Raiders came up with the idea of using it for our training ground. From then on, the outpost had hopscotched from owner to owner and functions to functions, not landing anywhere for too long. During the early stages of the War of 1812, the capture of Detroit was conceived and launched from the Fort, engineered by Sir Isaac Brock, a hero of the war and camp commander along with his partner in the successful siege, Tecumseh, the famous Shawnee chief. Fort Detroit surrendered without a shot being fired.

In 1813, the British were forced to burn and abandon Fort Amherstburg when the Americans sent large regiments to seize the key military post. Rather than let them have a healthy fort at the mouth of the river, they set it afire and fled. The Americans began to rebuild it until the war ended, and what was left of the garrison was re-occupied in 1815 by the British who continued the reconstruction and renamed it Fort Malden.

In the 1830s the Fort was once more on the national stage as a command post to help quash the Upper Canada Rebellion between 1837 and 1839. A decade later it gained notoriety once again but the activities at Fort Malden were of a secretive nature.

It became a haven for runaway slaves arriving under the cover of night from Detroit and other American launches along the river: by steamship, sailing vessels and rowboats by the thousands. It was one of, if not the most important, five Canadian stations along the Underground Railroad, contributing to the proud ancestry and history of the 'Burg and the surrounding areas, not to mention Ontario.

From 1859 to 1870, the Fort achieved much less notoriety as a mental institution called the Malden Lunatic Asylum, connected to a similar, sister-facility in Toronto. It housed about 250 male and female inmates who provided an astounding amount of unpaid labour to help restructure the grounds and produce crops from over sixty acres of the surrounding lands. When the Asylum's population was moved to London, Ontario, the compound was transformed into a large lumber mill. Then most of the Fort's grounds were subdivided for private homes until what was left was protected in 1921 when the Historic Sites and Monuments Board of Canada designated it as having national significance. Since then, it has been restored and rebuilt to reflect its unique stature and contribution to Canada's history.

It was then time for our last phase of the operation before the actual exploit: casing the compound after dark. It was shaping up to be a smooth mission conceived and conducted by the Rankin Street Raiders. Our bandit faces were smeared with burnt cork, we wore dark clothes, runners and carried a penlight each. They were our preferred choice of illumination as the beam was small and concentrated, easy to carry with a clip like the pen they were named after and could be held in our teeth if we needed both hands to get out of a jam. We stationed ourselves at five viewpoints around the main building. These included the front and back doors, windows on two sides and Skeese had shinnied up a tree for a front-row balcony view of everything. We waited, observed and kept track of the timing.

Pitkowski liked to smoke cheap cigarillos, the kind with the plastic filter tips that tasted like rolled cardboard dipped in cheap wine with the aroma of a burnt-weenie sandwich. These were a delicacy for Cherry Pit. His preference for those stinking, smouldering embers kept him sitting outside in between rounds. Sure enough, when we arrived, he was camped in front of the museum, a rumpled cigar drooping from his rubbery lips.

It was usually around the hour that Pitts managed to wrestle himself to his feet and begin his slow-motion rounds. He began by inspecting the main building we were observing unlocking the door, then meandering about, splaying his flashlight lazily here and there then ascending the stairs to do the same on the second floor. The hands on our watches seemed to move backwards, but his plodding pace would give our Raiders' inside team plenty of time to get in and hide.

Our plan was for two of us to follow him into the Hough House but not until he climbed the stairs so his footsteps would cover any accidental noise our guys might make. He didn't bother to lock the door behind him, which was crucial to our mission. When he was on his regular route, the outside team would follow, familiarizing themselves with the pattern of his checkpoints. If, on the night of our strike, he broke from his routine and headed back early, two of the outside Raiders would be dispatched, shining their penlights into the museum window as they ran to alert the inside team to get the heck out.

Once inside, the idea was to make our mark by changing mannequins' hats, turning some uniforms inside out, pointing muskets and pistols at the door and laying some swords in a cross on the floor—but nothing really noticeable until daylight.

Then the two museum Raiders would have to sit tight for an hour until Cherry Pit made another round. When he climbed the stairs, Sticks and Whaley would vamoose silently into the shadows, making it look like the Fort Malden ghosts had been up to midnight manoeuvres and all behind locked doors.

Stickers and Whales were the inside agents, me and Rogie were the advance warning pair, stationed in the bunkers and Skeese was the roving scout, shadowing Cherry Pit. The deal was done, and it was going to be fun.

Walking cautiously back after 1 a.m., Stickler asked aloud, "When we were in the Hough House, I saw an old straitjacket on display near one of the windows. What was that about, is that how the soldiers kept some of the prisoners?"

"No, you git, didn't you know?" the Rogester laughed. "The Fort was a mental hospital for a while before it became a museum."

"You're kidding, man. That really creeps me out," Sticks said with start. "We're gonna be in there with it at night, not to mention all those stuffed dead troops."

"Hey, that gives me the willies, too," Whaley said. "I hadn't really thought about hiding in there in the dark with those dead souls all around us, especially the nut cases."

"Ooooh, it's the ghosts of insane inmates and dead military," Skeese taunted. "Are you gonna have your mummy read you a bed-time story and tuck you in the night before?"

"Maybe you two will get lucky and they'll only be zombie soldiers and crazy patients coming to life when they smell young, ripe, human flesh," I added.

"Jeezalou on a pogo stick," Whaley said. "Maybe one of you tough guys want to trade roles for this raid?"

"Nope, you two cased the inside, you know where everything is, so unless you want to set fire to the whole operation just like the Fort in 1813, you had better get the goblins and wee fairies outta your skulls and be Raiders," Rogie stated flatly.

After that, it would be a silent march back to Rankin, our shadows thin and wavering as we passed under streetlights.

Late the following Friday night, we re-grouped at Toby Park, near where we would launch our own assault on Fort Malden, the final phase of our plan. We had carefully conceived and organized the detailed enterprise and our confidence was at high tide. Huddling together in a shadow and whispering, we checked our watches and tested our penlights. But there was a false step at the outset—Skeese couldn't find his flashlight at home, so we were short one of the essential illuminating and signalling devices we were depending upon. We considered aborting but it was decided that we would go ahead with Skeeser having to use low whistles to alert the rest of us if there were any problems.

Upon arrival, we scurried to our separate stations and watched the time tick down to midnight. The ratty cigar-smoking Pitkowski was languidly puffing away in front of Hough House like a smouldering, crumpled pile of old rubbish on a park bench. Whales and Stickers crept behind shrubs near the entrance, while Rogie and I panther-crawled into the trenches.

Skeese laid back, keeping his eyes trained on his quarry—the Pitts. Finally, after what seemed like the Seven Year's War, the witching hour arrived. We Raiders had shivers in our timbers. Our night watchman coughed himself awake from his half-sleep, hurled a phlegmy gob into the darkness, slid the key into the well-lubricated museum front door and shuffled inside. Sticks and Whaley scampered up to the door, training their eyes on his wavering torch light. His thick footfall was heard on the staircase. They eased inside like silent shadows, sliding into their separate hiding spots. Pitkowski huffed down the stairs a few moments later and headed outside on his appointed rounds, locking the main museum door behind him.

Using their penlights, our inside guys began busily making mischief by rearranging the artifacts. Peering from the trenches, Rogie and I saw Cherry Pit lumber by, while Skeese shadowed him from a distance, deep in the darkness. All was going according to our well-oiled plan.

Then lightning struck, followed by a clap of thunder that sounded like the Almighty starting the human race. Rain waterfalled. The outside crew hunkered down, and the inside guys slipped quickly over to the trench-side window in the museum.

The deluge hit the windows, seemingly melting the glass and the flashes caused the room to blaze momentarily. The suddenly haunted Hough House shook and creaked to its ancient foundation. Sticks looked up and saw the spot-lit straitjacket and then it was gone. He found himself thinking about all the inmates who were put in the asylum by evil relatives or those who could not be bothered to care for them, toiling for nothing, placing one feeble foot in front of another as they trudged toward their death. Abused, caged, herded and worked like beasts, they were denied families, friends and freedom, deprived even of hope. Despair their daily food and drink. He was haunted by these grim images. He could feel their helpless pain: weak-minded people caught with no beginning, no present and a future that was only a bleak, vacant end. They existed between shadow and light, prematurely bodiless souls in life.

Whaley was feeling unsettled, too. The storm continued to assault the museum, threatening to blow it apart with the cannon fire of lightning then thunder, lightning then thunder. Echoes of soft moaning reverberated through the rooms, spirits seeking a sanctum. A burst of light gave a second of life to a stuffed uniform near him, still bravely on guard. He felt the fear of one of the British soldiers, perhaps an ancestor, quaking to the crack of musket fire, cowering to the blasts of heavy artillery, lying prone in the bunkers, the relentless rain pelting him as he prayed for protection. The spooky soul inside the long-dead soldier's outfit next to Whaley seemed to murmur mournfully, his last gasps crawling into the Raider's ears.

"We gotta get outta here, man!" Sticks whispered hoarsely.

"I know, I know but we can't see the lights from Rogie and Matt," Whaley said, waking from his nightmare. "Pitkowski could be just outside the door."

"Look, over above the bunker, two lights rising."

"Okay, that's our signal, but let's wait a second to see what happens, they seem to be coming toward us."

Sure enough, two small laser-like lights shone through the downfall, piercing the windowpane. The lightning flashed again, and a single figure was frozen in the glare. A jumble of bones, its torso draped in the shreds of a straitjacket, a torn bandage wrapped on its bare skull and iridescent eyes staring at the two cowering Raiders. Clots of caked mud dripped from its bones. They closed their eyes to make it go away but the thing climbed behind their eyelids, re-displaying itself, burning its features into their brains. They looked again but only the glowing orbs were visible. Another flash illuminated it once more as it jolted and swayed crazily toward them: a dancing re-death in the firefight of the storm.

"We're gone, Pitts or no Pitts," Stanks yelled at Whales.

"Way ahead of you man."

As they raced to the front door, they heard a shriek in between the howls of thunder. They looked out to see Pitkowski, falling and running between bolts of lightning, his flashlight waving everywhere. They heard him scream again and then he was gone. The outside Raiders were nowhere to be seen, nor was the hundred-year-old asylum skeleton. They ran to the rendezvous where all the outside Raiders were waiting, panting with exhaustion. All five brigands were spent, sapped of strength and energy.

"Where were you guys? What happened back there?" Skeese asked breathlessly.

"We heard Cherry Pit screeching and saw him running out the front gate so we figured you guys were safe and would meet us back here," Rogie added.

"We saw your two signal lights, so we headed out the door just after Pitkowski ran off," Sticks said.

"Signal lights, what signals?" I asked. "I dropped my penlight and Rogie's battery went dead in the rain."

Whaley and Stickers looked at each other like they had just seen more than a ghoul.

"You guys didn't see anything else?" Whales asked.

"Just the storm and a lotta lightning and thunder," Skeese replied. "Musta' scared the bejabbers outta Cherry Pits. He's probably still running or waddling away."

Walking slowly home, triumphant but saturated, Whales and Sticks lagged behind the others.

"Was that lunatic, zombie, bone rack back there on manoeuvres, too?"

"I dunno, could be he was trying to help us out."

"Hey, you think the Raiders have a friend on the other side?"

"You mean the underside?"

"Well, he saved our scared asses, that's for sure."

"Yeah, and maybe he's resting a little easier tonight."

"I wish him peace, he and his buddies."

"Me too, brother, me too."

Chapter 23

Moonshine Hockey

Rocketing down backroads into another county at eighty miles an hour, we were skidding into and sling-shotting out of curves, engine whining, dual exhausts blaring, in a jacked-up, metallic-tangerine Camaro on a brisk and bright winter Sunday morning. We might as well have been running some end-of-season moonshine.

At the helm and in the other bucket seat sat two tough but funny guys in their twenties with decks of darts tucked into their shirtsleeves, babe tattoos, slicked hair with duck tails in the back, big gem-encrusted signet rings, tight leather jackets and even tighter jeans. They wore shades and grins that looked like sneers. Despite being strapped into the back seat the three of us lurched with every yank of the wheel, desperately trying not to get thrown through the windows. Sunk low, we could feel the dirt and gravel kick our asses. Then we were momentarily airborne, closer to the treetops it seemed only to smash back to the frozen ground to pick up more speed.

Our ride soared into the wind, gobbled up the miles and spat them out. Bouncing like jelly beans, we screamed with delight. Part torpedo, part roller-coaster and part time-machine, it was unsafe and scary, and we couldn't get enough.

We were on our way to a little league hockey game. The cool dudes up front were our coaches. Equipment bags, hockey sticks and pucks, water bottles and skates thrashed and crashed around in the trunk behind our heads. We all drank colas and were eating chips. It was me, Wiry and a part-time Raider, Donny, "The Hat" Nevitt. The other team that day had Sticks and Skeese on it. Sitting low in the rear seat, we learned more about girls from listening to our coaches than we did from our parents or in health class. Ears and eyes wide open we didn't miss a word when it came to our pre-game female mind and anatomy lessons. We all would have scored A pluses on those tests.

The 'Burg didn't have an arena then, so we had to play our league games in other towns and the only ice-time available was on Sunday mornings. When I realized that I could get out of going to church by playing in a league, I ran faster than I could skate to sign up. When I told my parents that I was going to compete in organized hockey my mum was worried about me getting hurt but my dad was all for it.

"What if he gets hit with the puck or pushed into the boards? There's hitting and fighting in hockey. It's a rough sport," she said to my dad.

"No, no, they wear lots of padding, helmets and mouth guards," he replied quickly. "Besides, he's a good skater and he knows how to stay out of trouble. Right, Matt?" he said turning to me.

"Yes, sir," I said, nodding, almost saluting him.

"Well then it's settled," my dad said proudly. "I'll bet he'll be a good hockey player. I wasn't too bad in my day."

"Thanks a lot, Dad," I said, suddenly supporting anything he had to say on the subject. Of course, he was furious with me when he found out when the games were held, but by then it was too late. Eventually church didn't stop him from attending a lot of my games. And I did become rather good, like all the Raiders. We were a co-ordinated bunch.

The Camaro rumbled into the arena parking lot, the brightest jewel in the place with Johnny River's version of "Maybelline" all but blowing us out the doors. The old arenas we played in were drafty with a lattice work of wooden beams barely holding those cold caves together. The seating was hard and covered with peeling paint. A tattered scoreboard was run by some bored teenager who moved the numbers by hand. It was dreary work. Our dream arena job was that of Zamboni operator, the guy who flooded the ice before and after games, waving wildly to the kids in what little crowd had gathered. Perched high on a square watering and scraping machine the size of a dump truck, sporting a gold and black hockey jacket, precision cut and oiled hair and a ready wink for the gals, he cruised to his own tunes, rockin' that machine up and down and around the ice, centre stage. Some invisible minion opened and closed the broad doors at the end of the rink when he finished. He all but took a bow and a curtain call at the end of each performance.

I had a sprained ankle for that game but was going to play anyway and see how long I could last. Skeese and I were the starting centremen for our teams. As we lined up for the first face-off, he asked me how my ankle was healing?

"It's ok, just a little tender," I told him.

He gave me a smirk. When the referee dropped the puck Skeeser ignored it and gave me a sharp rap with his stick on the inside of my foot. I yelled in pain and he scooped up the loose puck and headed toward our net.

"That'll teach you," I heard Sticks shout at me from between the pipes behind me. "At least it wasn't a lead stick," he added.

He was referring to a minor incident from a few weeks ago. My dad had been watching me and The Hat take shots at an old door he set up at the end of our rink in the backyard. We were putting dents in the thinner panels but mostly the pucks just bounced off it.

"You guys gotta shoot harder and faster," he told us. "Your aim's good but you need more power. I've got an idea."

He disappeared for about an hour and returned with six shiny, black pucks. "Try these out and see what happens," he said, tossing them lightly on the ice. We shrugged and I wound up and fired. The puck moved sluggishly toward the door and barely bumped it. My dad laughed and so did The Hat. Donny was a good hockey player, smart around the net and fast. He skated over and wristed another new puck as hard as he could at the door. It too travelled in slow motion. Puzzled, we looked at my dad.

"Turn one over," he said. "Take a look at the other side."

We each picked up a puck. They were heavy and on the underside were some holes with melted metal shining up at us. We blinked and felt the weight again through our hockey gloves.

"I drilled some holes but not all the way through then melted lead into them," he explained with a raised eyebrow. "You should get some arm strength from shooting those pucks."

After school for three days and five doors from the dump later, we felt as if we had gorilla arms. A regular puck was light as a flicker's feather. This was the greatest invention since Pop Tarts.

Then the Hat had a thought. "Let's get Sticks over here and we can take some shots at him," he said, a crafty look in his grey eyes. "We'll keep the pucks lead side down until he figures it out."

I agreed. "What we need is a live target, and Stickwood will try to stop anything."

Our buddy was lugging his jumbo equipment bag and goalie pads over soon after. He was always struggling with that bundle like a kid who played the cello and had to transport it to and from lessons. Once he suited up, we had the six pucks all lined up at the far end of the rink.

"Hey, put your mask on, man!" I called to Sticks.

"Naw, I don't need it. Not for youse two."

"My dad has a rule, goalie masks on at all times," I told him, like we weren't already about to break a rink rule.

"Okay, but I'm not worried about your weak-ass shots."

I fired first and it hit his goalie pad with a muffled thud. The Hat snickered beside me.

"Wow, you got all of that one," Stanks laughed at us.

Then Donny leaned into a shot that went wide, hitting the door with the sound of a tomahawk biting into a tree.

The third shrapnel-puck shot Sticks deflected with his blocker, but it rocked him a little as we saw him wince behind his cage mask.

"Hey, guys back up some, will ya? This ain't target practice."

"You got padding, suck it up," The Hat taunted.

Then I lifted a high wrist shot that Sticks speared with his glove hand—only the puck kept going, taking his mitt with it.

"Wait a minute, what the hell is this?" he said, stooping to pick up his big leather trapper and the puck, exposed lead side up.

"You guys been shooting lead pucks at me!" he hollered at us.

Sticks ripped off his mask and came at us waving his goalie stick like a club. We scattered. Skating off the rink and then running on our blades in the snow.

"You guys are gonna pay for this. You could have broken some bones. I'll get you rats."

Donny headed home and I slid in our side door, careful to yank off my skates before my mum saw me. He started pounding on the door, still flipping out like a deranged attacker in a goalie uniform.

"What's wrong with Leonard?" my mother wanted to know.

"Oh, he's mad because he lost a bet. He'll get over it," I reassured her as I lowered the blind and locked the door.

But my mother must have seen or guessed something because those six lead pucks disappeared forever and they were never mentioned again, by me or my dad.

Sticks wasn't forgetting anytime soon. Days later in our league game he cursed at me and The Hat every time we skated near his crease, looking to chop us on our unprotected calves with his big goalie stick. We lost the game 4-0. But Sticks never said anything about it all to his parents. He was a Raider through and through.

The best hockey game we ever played was six hours long, like triple overtime. It wasn't winning the league title or a tournament championship or because we scored hat tricks or blocked seventy shots. It wasn't because we won anything or bested any other team or player. It was the coolest contest we ever played because it was just us, the Raiders, and some of our buddies out on a frozen creek.

It had rained the previous day, without wind and then the temperatures sunk overnight. Arriving with our equipment, lunches, pops, extra socks, mitts, sticks and pucks, the ice was polished, as sparkling and as hard as a diamond. When we laced up our skates and coasted out onto its perfect surface like sails unfurling in the breeze, we all knew it would be a good day, maybe even great. The pucks whistled on the ice; our skates glided in tune. The sheer blue of the crystal sheen beneath us met the dazzling sky at the edges of our own natural arena, boarded by snow and cattails gone to seed. It was hockey on high, the top of the world, up where it is bright, untouched and sanctified.

We were playing with and against each other, laughing, passing, scoring and defending all day. Our blades slicing into the ice, we felt like we were flying, unbridled, without boundaries. We played under a spell of hockey on the smoothest surface imaginable, reeling in great arcs, taking long, true shots that travelled forever. Our voices wafted into the great sleeping willows above us as we stickhandled smartly in our crystal palace of an open-air arena.

We didn't tire, kept no score, had no consistent teams and no notion of time. But the day did pass, a few of our own precious hockey hours shared with friends first and competitors second. The sun sank behind the willows, but we were able to play a little longer, still clutching the magic in our sticks, gliding on the energy of the experience, willing it not to end. A cold and full moon rose to allow us a few more shots, a few crisp passes. As we changed into our boots the moonshine splayed on our frosty creek, illuminating the 1,001 swirls our skates had carved into its surface. A portrait of and a tribute to one of the finest days the Rankin Street Raiders ever captured.

Chapter 24

Grave Scares

An aging vampire opened the lid of his creepy casket and slowly sat up. His waxen face was frozen in a sneer and his beady eyes burned like embers in the remains of a 200-year-old fire pit. He uttered an evil noise that penetrated our spines and made them shake. "Neeeeeyhaaaaahhhha," he howled and snarled at us. It was his sinister signature laugh. Lying in a semi-circle in the dark at midnight, stretched out on our sleeping bags, chins propped up by pillows, we stared back at the portable TV, transfixed in the glow and awaiting the terror that was soon to wash over us. Like hypnotized hamsters, we squirmed uncomfortably as Sir Graves Ghastly and his frightening friends introduced the scary movies we were about to witness.

Late on Friday nights, the haunting host climbed fresh from his crypt into our homes, closed the drapes, dimmed the lights and proceeded to give us goosebumps and force uncomfortable giggles. He brought us classic features from the golden and silver ages of horror. The early originals we loved included *Dracula*, *The Wolfman*, *The Mummy*, *Frankenstein*, *Dr. Fu Manchu* and *The Phantom of the Opera*, as well a host of other ghouls, zombies and mad scientists and their assistants invariably named Igor.

Two of our favourites were *Bride of Frankenstein* and *House of Dracula*. The first because of the welcome-to-the-cemetery special effects in almost every scene and the sympathy we have for the monster as well as Elsa Lancaster's grotesque and unforgettable appearance and scream at the end that was worth the entire film. The second classic had a crowd of creatures from a hunchback nurse (this time around), and the must-have mad doctor treating Wolfie, Drac and Frank. Lon Chaney Jr., John Carradine and Ludwig Stossel starred. What more could we frightfully hope for?

The silver age was dominated by two new forces: Hammer Films in Britain and the invasion of aliens in a new genre: science fiction. Hammer produced only horror movies, the first studio to do so, and others followed. Their productions were lighter and less shadowy than their fore films with lurid Technicolor portraying baroque sets and buckets of blood. Edgar Allen Poe tales ruled as Chaney, Bela Lugosi and Boris Karloff were replaced by Peter Cushing, Christopher Lee and Vincent Price (who had a summer home in Amherstburg down on the Detroit River).

Sci-fi films flew us into new galaxies, unleashing undreamt of beings and beasts. Little green men seemed to rain from the sky, intelligent extra-terrestrial life forms aimed their ray guns right at us and robots threatened to control our minds. Horrific monsters climbed out of the sea, from Godzilla to giant octopuses the size of Detroit. Rats, cats and bats grew to prolific proportions. We were even attacked by a colossal carrot and a fifty-foot woman. Many were cheesy productions with special effects created seemingly in someone's backyard, always during eternal twilight due to the lack of proper lighting. But we were crazy for them, signing up for every outer and inner space movie mission we could.

And scaring ourselves was always on our agenda. When we had sleepovers in the summer on Skeeser's or Sticks' front porch, we discussed the most potentially dangerous locations to unroll our sleeping bags. In the back of our fearful minds was the worry that a maniac would burst in with a machete and slaughter us all then disappear back into the night without a trace. Never once did we ever hear about or read of this happening, but that made no difference. Killers could be out there and we could be easy prey. We would be so tired from staying up late with Sir Graves whipping the hearse horses across our TV screens that we would be deep asleep. The murderer would have a whole room full of kids in a nightmarish slumberland, too exhausted to wake.

"No way. I'm taking the first spot by the front door," Wiry announced.

"Ok, I'll sleep there," Rogie stated. "If the psycho comes in, he'll probably trip over the first sleeper and fall full out, jabbing his knife into the third or fourth guy from the door."

"Yeah, it's not like he's going to kick the first kid and then kneel down and stab him," Sticks offered. "He'll just rush in and start slashing."

"So, the safest spots are right under or furthest from the door," I said.

"I'm sleeping under the sofa," Skeese declared.

"Oh right, crazy people always forget to look under the couches," Wiry said shaking his head. "That's the place they look after they're done so there are no survivors, no witnesses," he added.

"Ok, then the safest place to sleep is right at the front door. That's crazy," I said.

"I'm not sleeping there."

"Me neither."

"I'm under the couch."

"I'm not third guy in."

"I'm furthest from the door."

Eventually we gave up and slept wherever we could find room.

But one night we had so much energy, maybe from all the candy, sugar snacks and soda pop we swallowed, that we couldn't sleep. It was so late that even Sir Graves Ghastly was back resting in his sarcophagus, dreaming of sinking his fangs into a juicy rare steak or some gal's neck.

"Let's go out to the cemetery," I suggested.

"What, man? No, it's too late," Skeese said. "And with no one around at this hour, it'll be easier for the cops to spot us."

"We've never been out there at night, and we can tell the guys at school what it was like," Rogan said, agreeing with me and ignoring Thatcher.

"We can make it a mission, move from tree to tree and bush to bush, staying low and out of sight," I said quickly.

"I've got a flashlight for when we get out of town," Sticks joined in.

"I've got one, too. That should be enough," Rogie replied.

We gathered up our stuff and went into whisper and whistle signal mode. The Rankin Street Raiders were out on the prowl. Adventure ahoy.

This was no ordinary prank or plunder; it was a test for the team. We didn't know what to expect. None of us had ever been to a graveyard at 3 a.m. on a night darker than the tombs we were approaching. How long could we stay out in a place where the ground was full of dead people? Who would be the first to suggest we turn back? Once there, who would want to leave right away?

And what was lurking out there above ground: zombies, monsters, ghouls, lost souls and spirits in search of release, desperate mad-men or robbers sharing loot? These fanciful fears collided in our skulls as we leapt from place to place, hiding and tucking our shadows in behind us while whistling one another ahead in shifts in the half-light.

As the streetlights and suburbs gave way to fields and farmland, we were able to talk and walk, still wary of any sudden noises or lights. Everything looked and sounded different at that odd hour. All movement was changed and potentially dangerous.

Night birds hooted and screeched around and beyond us in the deep and grim woodlots we passed. We heard their dead trees, not the live ones, whine in the wind. Rickety and rusted wire fences, unnoticeable and uninteresting in daylight, grated and sawed in our ears. Everything seemed to speak menacingly to us alone. Mailboxes creaked, and loose and tattered wooden shutters banged sharply. We hunkered together, marching in a protective group.

Chatting seemed to help keep the frights at bay.

"How much further?"

"Yeah, I'm getting tired, and we're running out of time."

"I wonder if it's better to be buried at the foot of the cemetery hill where the ground is moist?"

"What the hell are you talkin' about? You're dead, so who cares?"

"Maybe my corpse lasts longer if I'm in wetter ground?"

"Or it rots faster."

"I'd rather be up on top above the rest."

"What for, a better view?"

"Because it's drier?"

"No, I would just feel better up on higher ground."

"The only thing you'll be feeling is worms and rats."

"Okay, not this escaped convict coming to kill us so what's the better location deal all over again?"

"Shh, what was that?"

"I think it was an owl."

"Either that or the murderer asking, who's there?"

"C'mon, let's get up there and get this over with."

Our march had slowed to a trudge as we headed, suddenly solemn, for the dreaded graveyard gates. As we entered in single file, it was quiet all at once, as though the dead were absorbing any noises. A few little lights blinked sparsely from the 'Burg in the distance. The first and last Raider used our only two flashlights, illuminating headstones as we climbed to the rise at the centre of the cemetery.

Wavering, sickly shades appeared behind some headstones, despite the lack of light. The whole place was grey and black, shrouded in decay and defeat. We gathered automatically into a circle, speaking wide-eyed in muffled whispers.

"I saw one from the 1800s."

"Look at the size of that monument. Guy must have been rich."

"See anyone you know?"

"This is like being at a funeral where the mourners are in the minority."

"We're not staying here long, right guys?"

"Let's look around a bit more and then get the heck out."

Some tombstones were in rows and others were random. A few were marble but most were chiselled stone. The older were more pockmarked by endless day and night and sun and rain in the same spot. Flowers, we realized, meant fresher graves and well-kept plots meant loved ones still lived. Some husbands and wives were buried beside one another. Close birth and death dates carved forever into the marker above meant children or babies. Their hopes and dreams entombed with them.

We just stood there shuddering and sharing our unspoken thoughts. A misty gloom settled on our shoulders, the eternal enormity of it all reaching up through the ground and grasping us. Everyone planted under our feet was dead, like trees that would never sprout leaves. There would be no harvest for those dried human seeds slumbering below. Generations of families were frozen in their time, locked endlessly underground, lost to disease and desperation, hardship and hazard, suffering and sorrow. We were alive but we were standing on their deaths.

Silently, we turned as one Raider and headed back down to our own world, shaken and humbled and still trying to figure why. A heavy mixture of fear and sadness walked with us. We said little, threw a few rocks on the way but strode quickly, like vampires racing against the dawn. As we neared the comforts of our hometown and began to prepare for our covert ops to Skeeser's front porch we heard a moan, a loud and too real moan.

All that was left of us on the street was our skins because we had jumped out of them. About twenty yards away we saw a guy slumped against a chain-link fence, his head down, bawling and breathing hard. We crept up to him. He looked to be in his twenties with matted hair and ripped jeans. Rogie shone a light in his eyes and before he could cover his face with his arms, we could see a big purple bruise like a duck-egg with a red slash through it on his forehead. He was bleeding from the mouth. We leapt away like lemmings moving backward from the cliff.

"Help me," he stammered. "Please, help me." Then he fell to one knee into the gravel at the side of the road.

From a safe distance we asked him what had happened but all he did was continue to plead with us for assistance. "I need help, I can't make it myself," he groaned and spat blood.

"We gotta get outta here right now," Wiry said.

"But what's wrong with him?" I asked. "Is he drunk?"

"Maybe somebody beat him up," Sticks ventured.

"And those bastards might be coming back for him," Wiry pleaded.

"Or he got hit by a car," I suggested.

"Or all of the above," Skeeser said. "But I agree with Wiry, we gotta beat feet now."

"We can't just leave him. We can't just run away. This guy's in trouble and we're the Raiders. Running away isn't always the answer. We have to do something," Rogan declared.

"Yeah, if he's hurt bad, we might be able to save him," Sticks added.

"I got an idea," Rogie said quickly, pointing at a small, dimly lit convenience store down the street that had been shut for hours. "There's a pay phone over there."

"Whadda we gonna do, call the Skeesester's mum to see if she's started breakfast for us?" Wiry said, jogging on the spot.

"Very funny, dummy. We can call for help," Rogie replied.

"Who are we gonna call, one of our parents?" I wanted to know.

"No, we call the cops and let them take care of him," Rogie explained.

"Are you nuts, man? Then we all get busted," Skeese said. "No way should we ever call the cops."

"Look, here's the plan. We call the police without giving our names. We tell them there's a guy in bad shape here and they'll have to come. If he's drunk at least they'll get him off the street, and if he's hurt, they'll have to call an ambulance to take him to emergency and get him fixed up," Rogie told us. "Then we hide over there behind that hedge to make sure they send someone and run home when help arrives."

We coughed up some change up as fast as we could. "I'll call it in," Rogan said, "and you guys help carry him over to the pay phone in the light."

We mostly dragged the poor guy, trying not to get any blood on us, and slumped him down, doubled over against the phone booth. Rogan hung up and we scrambled over to the shrubs to wait, carefully hidden of course.

Sure enough, in a few minutes a squad car showed up, red lights flashing like a lighthouse. A dumpy policeman tumbled out of his car and ran over. He checked our man out quickly and then ran back and radioed a message in. It looked like a scene from a gangster movie with the cop on the blower, lights flashing, and some mug crumpled like an empty pack of cigarettes against a cracked and dirty phone booth. But this was no horror movie.

Hearts pounding like ball peen hammers, feet itchy and eyes like moons we waited until we heard the unmistakable scream of an ambulance. That was our cue, all we needed to know. We were gone so fast we left our shadows still crouching there. Our shadows caught up with us a few blocks later. Covert or overt be damned, we ran like racehorses with their tails on fire until we piled onto the porch and huddled in our sleeping bags, shoes still on, adrenalin pumping steam through our veins, bathed in sweat and sweet relief.

"Hey, Matt," Skeeser turned to me after the other Raiders had quickly fallen asleep. "I think we should stop trying to scare ourselves so often, you know, on purpose."

Whaddya mean?" I asked.

"I think the world is going to take care of that for us."

Chapter 25

Brown-Eyed Girls and a Canoe Courtship

The Detroit River was never far from us. It wasn't just down at the end of Rankin Street; it was also always in our minds. It was where we boated, fished, crossed to Boblo, kicked about the shore looking for treasure but usually found only gross, long-nosed gar pike carcasses and decaying, slimy mud puppies, launched our firecracker depth charges, watched in dwarfed awe as the dirigible-sized Great Lakes freighters parted the river on their silent journeys 200 yards from us, threw rocks at cat-sized water rats and waved at pretty girls passing in speed boats or lounging and tanning in bright bikinis on their docks and waterfront lawns. It was part of our lives and we knew it up and down, above and below, and season to season. We also learned that the river was not to be trifled with—a powerful being with a will of its own, lazily meandering as it pleased but when in a rage, rushing and flooding with a vengeance. And always pulsing, in its veins ran currents and undertows, that took their toll in its depths.

It was January during one of the colder winters when our dads toiled in the backyard to water rinks for our hockey and skating pleasure, kids got their tongues stuck on frozen metal fence poles in the schoolyard, we awoke to Jack Frost murals of ice patterns on our bedroom windows and the river became a sea of ice floes, the Arctic for a week and a few days. One Saturday morning, drawn, despite all our parents' and teachers' dire warnings, by the strange new thing our waterway had become, we ventured down to its frigid banks at the foot of the Water Works Park. The whole Raider squad was in attendance, if one of us was going to risk it, we all might as well have and, of course, there was safety in numbers. There, before us, was a wonder. The river was transformed. Great cragged, slabs of ice were moving slowly, in unison in direction, yet crunching into one another. They looked like upside down clouds, forming and reforming in the bright blue of the stream that supported them. We could hear them cracking, the heavy and cold sounds of flat glaciers colliding, a natural traffic jam in the wintery watery swell.

"Holy cats, it looks like the North Pole," Stickers said.

This roused us from our trance.

"Yeah except for the part where there's no Santa Claus or Donner or Blitzen or Dasher," Wiry stated.

"And technically, there's no water at the North Pole," Rogie said.

"How do you figure that?" Stickers asked. "Have you been there?"

"Well, even if there was, it would be frozen because that's as far north as you can go," the Rogester replied.

"Hey, look over there," Skeese said. "I just saw an Eskimo harpoon a seal and drag it out of the water."

"Okay, enough of all this," I said. "Let's go down and have a closer look. This is pretty cool."

"Yeah, it's so cool, it's frozen," Wiry laughed.

We all inched closer to the massive collection of ice floes, one tentative step at a time. We could feel the crashing and hear the grating of the sheets of ice but aside from that, all was still and silent. The river's new winter power seemed to suck the air out of everything, including our chatter. We stood in a line on shore peering into a cracked crystal floe on the river's surface, a force we had never encountered. The watercourse was revealing to us some of the brutish strength it kept unseen in its belly.

"Let's find some branches and move the floes around some," Stanks suggested, breaking the trance.

We shook off our cold fears and scurried about searching for something to push or re-direct the islands of ice. Then we started shoving those that drifted closest to us.

"Wouldn't it be boss if we could ride one?" I wondered.

"That would be righteous man," Wiry said, "like a frozen magic carpet."

"Yeah guys, like those French Canadians poling down the river, rolling on logs," Sticks said.

"That's dangerous. What if it cracked open and we all fell in?" Rogie said slowly.

We all eased closer anyway.

That's when, for some reason, I looked up and back over my shoulder.

My father was standing on the shore with a look in his eye that I had never seen before or would ever witness again. It rocked me; a slap shot to the chest. He was frightfully mute and rigid, feet apart with his arms crossed and his face was fixed in a teeth-grinding grimace. His stare went right through me, as though he was looking beyond, into my future, glaring at someone else, a person he didn't know and didn't like. My dad's black eyes blinked and narrowed slightly, shifting in their intensity, like a magnifying glass frying an ant in its sun laser beam. Then he did something I didn't expect, he reached up and wiped his face with his sleeve and looked at the sky, his mouth open, gulping air. I realized years later that he was fighting to control himself between his fury and his love for me, having arrived at the river in time not to see my death. But he had experienced it. For an eternal moment, branded into him, he held the vision of life without me in his mind. And it rocked him too.

Then I heard Terry say from behind me, "Oh, oh, Matty, your old man's here and he looks really, really pissed off."

"Thanks a bunch, Skeese, I am painfully aware of that fact."

"He's so mad, he isn't even saying anything."

"Caught that one, too. Can you stop helping me after the horses are out of the barn?"

My dad suddenly barked like a German shepherd on a chain. "All of you go home right now! If I ever see you by the river in winter again, I will call your parents and tell them what happened here today. Matt, you're with me."

Then he turned around and marched to our house. He didn't speak to me for longer than my track record for broken windows. It was worse than being grounded and having my allowance taken away rolled into one.

About a month later, after I was finally allowed to leave the house after school and on weekends, another cold snap hit the 'Burg. The temperatures sank and the ice floes returned; it was that kind of rare winter. Terry and I had just finished our paper routes after school and, we were eagerly counting our moolah, calculating how much we were going to tell our parental units we had collected and where we were going to spend the rest. We were strolling, cold but contented, by the Water Works when we saw some movement down by the edge. It looked like people were walking up and down the shore. We looked at each other, exchanging the same thoughts.

I am just recovering from my severe and extensive groundation, Skeese read my thinking.

Your dad is gonna call my dad if he sees me down there again, I understood his unspoken concerns.

"Okay, my father isn't home from work yet. Let's just take a peek anyway, just to see what's going on," I said.

We stashed our cash and hustled down to the river. As we drew closer, we saw that it was two girls about our age, laughing lightly and throwing rocks onto the slabs of ice. Being the gentlemen we were, we decided to introduce ourselves. Adjusting our toques into stylish angles and straightening up to appear taller, we ambled down like we owned the place. Shirley was Black with big brown eyes, a full mouth and curly hair that sparkled in the sunlight sprouting up from in between her earmuffs. Her friend Kelly had freckles, auburn hair and inquisitive eyebrows over greenish eyes.

Skeese and I told them we were Terrence and Matthew and almost bowed as diplomats representing the area.

"Where you two girls from? We haven't seen you around here before." I asked.

"We live in Anderdon, just between LaSalle and Amherstburg," Kelly said.

"We know where that is," I said all at once. "I play hockey with a guy from there, Rod Banes, he's on my team."

"He's my cousin, that's cool," Kelly said.

"Yeah, that's cool," Skeese managed to blurt out.

I gave him a side-long glance to maintain.

"What are ya doin' in the 'Burg?" I asked calmly.

"My mum is visiting my aunt just up the street, so we thought we'd come down here and play with these ice floes. The river never gets like this," Shirley told us. "In fact, we were just about to stand on one, just to feel what it's like to ride it."

Terry and I looked at each other, trying not to look alarmed.

"Hey, you gotta be careful. They could break apart and you could fall in," he said.

"Are you guys… chicken? This slab here's solid as a sidewalk," Kelly said.

"We're gonna step on with or without you scaredy cats," Shirley added.

"Whoa, whoa, if you fall in, there're fast currents below and the water'll freeze you if the undertow doesn't get you," I warned them.

"See ya later, afraidy gators," Shirley said and stepped onto the big, jagged floe.

We gasped and froze like the floes.

"Welcome aboard, c'mon over Kell, you can feel the water running underneath, like I'm skating without moving my feet."

As she reached out to pull her friend onto the ice, there was a sudden rifle shot crack. The ice broke beneath her and Shirley fell onto the main floe, her legs dangling off the side into the numbing river. Kelly screeched and dived back to shore. I grabbed and pulled her up, boots soaked, shivering, knees shaking and crying into my arms.

Skeesester waded into the frigid river, trying to reach Shirley's hand but she was just beyond reach on the floe that had yet to break free.

"Mattie, see if you can find one of those branches we had out here a few weeks ago. I'll stay with the girls."

I knew where we had left one or two of the small, driftwood poles and dug it out of the snow just down the bank then ran back like there were junkyard dogs on my ass. I heaved it to Skeese then took off my coat and wrapped it around the sobbing Kelly.

Shirley was wailing and waving as Skeese waded back in toward the drifting ice floe.

"Don't move," he shouted. "It might break up."

In between Shirley's screams, we could hear that monstrous crunching sound, floe against floe, the polar river's jaws opening and closing. Kelly hid her face in my parka.

With a last lunge, Shirley grabbed the other end of the life-stick.

"Now just hang on, I'm gonna pull you into shore but nice and slow and steady," Terry said soothingly, with an older voice. "Hold on with both hands and whatever you do, don't let go."

Shirley nodded, frosty tears streaming down her face.

We huddled and watched as Terry, like the anchor in a tug-of-war, hauled Shirley in as he retreated step-by-step to shore. The frigid and nasty current was fighting them. Finally, he lifted her off the deadly frozen float and knelt with her on the riverside. She cried into him as he, too, removed his jacket and wrapped her.

We brought them quickly up to my house at the top of the Water Works' lane. My mum warmed them up with blankets, called Shirley's aunt down the street and served us all hot chocolate. Shirley and Kelly were then rushed to Hotel Dieu Hospital in Windsor to be checked for frostbite or hypothermia. We learned later in the afternoon that they seemed to be fine but had to be held overnight for observation and as a precaution.

I got a phone call from Skeese early the next morning.

"Hey man, I was thinking of taking the bus in to see the girls today."

"That's a damn righteous idea, Pipster. I'm kinda keen on Kelly."

"Yeah, Shirley's pretty sweet, too."

"I should have the green light from my oldsters as, all of a sudden, I'm a hero around the house."

"Me too, Mattie. I can do no wrong, even pizza late with Senior Bowl Cutter last night."

"I got to stay up way past my bedtime for a movie with popcorn and extra butter, no margarine."

"What about bringing them some chocolates?"

"Even better, man. I'm sure my dad will cover the cost."

"Mine too. See ya at the bus station, 10 a.m.?"

"Coolosity, brother."

At the hospital we were directed to Shirley's room and it was our good fortune that Kelly was visiting as well. They were obviously completely surprised to see us, particularly with our hair combed and sporting striped, high-collar shirts and gleaming penny-loafers. And, if it had been a competition, the boxes of chocolates pushed us first over the finish line.

"Well, what are you guys doing here?" they wanted to know.

We shuffled from loafer to loafer and mumbled something about wanting to see if they were all right.

"I'm fine," Kelly told us. "Shirley has a little frostbite, but the doctor said it would clear up soon and won't leave any scarring."

"Yeah, and that's thanks to you guys," Shirley said in a high voice. "We could have been goners, especially me."

"You two are lifesavers," Kelly added, "Our heroes."

Then we chatted for a while about music and movies until a nurse came in and told us that visiting hours were over.

"Can you give us another minute or two?" Shirley pleaded.

The nurse nodded and left quietly.

"Hey, Terry. Come over here," Shirley said. "This is my phone number in case you want to give me a call sometime." Then she drew him close and gave him a peck on the neck.

I looked at Kelly. She smiled, handed over her number and gave me a hug and a warm kiss on the cheek.

We pretty much floated out of Hotel Dieu, lovesick and deliriously in need of our own urgent care. On the front steps Skeese released, at his highest register, one of his should-have-been patented "*Eeee-heee-Orreeetes*," to the obvious dismay of two paramedics nearby.

The winter passed and we exchanged a few phone calls but that was it for our brief ice floe girlfriends.

Skeese and I didn't see them again until two seasons later when it was brightly raining sunfish. So much so, there should have been a rainbow. But this was a Raider-made sunfish shower. They were floppin' and ploppin' all around a dock where two girls in colourful and scanty swimsuits sat screaming and laughing. We didn't know what that meant, and we couldn't believe they could do both at the same time so we just kept firing the brightly coloured little fish: overhead bombs, horseshoe end-over-ends, lob-balls and skipping their pancake, spiny bodies sideways like stones. Anything over four skips was cause for celebration in our books.

Congratulating each other and reaching into our bucket for more panfish ammo we looked up to see them, beach towels over their heads, climb down into a canoe and begin paddling an escape. Our two-part plan was to get their attention by launching a barrage of bluegills at them and then cruise over in our own canoe and save them, you know, from ourselves. It wasn't the best Raider plot in our logbook, but to us, girls were skittish and unpredictable, yet alluring so we were willing to try anything to see if it worked.

We had started that summer day by sleeping just long enough to watch Rita Bell's prize movie after a sleep over at Skeester's house. By the time Rita had given away a toaster and a waffle iron, we were getting sent outside by Terry's mother. It seems that it was too nice a day to be sitting inside, glued to the boob tube. His uncle had a place on the river with a dock, a canoe and the promise of jumbo perch for lunch if we got lucky. We picked up our poles and peddled the long ride out to just this side of LaSalle.

It was as humid as a sweatbox in the Perspirationville county jail, but cooler out on the dock. We dug for worms in the shade, hooked up our red and white bobbers, stretched out on the weather-beaten wharf, tipped our Detroit Tigers ball caps south and waited lazily for nibbles, legs drooping above the water. The only time you can productively loaf is when you're fishing. We had a big bucket full of river water tucked under a leafy tree in case we caught any keepers. But all we hauled in were mini panfish: pumpkinseed and crappies. Although they weren't worth a pinch of coon crap, we decided to keep them to see how many we could collect. Besides, there weren't nuthin' else biting.

It was then that we noticed the bathing beauties a few docks down and launched our panfish barrage. After they made their escape attempt, we paddled harder. Suddenly, as we drifted closer, we realized in shock, that we might have been making a horrible mistake.

"Hey," Skeester said. "Isn't that Kelly and Shirley, the girls from the ice floe, two winters ago?"

"Ahhh, yeah, you could be right," I replied. "And that ain't good."

"No guff, wise ass, what'll we do now, try to hide in plain sight in the middle of the river?"

"Let's just fess up and apologize. I get the feeling that those two don't take kindly to lying."

We called out their names and they stopped paddling.

"Terry and Matt?" they called back over their shoulders.

"We're sorry, we didn't know it was you, you know, without your winter coats or hospital gown."

"So, is this how you spend your time, hanging around the river, distressing damsels and then saving them?" Shirley demanded.

"Ah, it was just a misunderstanding, and it was Matty's fault."

"No way, it was Terry's call."

We quickly dumped the rest of the fish in the drink and sidled up beside their canoe. We asked if they were fully recovered from the icy incident. They both said yes.

"It's a lot more fun floating on the river in a canoe than on an ice floe," Kelly said.

"You want to hang out?" Skeese asked. "We've got the rest of the day."

"Sure, we're just catchin' some rays and tunes," Shirley said.

They were listening to the latest hits on a transistor radio and we had one too so we both tuned into CKLW and cranked up our volumes. We sang along with everything from the Stones' "Paint it Black" to the Circle's "Red Rubber Ball." Then Van Morrison's "Brown-Eyed Girl" kicked in.

"I just love this song," Kelly giggled.

"I wonder why?" I laughed.

The shoreline slipped gently past, a blur of soft scenery giving focus to the young maidens suddenly in our care. The sun seemed to bounce off their lovely and happy youth. Our little vessels safely lashed together, our fingers entwined, our young hearts beating boldly. We floated on the new and refreshing current of a canoe courtship.

The Raiders were turning their tides on a river of love and on the corners of Rankin Street.

Chapter 26

Rankin Street Raiders' Logbook - Final Entry

Life is full of endless roads, opportunities and possibilities. It fires a load of puzzling pieces at us. It isn't about connecting the right, the best or the ones that result in drawing the most attention; the secret is to choose those paths and make the decisions that have meaning, for us and those whose lives we affect.

We shared our growing years. Not just any adolescence but one forged in friendship and somehow designed for a special, enduring purpose. The Rankin Street Raiders discovered our own fountain of youth. When all our tireless plotting and adventures came together, we were in a hallowed place. Our mischievous ideas and energy allowed us to be detached from the regular dictations of boyhood. In that short period of our lives, we created our own existence, and it was instantly everlasting.

We stayed in touch for a few years to the end of secondary school and then each of us began to drift apart, some moving away from the Burg, starting our own families and acquiring new friends. Many rising moons later when even a couple of us would get together, there was always a Raider adventure to be recalled with much laughter; our friendship shining and waving over us as an undiminished beacon from the past.

Some of us are gone now, called by a greater power. Others are infirm, battered by the rigours of illness. And the rest of the team are simply growing old, bowing to time's demands. But we know that we will always live on Rankin, then, now and forever, as the eternal Raiders, because our souls are still playing, running and soaring along and above that treasured little street.

Acknowledgements

This book is dedicated to Bill Wigle, John Rodgers, Pat Thrasher and James Stickings.

I would also like to express my deep appreciation to my editors Wendy MacMillan, Matthew Beatty, Laurie Monsebraaten and Jessica Kirby for their enthusiasm, insights and professionalism.

There are many, many people who have helped me along the way, in and out of time, to accomplish this novel. For their friendship, love and support I would like to thank Robert and Margaret MacMillan, Sara, Joe, Henry and Nolan Hawkins, Collin and Jasmine MacMillan, Les and Carolyn Thrasher, Jayne Thrasher, Wes and Karrie Thrasher, Becky and Jamal Banks, Lindsay and Mike Gyori, Brady Thrasher and Jessica Mastronardi, David Goldman, Ricky Stewart, Dan and Debbie Nedin, Joe Bondy, Jack Thrasher, Ron Nedin, Gordon Bailey, Mark Johnson and Larry Harris.

Manufactured by Amazon.ca
Bolton, ON